The Other Side of Goodbye

WELCOME TO REDEMPTION, ALASKA

The Other Side of Goodbye

HEIDI MCCAHAN

The Other Side of Goodbye
Welcome to Redemption, Alaska - Book 1

Published by Sunrise Media Group LLC

Print ISBN: 978-1-966463-18-4

This book is a work of fiction. Names, characters, places, and incidents are either products of the author's imagination or used fictitiously. Any similarity to actual people, organizations, and/or events is purely coincidental.

Scriptures taken from the Holy Bible, New International Version®, NIV®. Copyright © 1973, 1978, 1984, 2011 by Biblica, Inc.™ Used by permission of Zondervan. All rights reserved worldwide. www.zondervan.com The "NIV" and "New International Version" are trademarks registered in the United States Patent and Trademark Office by Biblica, Inc.™

For more information about Heidi McCahan please access the author's website at the following address: HeidiMcCahan.com.

Published in the United States of America.
Cover Design: Sunrise Media Group LLC

For my mom, Nancy,
who taught me everything
I know about baking pies.

One

S HE HAD NEVER FORGOTTEN THE FEELING OF Redemption.

Tisha Binford slowed down as she cruised into town on a cold Saturday afternoon, pausing at the blinking caution light. A green-and-white sign protruded from the snowbank, declaring that this small Alaskan town had won last year's high school basketball championship. Drumming her thumb on the steering wheel, she quickly surveyed her surroundings and braced for the onslaught of memories. The same bank, gas station, motel, and gift shop claimed each of the intersection's four corners. As she picked up speed and headed down Main Street, Sadie, her seven-year-old daughter, squirmed in the passenger seat.

"Are we almost there?"

"We're here. This is it." Tisha smiled, then pointed through the windshield. "In a few minutes, we'll drive up that hill over there, and then we'll be at Grandma and Grandpa's place."

Sadie craned her neck. "Where's their restaurant?"

"The café?" Tisha slowed to a crawl and gestured to a one-level building barely visible one block off Main. "Quick, peek down that street. It's the blue one with the gray roof."

Sadie twisted in her seat. "Where? I didn't see it. Can we go back?"

Tisha hesitated. Oh, how she wanted out of this car. It had been a long, tedious five-hour trek from Anchorage. She wasn't used to driving on snow-covered roads or traveling for several miles without passing another car. Or gritting her teeth to keep from complaining about the playlist Sadie had curated and insisted they listen to on repeat.

"I'll take you by tomorrow. Since I'll be helping with the baking, you'll spend plenty of time there."

Too much time, probably. She tamped down the guilt already trying to rear its ugly head. A few minutes later, she turned onto Hillside Drive, wound her way around a curve, then pulled into her in-laws' driveway and turned off the engine.

Sadie pointed. "Mama, look. The snow is almost as tall as their windows."

"It sure is." Tisha peered through the windshield at the snowbank. "Your grandpa has to use a special machine called a snowblower to clear the driveway. He zings the snow back into his own yard."

"A *snowblower*?" Sadie giggled. "That's funny. Can I see it?"

Tisha smiled, then reached across the center console and gently tugged on one of Sadie's long braids. "I'm sure he'll be happy to show you how it works."

"Right now?"

"Let's go inside and say hello first."

Tisha unbuckled her seatbelt. "Come on, sweetie. You're going to love it here."

She climbed out of the car, the cold air biting at her cheeks as she slammed the door behind her. After she gave the hood of the new-to-her SUV an appreciative pat, she zipped up her coat, shivering as a brittle January wind swirled across the driveway. Though she and Chase had visited his parents in winter before, the sheer volume of snow blanketing everything gave her pause.

Are you out of your mind?

Her mother's critical voice echoed in her head. Tisha pushed the thought aside and took Sadie's hand.

"Wait. I need Ollie." Sadie tugged free and turned back toward the car.

Tisha bit back an impatient sigh. Ollie the stuffed Orca whale Chase had given Sadie as a birthday gift—their last one together—went everywhere Sadie went.

"Ollie will be safe in the car for a few minutes. We'll be right back to grab our things."

Sadie tugged the car door open. "What if he gets scared being alone? This is a strange place."

Hard to argue with that. Tisha jammed her hands into the pockets of her teal green puffy winter jacket, purchased exclusively for this grand adventure, and waited while Sadie collected her beloved stuffed animal from the front seat.

"Got him." Sadie slammed the car door, then closed her eyes, tucked the black-and-white killer whale under her chin, and whispered something Tisha couldn't hear.

A prayer? A pep talk? Who knew. Was it weird how much Sadie talked to her stuffed animals? Add that to her list of problems to worry about later.

"All right, Sadie and Ollie, here we go." Tisha took Sadie's hand in hers again, and together they hurried up the freshly cleared driveway, the crunch of snow beneath their boots punctuating the silence of the winter landscape. As they approached the one-level ranch house, painted a muted gray with crisp white trim, the door swung open before either of them could ring the bell.

"There's my girls!" Melinda Binford stood in the doorway, her salt-and-pepper hair pulled back in a loose ponytail. Her ice-blue sweater mirrored the color of her eyes, which crinkled at the corners with warm familiarity. Those eyes—Tisha's heart pinched at the reminder of Chase.

"Hey, Melinda." Tisha swallowed hard against the tightness in her throat as she stepped into her mother-in-law's warm embrace. The comforting scent of detergent wafted in from the laundry room just off the entryway.

"I'm so glad you both are here." Melinda's soothing voice wrapped around her like a soft blanket.

"Well, well, if it isn't my sweet Sadie!" Tom Binford joined them, adjusting his wire-framed glasses on the bridge of his nose. His hair, what remained of it, had turned completely white. Maybe grief had aged him too.

"Hi, Grandpa!" Sadie flung her arms around his waist. "We saw piles of snow taller than our car today."

"How about that? Quite the change from North Carolina, isn't it?" Tom patted Sadie's shoulder, but his gaze shifted to Tisha, a flicker of empathy shining in his clean-shaven face.

"Hey, Tom." She offered him a wobbly smile. Had she made the right decision? Moving in with the Binfords so she could keep Chase's memory alive for Sadie wasn't the worst life choice. But uprooting her daughter from everything she knew in North Carolina might be even harder than she'd expected.

"Welcome back." Tom kept one hand on Sadie's shoulder, then leaned over and gave Tisha's cheek a quick peck. The tender gesture from a stern man who rarely expressed his emotions startled her.

Thankfully, Melinda didn't miss a beat. "We've got the cabin all ready for you. Want to come inside for a snack or get settled first?"

"Oh, I love snacks." Sadie hopped from one foot to the other, thrusting Ollie into the air.

Tisha reached down, tucking a strand of her daughter's blonde hair behind her ear. "Let's settle in, and then we can focus on food. Remember, you just had a snack in the car."

"I know, but I'm hungry again," Sadie said. "Ollie and I need more Goldfish crackers."

Melinda chuckled and retrieved her coat from the hall closet. "Let's go out to the cabin and I'll show you, Ollie, and your mother where I put the groceries. I bet we can find something delicious. Tom, why don't you grab their bags?"

"Absolutely." Tom gestured to his slippers. "Let me change into my boots and grab my coat, then I'll be right out."

"Thank you so much for letting us stay with you," Tisha said, leading the way outside. "This means a lot."

"Of course." Melinda pulled the door shut behind her. "We're thrilled to have you, and when you're ready, our café customers will be glad you're here as well. We've had trouble keeping up with the demand for our baked goods since two of our employees up and quit before Christmas."

"Sorry to hear that happened." Tisha zipped her coat up to her chin. "I'm excited to get started."

"Mama, did you pack my hat?" Sadie's teeth chattered. "My ears are cold."

"Let's try this for now." Melinda gently covered Sadie's head with her coat's hood. "We're only going to be outside for a minute. Take my hand."

Melinda offered her hand to Sadie, and the little girl eagerly threaded her fingers through her grandmother's.

As they walked along the wide path Tom must've cleared with the snowblower, Tisha paused, looking up at the stunning sunset. The sky was awash in glorious shades of cotton-candy pink, casting a soft glow over the snow-covered landscape. Tears pricked at her eyes, but she blinked them back.

Melinda stopped walking and looked over her shoulder. "You coming, Tisha?"

She gave a quick nod because she didn't trust herself to speak. Falling apart right now would scare Sadie.

"Everything all right?" Melinda asked, her gaze steady and concerned.

She hesitated, then cleared her throat. "Chase loved it when the sun hit the mountains like that."

Melinda tipped her head to one side, her smile bittersweet. "He sure did."

"Are you talking about my daddy?" Sadie chimed in, looking between Melinda and Tisha.

"We are. We talk about him all the time, don't we?" Tisha pointed to the snowcapped mountains that ringed the small coastal community. "Your daddy loved that pink light on the mountains. It was his favorite."

"Grandma, can you tell me about his other favorites?"

Melinda winced, then turned toward the cabin. "You bet. Let's start with this cute little place back here. Your daddy loved to stay here when he came to visit."

The Craftsman-style bungalow tucked against the tall spruce trees at the back of the Binfords' property had the same gray and white paint as the main house. Lamplight spilled through the curtains hanging in both of the square windows flanked with white shutters. When they climbed the three wide steps, Tisha took Sadie's hand as Melinda pushed open the door. The scent of pine mingled with something sweet and warm in the air.

"I brought fresh towels out here earlier. We had the place all fixed up for Jennifer, but then she surprised us and took that job in Wyoming, so now it's all yours."

"I hate that she's not here. I bet you miss her, but it's nice for us. Look, Sadie. We have a cozy place to live." Tisha turned slowly, taking in the space. "Oh, you still have the Christmas decorations up."

A small tree sat in the corner, adorned with a strand of lights that weren't plugged in. It was topped with a gold star, and traditional silver and gold balls along with vintage icicle ornaments hung from its branches. The exact same decor had been in here when she and Chase and Sadie had stayed in the cabin two years ago.

"Yes, Jennifer loves Christmas, especially her grandmother's old ornaments. She didn't want to take the tree down before she left, and I just haven't gotten around to it," Melinda said.

Tisha's gaze swept over the cozy furniture—a gray microfiber love seat and a recliner, a sturdy wooden coffee table, matching side tables, and a fireplace with a stone hearth that beckoned for a fire. It felt like a place they could make a home, even amidst the memories.

An urn wrapped with a stunning watercolor image of a plane soaring over water sat on a small table pushed against the wall. More hot tears pricked her eyelids. Chase's ashes. She'd promised Melinda and Tom that when she and Sadie got to Redemption, they'd make plans to spread the ashes out at the lake. Together. But now that she stood here, staring at the urn, she wasn't sure she could follow through on those plans.

"I brought over some tomato soup and groceries—just a few basics. I thought you could have grilled cheese and tomato soup." Melinda pulled a lighter from a drawer and lit a candle nestled in the faux floral centerpiece on the coffee table. "You both must be exhausted."

"Soup and grilled cheese sounds perfect. Thank you." Tisha ran her hand over the gray-and-white-striped blanket draped neatly over the arm of the recliner. It had a thick, soft texture—perfect for snuggling under with a good book.

"Let me show you where I put everything," Melinda said.

Tisha crossed to the small kitchen. Stainless-steel appliances, an L-shaped granite-topped counter, and white Shaker-style cabinets provided all they needed. "Skye and Tyler gave me a case of bottled water plus two bags of cleaning supplies and paper products this morning before we left their house. I still can't believe they gave us their car."

Melinda opened the pantry cabinet. Sugar, flour, coffee pods, honey, tea bags, a couple of boxes of crackers, granola bars, and a box of cereal sat on the shelves. "Tyler really misses Chase. He's had a hard time dealing with the loss of his brother. I'm sure he and Skye will do whatever they can to help you and Sadie make a fresh start."

"I really appreciate this. All of it." Tisha gestured toward the food. "I don't know what I would have done without you."

"Well, you're a godsend, stepping in and offering to bake pies for us." Melinda closed the pantry door. "It's not easy to find reliable, skilled help. Especially this time of year."

"Happy to do what I can," Tisha said. "Sadie, please put your coat on the hook by the door."

"Oh-kayyy." Sadie dragged her coat from where she'd dropped it on the sofa and plodded across the room, her shoulders slumped.

Melinda gave Tisha a questioning glance.

"I've probably pushed her a little too hard," Tisha said quietly, then joined Sadie by the door. "Here, sweet pea. After you hang up your coat, you can put your boots on this cute tray. See?"

"When Tom comes in, I'll have him start a fire," Melinda said. "That will make everything feel extra cozy."

"There are a lot of pictures of my daddy here," Sadie said after hanging up her coat and tugging off her boots.

"There certainly are." Tisha hung her coat beside Sadie's and lined up their boots on the tray.

"Look at that one." Sadie's eyes lit up as she pointed to a gorgeous photo of Chase standing beside his seaplane out at the lake. His close-cropped blond hair, bright blue eyes, and charming smile instantly took Tisha back to that perfect summer.

"He looks so young," Sadie said.

"That's because he was." Tisha turned away from the framed photo. "It's been almost ten years since that picture was taken. Want to help me plug in the lights on the Christmas tree?"

"Sure." Sadie skipped over to the tree in the corner. "I can do it by myself."

"All right." Tisha hovered while Sadie fumbled with the plug in the outlet. Then the lights turned on, casting a golden glow into the room.

"Yay." Sadie clapped her hands. "I'm glad Christmas can last a little bit longer."

More framed photos were scattered throughout the room, a mix of black-and-white and color images capturing Chase on a fishing trip, on a hike, hunting for moose, and riding four-wheelers with Tyler.

"I pulled out some of his old artwork, and Jennifer helped me frame it," Melinda said, smiling as she pointed to a trio of framed drawings hanging on the wall above the small round table and three chairs. All three featured airplanes flying over what looked like mountains.

"That's sweet." Tisha rubbed at the dull ache forming behind her sternum, but she forced herself not to dwell on it. If she wanted to keep Chase's memory front and center, surrounding themselves with photos and artwork was the way to go.

Just then, Tom came in, stomping the snow from his boots. He had a backpack hanging from each shoulder, and a suitcase in each of his gloved hands.

"Oh my goodness, Tom, let me help you." Tisha hurried to take the luggage from him.

"No, no. Stay in where it's warm. I'll just make a couple of trips," he said, his voice warm but dismissive. He piled the backpacks on top of the suitcases, then went back outside. Tisha winced. She had probably overpacked. The movers hadn't guaranteed when they'd deliver their things though. The Binfords had generously offered to provide most of what they needed, and Tisha and Sadie had crammed as much as they possibly could into their suitcases.

"Once your luggage is inside and Tom starts a fire, we'll give you and Sadie some space," Melinda said. "Is there anything else you need that I might've forgotten?"

Sadie yawned, rubbing her eyes. "Can I watch a show, please?"

"Let's go see your new bedroom." Tisha guided Sadie down the short hallway lined with more pictures of Alaska and the Binford family. They entered Sadie's room, where the white metal-framed twin bed was decorated with a new polka-dotted comforter, a matching dust ruffle, and a half dozen decorative throw pillows shaped like hearts and candies.

"Oh wow, Sadie." Tisha stopped in the doorway. "Look at those super-cute pillows. How did Grandma and Aunt Jennifer know you like polka dots?"

Sadie shrugged, then walked a slow lap around the room. A white dresser with pastel glass drawer pulls stood against the opposite wall. The matching nightstand and a small bookcase with books and three more framed photos of Chase, Tisha, and Sadie filled the adorable space.

"Jennifer gets all the credit." Melinda stood in the doorway. "She worked really hard to redecorate."

"It's beautiful." Tisha made a mental note to send her sister-in-law a photo of Sadie sitting on the bed.

Melinda towed a suitcase into the room. "Want me to heat up the soup while you unpack?"

"But what about my show?" Sadie whined, hugging Ollie close.

"Please find your pajamas, toothbrush, and your favorite blanket first, and then you can watch a show," Tisha said. "I'm going to help Grandma."

Later, after they'd said good night to Tom and Melinda and finished a quick meal of grilled cheese and tomato soup, Tisha tucked Sadie into her new bed.

"I need a night-light, okay?" Sadie said, her eyes wide and earnest.

"I'll see what I can do. We might just have to leave the hall light on for now. I didn't pack a night-light." They said their prayers, and Tisha kissed her good night, then turned off the lamp and stepped out into the living area.

Sipping a cup of decaf tea, she settled onto the sofa and propped her feet on the coffee table. Fire crackled in the fireplace, and the warmth made her drowsy. She reached for her phone and scrolled to the group chat she'd started with her sisters, Natalie, Cami, and Kirsten.

Cami

Hey. Checking on you. Did you make it to Redemption yet?

Tisha

Hey. Thanks for checking in. All good! Sadie and I got here a little before supper.

Natalie

You're up late.

Tisha

It's not that late in Alaska but I don't want to go to bed.

Kirsten

Memories of Chase?

Tisha

He's here. Everywhere I look, he's here. And of course the last time I stayed in this cabin, we were together and married. Just don't want to sleep in the bed alone.

Cami

"Mama, help!"

Oh no. Setting her tea aside, she pushed to her feet, then hurried down the hall. Sadie sat up in bed, tears streaming down her cheeks.

"What's wrong?" Tisha rushed to her side.

"I had a terrible dream about Daddy. He was waiting for me in a field of pretty flowers, and I was running to him, but no matter how far and how fast I ran, I just couldn't get there."

Tisha swallowed back a sob. She'd held it together all day, but Sadie's heartache threatened to unravel her. "Oh, sweet girl, come here."

She lifted Sadie into her arms, grabbed Ollie and the tattered blanket Sadie had clung to since infancy. "Let's snuggle on the sofa by the fire."

Sadie swiped at the tears on her cheeks. "Now?"

"Yep. Here we go." Tisha carried her out into the living room. They pulled blankets from the cedar chest under the window, and Tisha quickly stoked the fire with another log. Then they constructed a cozy fortress, piled under layers of quilts and blankets.

"Tell me a story about Daddy," Sadie said softly as she nestled against Tisha.

"Sure, which one?"

"One where he's flying his favorite airplane." Sadie yawned, then balanced Ollie on top of their blanketed laps.

"All right, one where he's flying."

Tisha began to weave a tale about how she had been staying at a friend's cabin beside a beautiful lake, thinking she would have the place to herself, when a handsome guy with an incredible smile had landed his plane and declared he wanted the cabin too. At first, they had argued, teasing each other just like they had when they knew each other in college. But somehow that summer, they had forgotten all their disagreements and instead, they had fallen in love.

Tisha trailed off, then glanced down at Sadie. She'd closed her eyes, her breathing steady and peaceful. She had fallen asleep, but Tisha was wide awake, memories of Chase flitting through her mind like fireflies in the fields surrounding the farm back home in North Carolina. One thing was for sure: she'd come to Redemption for a fresh start and to help Sadie remember that she'd had an amazing dad. Cute stories, sentimental songs, a hundred photos—whatever it took—she'd keep Chase front and center. And somehow she'd learn to accept the hard truth that not all happy endings last forever.

No doubt about it, he was made to fly.

Ethan McGuire eased the helicopter onto the mountaintop plateau. The skids kissed the snow, and the rotors churned up a glittering storm of fine powder. Staring out at the glorious blue sky and the razor-sharp peaks, he adjusted the cyclic as his brother Luke flashed a grin and a thumbs-up. Ethan responded with a faint nod, his attention still half on the chopper and half on the view. He'd only been back home in Redemption, Alaska, for about a month. But soaring over the untouched wilderness and navigating the ridges and angles tapped into his innate skills—and offered freedom. Up here, the weight of everything else stayed grounded. Up here, he didn't have to wrestle with himself.

"You guys ready?" Luke's voice crackled through the headset, pulling Ethan from his thoughts.

He swiveled in his seat. The chatter of excited clients, three men from Utah, filtered in from the back. When Ethan gave the go-ahead, they climbed out of the helicopter, laughter and awe trailing behind them. While Luke opened the cage and retrieved their gear, Ethan checked the fuel gauge. More than enough. It would take at least ninety minutes for these fellas to make their way down the mountain, giving him plenty of time to scout the area he'd reviewed on the map.

Luke climbed back into the helicopter, his cheeks flushed from the cold. He tugged the door shut, then slid his headset into place. "All right, they're all set. We're planning on a twelve-thirty pickup."

"Roger that." Ethan lifted off, the helicopter hovering momentarily before soaring west.

"Hold up. Where are you headed?" Luke shot him a questioning glance.

"Relax. I know what I'm doing."

"You're going to look for Trevor's plane, aren't you?"

Ethan nodded. "Of course I am. We're already out here, so why not?"

"Dude, he went down six months ago. They've searched high and low. You're not going to find him."

"What you meant to say is, nobody's found him *yet*." Ethan fought to keep his voice even. "I spent twenty years in the Coast Guard, Little Bro. Locating missing things is what I do."

"Slow your roll there, big guy. We've had the best of the best out here, combing every inch."

"There's no way anyone has scanned every nook and cranny of these mountains." Ethan's breath fogged the window as he studied the jagged rocks protruding from the snow-covered hillside. "That's not possible. Besides, it doesn't hurt to keep looking."

"You don't have an unlimited amount of fuel," Luke said.

"Correct. But I did file a flight plan that said we'd be gone three hours." A frozen stream that fed into an ice-covered lake caught his attention and earned a second look. "I can't let his story end this way."

"I know this brings up memories of losing your bestie, MJ," Luke said. "But maybe you should focus your efforts elsewhere."

"What's that supposed to mean?"

"How's Brody doing?"

"He's fine. He's great. Everything's great."

"Um, that seems highly unlikely. You moved across the country, put him in a new school, and left his grandparents in Florida."

"I didn't leave them. They wanted to move into an assisted-living place. That was their choice."

"I'm just saying, Adeline's only been gone a little over a year. Brody's been through a lot. He can't be fine. Not after all that."

Ethan gritted his teeth. Since when had Luke—who'd never married or had children—become the local expert on coping with grief and being a single dad?

"All right, so maybe he's not great. But that's okay because we're home now. No more moving around. We've got lots of family support, and I'm going to fix everything. You'll see." He scanned the endless expanse of snowy peaks below. Trevor's older brother, MJ, had drowned along with their dad on a fishing trip decades ago. Which meant Mrs. Kelly had lost her husband and both her sons. Ethan couldn't let her go forever without closure.

"Uh-oh," Luke said, his tone shifting. "You need to head back."

"Why?"

Luke held up his phone. "Got a text from Mom. Looks like the school called. Brody's not having a great day."

Ethan stifled a groan. "All right. Headed back now. On our way, I want to fly over Townsend Glacier."

"All right." Luke nodded. "It's changed quite a bit. Remember when we were kids and we could take a boat right up to the face?"

"And your friend Cal's dad would blow the horn and ice would calve?" Ethan glanced at Luke and grinned. "That was the best."

Ethan adjusted their course, flying east toward the glacier and then Redemption. Below them, jagged ice stretched for miles, a frozen river of glorious blue crevasses and dirt-crusted icebergs spilling through a valley between two mountains.

Luke let out a slow whistle. "Check that out. On the far left. Looks like it's about to calve."

Ethan leaned over and stared out the window. The water in the bay was littered with icebergs. He scanned the jagged edge of the glacier's face where a blue-and-white chunk of ice tipped forward, ready to splinter off. "Just a matter of time before it goes, right?"

"Yep," Luke said. "If only we'd brought the air horn."

Ethan headed for Redemption, trying to ignore a strange unease settling in his chest. Right now he had bigger problems than a calving glacier. Like getting to the bottom of whatever trouble Brody had gotten into at school.

Thirty minutes later, he set the helicopter down on the landing pad. The McGuires' sprawling two-story log resort loomed before him, its rustic charm a stark contrast to the dense evergreen forest climbing the mountainside behind their property. With its wraparound balcony, icicles hanging from the edge of the roof, and snowdrifts in the yard, he sort of felt like he'd wandered into a Hallmark movie. Behind the resort, the building known as the shed, which his dad and grandparents had built years ago, stood strong, its red metal roof a beacon against the backdrop of white snow. They'd spent hours in there playing basketball, soccer, touch football, and Ping-Pong. Pretty much anything that involved a ball. Well, except for freeze tag, and they only played that when his little sister Megan whined about being left out. Sure, there'd been some squabbles and hard feelings, but mostly good memories. Memories he'd hoped to recreate with Brody.

Except they were off to a rough start.

He powered down, thoughts of his son interfering as he logged flight time and fuel.

"If I'm with Brody, who's going to pick up the skiers?"

"I'll take care of it." Luke left his headset on the hook over the console and climbed out of the chopper.

Ethan followed and inhaled sharply, the cold air biting at his cheeks. It was a sensation he still hadn't fully acclimated to. He missed the warm, humid breezes of Florida, the salt in the air, the ease of wearing shorts and T-shirts year-round. He shook off the thought as quickly as it came. Florida wasn't for them anymore—not without his wife.

Snow crunched beneath his boots as he crossed to the back door and pushed it open. The resort's interior enveloped him in familiar warmth. The inviting scent of cedar mingled with the faint aroma of freshly baked cookies from the kitchen. Wooden beams spanned the high ceiling, and the walls were adorned with photographs of three generations of family gatherings, ski trips, and vacations in the lower forty-eight. The spacious living area, with its leather couches and stone fireplace, still felt like a refuge.

Brody's backpack lay abandoned on the floor. Sighing, Ethan stepped over it. His mother, Cassie McGuire, stood behind the desk where they usually greeted customers, her dark hair twisted into a neat bun, a few stray strands framing her face. Country music played softly in the background, a soothing contrast to the tension in the air. She turned, offering a smile that didn't quite reach her eyes. Dangly earrings caught the light from the rustic chandelier overhead.

"There you are. How'd it go?"

"Fine. Luke says he will handle the pickup. What's going on?" He leaned both elbows on the desk's worn surface. "Where's Brody?"

"He's out in the shed. Blowing off steam." She gave him a knowing look. "Kind of like you used to do."

"I don't like the sound of that at all."

Mom glanced back at her laptop and clicked out of whatever she'd been working on. "I had to pick him up. He was a mess, so I brought him home early."

Ethan pinched the bridge of his nose. "But he's not supposed to miss school. His teacher already said he was behind."

"Honey, relax. I spoke to the principal. You know, Mr. Price. You guys were teammates back in the day."

"Yeah, yeah. I heard. Can't believe he's the principal now."

Mom reached across the desk and gently squeezed his arm. "Why don't you go talk to Brody? Get his side of the story."

"On my way." Ethan forced a grateful smile. "Thanks for helping me out."

"Anytime," she said. "That's what family's for."

He turned away and walked back outside. A minute. That was all he needed. A minute to collect himself. Just as he steadied his thoughts, the door opened and a familiar voice broke the silence.

"Hey there, Clutch! Long time no see."

Ethan turned to see Hank, the resort's maintenance man. A burly guy with a friendly smile, Hank had been part of the fabric of Redemption for as long as Ethan could remember.

"Hey, Hank." Ethan reached out and shook his hand. "What's up?"

"Just working on the hot tub. Heard you were back in town. You know, the kids still talk about how you used to sink three-pointers like it was nothing. Some say you never missed."

Ethan felt a pang of nostalgia, mixed with a bittersweet sting. "Yeah, those were some good times."

"Good times, indeed! You should teach Brody some of your moves. Kid's got potential."

"He's not really into basketball, Hank."

"Aw, come on. You were made for it. He just needs some encouragement. Maybe he could be the next Clutch McGuire."

Ethan glanced toward the shed. "I'd love to, but Brody's not interested. He's more into skateboarding these days."

Hank shrugged, his grin fading slightly. "Kids can be stubborn. But you know, it's not just about the game. It's about spending time together, making memories. I'd give anything to have my son interested in something I love."

Ethan's chest tightened. That was exactly what he wanted for

Brody, but the gap between them felt insurmountable. "Yeah, I get that. Just . . . trying to figure things out."

"Hey, you're back home now. That counts for something. You'll find a way," Hank said, clapping Ethan on the shoulder. "Just don't give up on him, all right?"

Ethan nodded, but the weight of Hank's words lingered in the air, heavy with unspoken fears. He watched as Hank walked away, whistling a tune Ethan couldn't quite place.

"Just don't give up," he whispered, but the words felt hollow. How could he reach a boy who seemed set on pushing him away?

With a deep breath, he turned back toward the shed, its presence a reminder of everything he longed to share with Brody. But as the echoes of Hank's encouragement faded, the reality of the situation settled in—for now, he was still just Clutch, a name that felt like both a badge of honor and a painful reminder of what he used to be.

His breath left white puffs in the air as he cut long strides across the yard. Someone had rolled up the garage-style doors for Brody. Ethan caught a glimpse of his son sailing across the gorgeous parquet floor on his skateboard.

"Oh my word." Ethan broke into a jog. "Brody, what are you doing, man? You can't skateboard in here."

Brody hopped off the board, tapped the back end with his toe, then grabbed the nose with his hand. He glared at Ethan. "Why not?"

Ethan planted his hands on his hips. He opened his mouth to admonish the disrespectful tone, but his son's sullen expression made him choose his words carefully. Brody wore a black hoodie with sleeves pushed up, gray cargo pants, and black-and-white checker-print sneakers that seemed out of place in Alaska in January. With his flushed cheeks and that stubborn set to his jaw, they might be in for a tough conversation.

"The wheels aren't good for the floor," Ethan said quietly.

"But there's nowhere else." Brody glared at him, suddenly looking more like a frustrated teenager than an eight-year-old.

"When the snow melts, you'll be able to skateboard outside. There's plenty of asphalt. Come on. Let's shoot some hoops."

Brody shook his head. "I don't like basketball."

Ethan raked his hand through his hair. "Son, what happened?"

He dipped his chin. "I don't want to talk about it."

"Your grandmother said she had to pick you up early, so it sounds like we need to talk about it, whether you want to or not."

Brody's chin shot up, his brown eyes glossy with tears. "I said I don't want to talk about it, and I don't want to play basketball! You wrecked my life. You wrecked everything. I hate it here! I want to go home."

He let his skateboard hit the floor with a *thunk*. Crying, he ran out the door and back toward the resort.

His heart hammering, Ethan stalked over to the old metal rack that held their gear. He grabbed a basketball, bounced it three times—hard—then hurled it across the shed with a guttural yell.

Then he doubled over, breathing hard, and clutched his knees with his hands. Brody's words knifed through him, as precise as a surgeon's blade, straight across his mangled heart. The kid wasn't wrong. Everything about their life felt wrecked. And Ethan wasn't sure he could fix any of it.

Two

FIRST DAY AT A NEW SCHOOL. HOW BAD COULD it be?

"Here we are." Tisha stopped outside the doorway of Sadie's assigned classroom at Redemption Elementary.

"But, Mommy, I don't want to go in there." Sadie tightened her grip on Tisha's hand. "I want to stay with you."

Uh-oh. They'd had this talk twice already. Tisha gulped back a sigh and offered a bright smile. "I need to start my new job baking at Grandma and Grandpa's café. Besides, you're going to have so much fun that I bet the day will fly right by."

Excited chatter filled the air as the other second graders filed in, hanging up their backpacks and coats, the sounds of zippers and laughter mingling together. A woman in her late twenties greeted each child with a warm smile, her strawberry-blonde hair woven into a neat French braid tied off with a festive navy-blue bow. She wore stylish jeans with flared bottoms and a bright yellow cardigan over a navy-and-white-striped T-shirt. Even her leather clog-style shoes looked trendy.

Tisha knelt down to her daughter's level and gently clasped

Sadie's shoulders with both hands. "Look at your teacher, Miss Johnson. Look how she did her hair. Maybe tomorrow I can French braid your hair like that. Oh, and she loves bows. You like bows, don't you?"

Sadie's brow furrowed, a hint of defiance in her large blue eyes. It had been a struggle, but Tisha had convinced her to wear her hair in two adorable pigtails, though Sadie had shown little enthusiasm for the idea. Thankfully, Tisha had won that skirmish and acquiesced on the outfit—Sadie's white dress with purple polka dots and hot-pink leggings were a small victory in the battle of wills. But the refusal to wear her snow boots had become a familiar refrain; instead, she insisted on her white sneakers that lit up with every step.

"Come on," Tisha urged, planting a kiss on her forehead before pushing to her feet. "You're going to have an awesome day, and I can't wait to hear all about it when I pick you up in a few hours."

Oof. That came out a smidge too enthusiastic. Maybe she needed to dial back the sales pitch. Just then, Miss Johnson appeared at the door, her smile radiating warmth. "Hi! You must be Sadie Binford. Welcome to my class. I'm Miss Johnson."

"Hi," Sadie whispered, then nibbled on her thumbnail and scooted closer to Tisha.

Miss Johnson motioned for Sadie to follow her as if she were offering a safe harbor. "Give your mom a hug or a high five and then come on in."

Tisha hesitated. *Really?* They were going to part ways out here in the hallway? Sadie looked up at her, her lower lip trembling, and Tisha's chest tightened. But maybe a quick getaway was exactly what they both needed. She kissed her daughter one more time, the familiar scent of Sadie's shampoo—sweet and fruity—lingering around her, and headed for the exit. She'd pop into the office to make sure all the paperwork she'd just dropped off was in order, and then she'd be on her way.

A few minutes later, Tisha was back in the car, pulling out of the parking lot. School buses rolled in, their bright lights flashing in the gray morning, while a long line of cars snaked through the lot. Tom and Melinda had told her the bus stop was at the end of their street and she could arrange for Sadie to ride. Or maybe she could find a way to get Sadie dropped off at the café. That was a problem for another day. For now, she'd drop off and pick up. At least until Sadie's anxiety about going to a new school faded.

She reached for her insulated coffee mug and took a sip. Melinda had been so kind to buy her favorite brown-sugar oat-milk creamer and leave it in the cabin's fridge. What a sweet surprise during a stressful morning.

Driving slowly through town, she eased past a small group of guys in winter parkas standing beside a utility truck. They'd raised a basket overhead, where two men removed the last of the Christmas decorations from the lampposts. It wouldn't be long and they'd probably be back to install the Love Is in the Air decor for Redemption's annual February festival. She slowed at the main intersection, waiting for a woman walking her dog to cross the street. The husky's pink tongue lolled and its graceful bushy tail bounced as they kept up a brisk pace.

Turning left, Tisha pulled into the parking lot of the Homestead Café, a long-standing Redemption business that Chase's parents had purchased a few years back when they'd moved from Anchorage. The café's four wide windows were trimmed in white, and an old-fashioned Open sign suction-cupped to the window closest to the front door invited customers to come in. She turned off the engine and glanced around the parking lot. Not crowded yet. Good. She needed a few moments to gather her thoughts.

Okay, God. Please help me get this right. Tisha grabbed her purse and coffee and headed toward the café's entrance.

Melinda greeted her with a bright smile. "Good morning! How'd Sadie handle drop-off?"

Tisha winced. "Not great."

"Oh dear." Melinda gave her arm an empathetic pat. "It's a big change, starting a new school. I'm sure it will get easier."

"Hope so." She followed Melinda past the counter with a register and a stack of menus, then stepped through the swinging doors to the kitchen. The delicious aroma of bacon wafted through the air as she entered, and her stomach growled in response. Yikes. She'd quickly eaten a slice of peanut-butter toast at the cabin early this morning. Must not have been enough.

"I'll give you a quick tour. That's Owen, our line cook," Melinda said, nodding toward a gray-haired man wearing a stained apron layered over a T-shirt, faded jeans, and sneakers. He adjusted his hair covering and waved, then went back to turning the bacon on the grill.

"This will be for you." Melinda motioned to a stainless-steel counter with an industrial-sized mixer at one end. "I've stocked the cupboard pretty well, but if you need anything, just make me a list and we'll place an order."

Tisha nodded, taking in the neatly labeled bins of flour and sugar on the shelves beneath the counter.

"No one expects you to bake a pie today, but whenever you're ready, the kitchen is prepped for you." Melinda smiled. "No pressure or anything."

"Well, pies are kind of my thing, so as soon as I get settled, I'll get to work."

Just then, a young woman probably around thirty walked in, tying an apron around her waist. Her long, sleek black hair was pulled back in a neat ponytail. Thick lashes framed her golden-brown eyes, and she flashed Tisha a wide smile.

"You have the most beautiful eyes I have ever seen," Tisha blurted out, surprised by her own boldness.

"Well, you are my new favorite coworker. But don't tell Owen." Her exaggerated whisper drew a laugh from Melinda. "This is

Charlie. She works the day shift as a server. She's also a lifelong Redemption resident, so if there's anything you need to know, she's probably your girl."

"It's nice to meet you, Charlie." Tisha shook Charlie's hand, then took the apron Melinda handed her. "I'm Tisha Binford."

"Glad to have you on board," Charlie said, tucking a pen and a small notepad into the pockets of her own apron.

"Charlie will show you the ropes. I've got a truck coming with the grocery delivery out back, so I'm going to run. So glad you're here, honey." Melinda pulled Tisha in for a side hug before hurrying away.

"All right, first thing you really need to know is today's special." Charlie pointed to the dark chalkboard mounted on the wall beside Owen's service window. "This morning we're going to be taking standard breakfast orders from our usual menu. For lunch, our specials are two kinds of soup: broccoli cheddar and chicken noodle. We often sell out of the sourdough bread bowls."

"Two kinds of soup, sourdough bread bowls are a winner, and—"

She trailed off as the door opened and a man stepped in—tall, with broad shoulders and dark hair, shorter on the sides and longer on top. He chose a seat in the middle of the L-shaped counter, shrugging out of his puffy jacket to reveal a long-sleeve gray Henley. Even though he was clean-shaven, he exuded a rugged appeal that was hard to ignore.

Charlie offered a curious smile as she nudged Tisha's shoulder with hers. "He's a handsome one, isn't he?"

"He looks familiar," Tisha whispered, checking her reflection in a small mirror on the wall. "Do you know him?"

"That's Ethan McGuire. Moved back to town from Florida about a month ago. His family owns Redemption Resort."

"McGuire?" Tisha's breath hitched. "My late husband, Chase, was good friends with Luke."

"Ah." Charlie's smile faded, and empathy filled her eyes. "Sorry for your loss."

"Thanks. It's been two years. I'm grateful to Tom and Melinda for making space for me here. It's going to be the fresh start I desperately need." She pressed her palm to her forehead. "Good grief, that was way too much info. Forgive me."

"Not too much info at all. I have some deets to share with you. Compared to Luke, Ethan's quite grumpy. Maybe he's still getting used to living here after being away so long. Or maybe he's struggling to adjust to our weather. Anyway, he's been in a few times, usually sits down, orders coffee, then stares at it. Or reads something on his phone," Charlie said. "Why don't you take his order? Should be an easy first one."

"Coffee? That's not very exciting."

"If you can persuade him to get anything else, I'll be impressed. He's kind of broody."

"Huh. Well, I believe there's a perfect flavor of pie for everyone."

"Good luck with that." Charlie arched a dark brow and handed Tisha a pad and paper.

"Good morning," Tisha said, her voice steady as she approached Ethan. He looked up from his phone, his expression unreadable.

"I'm Tisha." She extended her hand, and his eyes flicked to her palm before shaking it.

"Ethan."

"What can I get you?"

"Just coffee." He returned to scanning his screen. "Black."

"Just coffee? Nothing else? I hear Owen makes a mean omelet."

"I already ate."

"How about some pie?"

Frowning, he scrolled some more. "It's literally nine thirty."

"Oh, come on." She tilted her head toward the glass case. "One slice. Live a little."

"All right. Pie it is, then. Just a small slice, please."

"Perfect." She wrote down coffee and pie. "I'll be right back with your coffee."

"No worries. I'm on it." Charlie appeared behind her with a mug and a carafe. "Hey, Ethan."

"Hi, Charlie." He gave her a firm nod as she filled the mug and set it down.

Tisha stood in front of the glass bakery case at the end of the counter. "These pies look sad," she said, her heart sinking a little at the sight.

"Well, that's because they're brought in frozen. We plate and serve them." Charlie stopped in front of the service window and clipped a new order into the turnstile. "There you go, Owen. Over easy on those eggs, please."

Owen nodded. "Got it."

Tisha opened the door, then pressed up on tiptoes to get a closer look. "This isn't right."

"That's why you're here. To overhaul our pie game, remember?" Charlie opened a cabinet under the counter and handed over a small plate and pie server.

"What are my options?"

"Um, chocolate cream, banana cream. I think there might be some pumpkin." Charlie frowned. "Everything else is still frozen, sorry."

"Okay, well . . ." She lowered her voice. "A guy that grumpy needs some banana-cream pie in his life."

Charlie bit her lip, shaking her head slightly. "Girl, you don't even know."

Tisha plated a slice of banana cream, and after Charlie showed her where the forks were kept, she carried the pie out to Ethan.

"Here you go," she said, giving Ethan her best smile as she set the plate next to his coffee. He studied her, his brow furrowed. Oh, wow. Warmth heated her skin. His piercing green eyes and ruddy cheeks were quite attractive. Or maybe he just had that whole strong, independent Alaskan-male thing going on.

"Have we met? Before today, I mean?"

She hesitated, clicking the end of her pen. "Rumor has it we have some mutual connections."

He used the side of his fork to separate a sliver of pie. "Who?"

"I used to be married to your brother Luke's best friend."

Ethan paused, his fork halfway to his mouth. Something she couldn't quite identify flashed in his expression. "Chase Binford."

She nodded. "He passed away unexpectedly. Two years ago. I'm sure Luke told you all about it."

"I'm sorry for your loss," he said, his tone softer now.

"Thank you." Tisha drew a deep breath, then leaned her elbows on the counter. "So, how do you like the pie?"

He took a bite, chewed thoughtfully, his expression masking any hint of pleasure. "It's okay."

She straightened. "Just okay?"

"Yeah, not a fan of pie."

"Really? Not at all?"

"Not a fan of bananas either."

"Seriously? Who doesn't like bananas?"

He picked up his coffee and shot her a look over the rim of the mug. "People who've lived in places with better options."

"Huh. Noted." She tore his bill from her new pad, then tucked it between the salt and pepper shakers in front of him.

"Tisha?" Charlie stood at the cash register. "Let me show you how to use our system."

"Be right there." Tisha gave Ethan a polite smile. "I'm going to figure out what kind of pie you like."

"Good luck."

Wow. Okay, then. "Challenge accepted."

The rest of the day moved quickly. Lunch brought a flurry of soup orders, a café full of chatty customers, and an overwhelming amount of onboarding info from Charlie. By two fifteen, her back ached and her feet throbbed in protest. *Note to self: Invest in more supportive shoes.*

The ladies in the front office at the elementary school had explained how to drop off Sadie and pick her up, plus she'd reviewed the instructions posted on the school's website. By three o'clock, she sat in line, listening to her favorite country-music playlist while sipping a hazelnut latte from the Copper Kettle. When she rolled to the front of the line, the passenger door opened, and Miss Johnson stood on the other side.

"Good to see you, Mrs. Binford. Sadie had a great day. We'll see you tomorrow."

"Thanks." Tisha waved, then waited while Sadie climbed in and hurled her backpack into the back seat. "Hey, pumpkin, how was your day?"

"It was fine." Sadie sniffed, tears streaming down her cheeks.

"Oh no." Tisha reached over, smoothing Sadie's pigtails. "What happened?"

"I don't want to tell you," Sadie whispered.

Tisha glanced through the window toward Miss Johnson, but she'd already moved on to help another student get in his car. "Can you tell me one good thing that happened? What was your favorite part of the day?"

"Leaving."

Oh dear. Tisha sighed. "Come on, let's go home. Grandma and Grandpa need some better pies at their café. You can help me make some."

"Okay. Can I choose the flavor?"

"Sure." Tisha gestured toward the sound system. "You want to put on some of your favorite songs?"

"Yes, please."

Sadie grabbed Tisha's phone from the console, swiping through a soundtrack from one of her favorite animated movies, filling the car with a cheerful hit they'd heard a hundred times. A few minutes later, they pulled up in front of the Binfords', parked, and got out.

"Grandma and Grandpa are still at the café. Let's go fix some hot cocoa and you can tell me what happened."

Inside, Sadie dropped her backpack by the door, yanked off her boots, and let her coat slide to the floor. "Can you get the fire going again?"

Tisha pointed to the pegs. "Remember, backpack and coat and boots here?"

Sadie nodded, her cheeks still flushed. Poor girl.

While Sadie put her stuff away and carried her lunchbox into the kitchen, Tisha stoked the fire. A few minutes later, golden flames licked the logs, casting a warm glow around their cozy cabin.

"Let's see what we have here in the cabin that we can make into a pie while you tell me about your first day of school." Tisha found two mugs and a container of hot-cocoa mix in the cupboard. "What made you so upset?"

"Some dumb boy called me Daisy." Sadie pooched out her lower lip, her eyes glistening with unshed tears.

"Oh, that's not so bad. Why did he call you Daisy?" Tisha plugged in the electric kettle to heat the water. "Maybe he thinks you're as pretty as a flower."

"No, he's dumb. That's why."

"Oh, I don't think that's true. Did you know that daisies are my favorite flower? Your daddy used to pick bouquets from the field and bring them to me."

"He did?"

"He sure did." Tisha bent down, grabbed Sadie's hands in hers, then met her daughter's gaze. Wow, her eyes were so much like Chase's. "So I happen to think daisies are lovely."

"Daddy was nice." Sadie's voice turned pitiful.

Tisha's heart pinched. *Please, no more tears.* She directed Sadie toward the sink. "Let's wash our hands. Maybe you can help me roll out the pie dough. I'm sorry to hear that this boy is bugging you. I had a difficult customer today too. He didn't like pie."

Sadie squirted soap onto her hands. "Everybody likes pie."

"Of course they do." Tisha floured the counter and got out a ball of dough, handing Sadie the rolling pin. "Can you put some flour on that, please? Just a little bit."

Sniffling, Sadie dried her hands, then pushed up her sleeves and sprinkled flour on the rolling pin like Tisha had taught her.

"You're good at this, sweetie." Tisha patted Sadie's back. "Do you want me to go in and talk to Miss Johnson about this boy?"

"No, what I want you to do is take me back to North Carolina!" Sadie dropped the rolling pin on the counter, then ran to her room and slammed the door.

Oh boy. Tisha pressed the back of her hand to her forehead. Was her mother right after all? Had she made a terrible choice, bringing her daughter here? For all her talk about how life was an adventure, and she'd certainly had plenty of adventures in Alaska over the years, she couldn't shake the nagging feeling that she was really going to mess this kid up.

⁓

Airport-shuttle run and online research about recent plane crashes—not the most exciting to-do list for a Wednesday morning, but he'd vowed to do his part to help with the resort. And figure out what happened to Trevor.

"Have a great trip home." Ethan stood outside the small airport in Redemption, shaking hands with the guys he'd flown up into the mountains the day before.

"Thanks, man! That was epic. We'll definitely be back." The taller one grinned, his sunburned cheeks crinkling as he adjusted his reflective sunglasses.

"Glad you enjoyed it." Ethan waved them off as they shouldered their packs and disappeared through the airport doors.

The exhaust from a nearby diesel truck idling at the curb wafted toward him. Turning back to the late-model Suburban that doubled as the resort's shuttle, he slammed the hatch closed. Then he hurried around to the driver's side, climbed in, and rubbed his gloved hands together for warmth before cranking up the heat.

He'd been stationed in cold climates early in his career, but after twelve years at warm southeastern air stations, this chill was a shock. It was as if he'd forgotten that Alaska was anything other than frigid and snowy. At least this time of year.

The sun crested the snowcapped mountains, casting a bluish hue across the landscape. Snow crunched under his tires as he navigated through the crowded parking lot.

He slowed at a stop sign, exhaling sharply. Reaching for the radio, he hesitated, opting for silence instead. Brody's mood from the night before nagged at him like a persistent itch. The kid had barely touched his dinner. He'd slumped in his chair and answered all of Ethan's questions with two- or three-word answers. Then he'd taken a shower without complaining—a sure sign something was up. They'd topped off their miserable evening with a half-hearted "Good night."

Ethan tightened his grip on the steering wheel and turned right, toward town. Heavy dollops of snow clung to the branches of trees lining the road. The salt and gravel put down by the highway department sprayed out from under his tires and spattered the sides of the Suburban. He spotted a moose ambling through the trees and slowed, admiring the majestic creature.

When was the last time he'd bothered to admire gorgeous scenery? Or an animal in the woods? Almost never. But there was nothing wrong with embracing a slower pace, right? He glanced at his phone, tempted to pull over and take a picture for Brody.

So far the kid had hated pretty much everything about Alaska. Maybe a moose in a snowbank wouldn't be all that impressive.

Sighing, Ethan sped up. This fresh start was supposed to be good for both of them. A small business, with grandparents, an aunt, and two uncles close by, Ethan was banking on the strength of his close-knit family to help Brody heal.

But was it going to help him?

He punted that thought right back where it came from, doubling down on his fierce determination to outrun his own grief.

At the next intersection, he eased to a stop. Straight ahead led to the resort and plenty of time to scour the Internet for details about planes going down in the Chugach Mountains. But a right turn would take him past the café. Frankly, yesterday's chat with the pie lady had made him feel like a normal guy for the first time in ages. He still wasn't a fan of bananas in his pie, but something about her piqued his interest. Besides, Charlie knew several customers who came into the café, so maybe she'd point him toward someone he could talk to about Trevor.

He turned right, then headed for the Homestead Café and claimed a parking spot near the front door. Adeline would've encouraged the last-minute change of plans. "You've got to live a little, Ethan," she'd say, rolling her eyes at his predictability. Memories of his late wife still provoked an ache in his chest. At least the pain didn't flatten him the way it used to.

He stepped inside the café. The savory aroma of melted cheese mingled with fresh coffee and an overpowering floral perfume. Ethan frowned. An older woman in a faux-fur jacket hustled ahead of him, snagging the stool he had his eye on. He picked a spot farther down the counter, trying to avoid the heavy scent that clung to the air.

The grill cook glanced his way, offering a friendly nod before returning to his task. Tisha, the pie lady, emerged from the kitchen.

She wore her hair in a long, smooth ponytail and her blue eyes sparkled when she smiled. A crazy warmth spread through him.

Wow, okay. One pretty smile shouldn't have that much of an effect.

Should it?

He shrugged out of his coat, then set his phone face down on the beige-and-white speckled Formica countertop.

Tisha held up a mug. "Hey. Coffee?"

"Yes, please."

She filled the mug, then set the carafe on the counter and leaned closer. "Might I interest you in a *homemade* pie? Just a tiny slice."

He cast a sideways glance toward the woman with the faux-fur jacket, who wasn't even trying to hide the fact that she was listening to their conversation. "What's the catch? And why are you acting like this is a covert mission?"

"I haven't been here long enough to know the ins and outs, but allegedly I'm not supposed to serve anything that wasn't made in a health-inspector-approved kitchen."

He dropped his voice to a hushed whisper. "Clearly a federal crime."

Tisha hesitated, drumming her polished nails on the counter. "My daughter and I made something incredible at home last night, though, and I think you should try it."

He slid the steaming coffee closer. "Only if you promise to come and visit me in prison."

She laughed. "Pretty sure I'm the one who would get arrested."

"Well, is it worth it? How much time would you do for illicit pie sales?"

Her conspiratorial smile made him want to lean in. What in the world? Was he *flirting?*

"I don't know." She shrugged. "Five to ten? But only if they can prove it."

"I'm in."

"Perfect." Tisha's smile widened. "I'll be right back."

Ethan nodded, then took a sip of his coffee and forced himself not to stare as she walked away. His phone hummed. He picked it up and glanced at the screen.

<u>Kaylee</u>

If you won't do it for me, please do it for your in-laws. We all loved Adeline too, you know. She deserves to have her story told.

The text message from Kaylee, his late wife's best friend, hit him square in the chest. The woman had been angling for him to grant an interview about everything Adeline had done for the women in the Coast Guard community in Florida. Kaylee was right. Adeline's commitment to helping others thrive was a story that needed to be told, but he just couldn't bring himself to go there. The grief was still too raw, too fresh.

"Ta-da." Tisha set down a piece of pie with a crisscross lattice top and a purple fruit concoction peeking out from between the little squares. The crust looked flaky and moist, and his stomach rumbled.

"I heard that," Tisha said. "I'm determined to figure out your ideal pie flavor, so we're gonna overlook the misstep with the banana cream and I want you to try this instead. My daughter calls it jambleberry but the proper name is jumbleberry."

"Jumbleberry? What's in it?"

She lifted one shoulder. "Don't let the name distract you. It's a concoction of ingredients we found at the house."

There was that playful gleam in her eye again. He spread his napkin on his lap but didn't reach for his fork. "Hmm. You're not exactly selling it."

"Here you go, Mrs. Dawkins." She pressed a plastic lid on a to-go cup of coffee and handed it to the woman with the healthy affection for perfume and faux fur. "Enjoy."

The woman's mouth puckered. "I certainly hope you're not serving desserts that weren't made in a commercial-grade kitchen."

"Of course not. Ethan's my official taste tester. He's agreed to sample any new baked goods before we make them widely available to the public."

"I have?"

She gave him the side-eye, then scooped up a handful of packets from under the counter. "Did you need extra cream and sugar?"

Still frowning, Mrs. Dawkins took all of the packets and shoved them into her pockets.

"Charlie will take your money at the register." Tisha smiled sweetly. "Thanks for coming in."

When she turned back to face him, he couldn't help but smile.

"What?" she said. Her brow furrowed. "What'd I say?"

"Official taste tester, huh? Do I need to sign a waiver?"

"No paperwork, I promise. Just try the pie."

He took a small bite. Chewed slowly. It was tart but sweet, and the crust was everything he'd imagined it would be.

"Well?" Tisha rubbed her hands together. "Survey says?"

"Flaky crust. It's quite delicious. Jambleberry? Jumbleberry? Whatever those are, they're a little tart."

"Yeah, we probably should have added more sugar. Sadie can be heavy-handed in that department, though, so I tried to hold her off."

"Could use a little Cool Whip."

"Could it now? Wow. Tough crowd today."

Ethan grinned. "Just being honest. I take my duties as the official taste tester very seriously."

"Yeah, don't make me sorry I appointed you to the position."

"Tisha, order up."

She turned and lifted an omelet with a side of hash browns and sausage links from the service window. "Enjoy the rest of your pie."

His gaze lingered a little longer than it probably should as she walked away. Maybe it was the sway of her ponytail that matched her bouncy steps. Or the way she'd bantered with him. He hadn't expected that. Or the pie. His phone hummed again before he could take another bite. This time it was a call.

Uh-oh. Brody's school. "Hello?"

"Hi. May I speak to Ethan McGuire, please?"

"This is he."

"Ethan, this is Aaron Price over at the elementary school."

"Aaron. Hey. What's up?"

"I'm glad to hear that you're back in town. Um, listen, I'm going to need you to come by the school."

"Sure, what time?"

"How about now? Your son Brody's been involved in a conflict."

"You've got to be kidding me." He sighed. "All right. Thanks for letting me know. I'll be there in a couple of minutes."

Ethan ended the call, then fished a few bucks from his wallet and tucked them under a plate. Shoot. He hated to run out, but he had to get to Brody.

The dour gray sky matched his mood as he made the short drive to Brody's school. Maybe he should've asked Aaron a few more questions. What kind of a conflict? A fist fight? Had anyone been hurt? Surely Aaron would've mentioned any severe injuries. Right? Or had he been vague on purpose so Ethan wouldn't panic?

He pulled up in the parking lot and snagged the closest empty space. Adrenaline surged through his veins as he jogged toward the school's entrance, then jabbed the buzzer at the door.

"May I help you?" A woman's voice came through the intercom.

"Ethan McGuire. Mr. Price called and asked me to come by."

"Come on into the front office, Mr. McGuire."

The door unlocked. He pulled it open and hurried inside. The smell of cafeteria-style pizza greeted him. Probably the same stuff he'd eaten years ago.

Aaron met him at the entrance to the office. In his

three-quarter-zip pullover, chinos, and lace-up brown dress shoes, Ethan barely recognized his former classmate. He wore his salt-and-pepper hair close-cropped, and fine lines crinkled at the corners of his blue eyes when he smiled.

"Ethan, it's great to see you, my man."

Ethan shook his outstretched hand. "Wish it was under different circumstances."

"We'll get this all worked out." Aaron headed down a short corridor. "Come on into my office so we can chat for a minute."

Oh, he did not like the sound of that. A young girl, probably six or seven years old, sat on a sofa across from the assistant's desk. She kicked her heels against the furniture, and he guessed from the blotches on her cheeks that she'd been crying. She held a damp paper towel on her palm.

"I can't believe you're the principal," Ethan said as he took one of the open seats across from Aaron's mahogany desk.

"Yeah, sometimes I can't believe it either." He gestured to the framed diplomas on his wall. "It's been a journey, but I'm glad to be here and grateful to give back to the community. I wouldn't be who I am without the people in this town."

"Same." Ethan rubbed his palms on his jeans. "So, what happened?"

Aaron sat down in his leather chair. "I'll bring Brody in in just a minute. He's sitting in the other room with our school counselor. I had to keep the kids separated."

Ethan swallowed hard. "Kids? How many were involved?"

"Just two. The little girl that you walked past—she and Brody got into it. I was going to ask you to bring me up to speed with what's been going on at home, but I think I'll let him tell you the story first. Hang on."

Oh boy. Ethan dragged his hand across his face, then leaned forward and rested his elbows on his knees.

Aaron stepped out of the office and then returned a couple minutes later with Brody trailing behind him.

Brody flopped down in the chair beside Ethan and stared at the floor.

"Hey, buddy, what happened?"

"She started it, Dad."

Huh. Interesting. Ethan shifted toward his son and draped a protective arm on the back of the straight-backed chair. "Start from the beginning, and tell me exactly what happened, please."

"Daisy or Sadie or whatever her name is. I didn't mean to call her the wrong name. I didn't know I'd said the wrong thing. But she got mad and she kicked me really hard, and you've always said to stand up for myself. So I pushed her. Except she fell back and scraped her hand and started to cry, and then I was hosed."

"Whoa, whoa, whoa. What do you mean she kicked you?"

Brody pulled up the cuff of his black jeans, revealing a nasty, swollen bruise already turning red and purple on his shin.

Ethan sat up, flames licking at his insides. He gave Aaron a pointed look. "You need to call that little girl's dad."

"That's going to be impossible seeing as how he's no longer with us." Tisha stood in the doorway of Aaron's office, her hands clamped on a petite blonde girl who looked every bit as angry as Brody.

No. No way.

His mouth ran dry. Pie lady was her *mom*?

A few minutes ago, he'd been sitting at the café, thinking pie lady just might be a bright spot in a foggy, frustrating return to Redemption. She'd smiled. They'd chatted. She'd asked him to be a taste tester.

Meanwhile her daughter had kicked Brody in the shin.

"I haven't seen your daughter's hand, but I bet it's nothing like that bruise on his leg. What's she doing kicking people like that?"

She tipped her chin up. "What's your son doing shoving little girls?"

"Okay, okay." Aaron stood and held up both palms. "Folks, let's take it down a notch. It sounds like there was a bit of a misunderstanding. Sadie, you go first. What would you like to say?"

"He didn't call me the right name. I'm *not* named after a flower." Sadie glared at Brody, then stomped her foot.

"Don't stomp, sweetheart," Tisha said softly. "That's not polite."

"Neither is kicking someone," Ethan said.

Her frigid glare turned downright glacial. He refused to look away.

"I didn't know," Brody said, thrusting both hands in the air. "All you had to do was tell me, 'Hey, my name's Sadie.' Simple as that."

Ethan covered his mouth with his hand to hide his smile. Brody's pragmatic approach deserved a high five, but something told him he'd better keep a lid on his praise. For now.

"Everyone's names are written in like three places in our classroom plus mine's on my desk in huge letters," Sadie said, spreading her hands wide.

Brody pressed his lips together and ducked his head.

The defeated posture planted a hollow ache in Ethan's stomach. Was Brody ashamed?

Tisha shifted her attention to Aaron. "There has to be a way we can work this out."

"I agree." Aaron ran his finger across his laptop's touch pad to wake it up. "We have instituted something here called restorative practices."

Ethan laughed.

Aaron shot him a look. "Is there a problem?"

"Restorative practices? What does that mean? We used to empty trash cans. Or wipe down the whiteboards. What happened to writing sentences?"

"I don't feel that extra chores will resolve the deeper issue here," Tisha said.

He had no words. This couldn't be the same woman who'd just low-key flirted with him until he agreed to taste her random pie. Could it? Where did that woman go?

When he didn't respond, Tisha cleared her throat. "Mr. Price, Sadie and I are happy to be part of the solution."

"Yeah, I'll bet," Ethan scoffed. "Maybe you can bake us all more pie."

She cut him a murderous look.

Okay, so maybe he could've kept that last part to himself.

Aaron turned away from his computer and rested his hands on top of his desk. "In case you're not familiar, *restorative practices* means we bring both students and their guardians in for a series of meetings."

Ethan groaned. "Seriously? And what are we going to talk about at these 'meetings'?" He made air quotes with his fingertips.

A muscle in Aaron's jaw twitched. "The intent is to foster teamwork, collaboration, problem-solving, and working through our big feelings."

"Yeah, no, we're out. Come on, bud." Ethan gently tugged on Brody's sweatshirt sleeve, then stood. He gritted his teeth to keep from saying anything he'd really regret later.

Aaron stood and rounded his desk. "Where are you going?"

"We're not into that. At all. My son did nothing wrong." He glared at Tisha. "Excuse us, please."

Her mouth dropped open, but she and Sadie moved aside to let him walk by.

The administrative assistant frowned at him from behind her post at the front desk. "Sir, you can't just leave with your child."

"I can't? Why not? He's mine." Ethan looked at Brody. "Do you have your stuff?"

Brody nodded, his eyes wide with disbelief. Then he hurried

to the sofa and scooped up his backpack, probably from the same place where he'd flung it when they sent him to the office.

"Ethan, wait." Aaron came out into the corridor. "We need to talk about this."

"No, we don't." Ethan guided Brody toward the exit. "I said all I need to say."

"Good." Brody slung his backpack onto his shoulders. "I didn't want to be here anyway."

Warning bells clanged in Ethan's head. Was he doing the right thing? Together they walked out to the Suburban in silence. Maybe this wasn't the best coping strategy, but he'd made the decision and now they had to own it. So much for helping his son fit in.

He got in the car and started the engine. Brody climbed in the passenger side, dropped his backpack at his feet, then slumped against the seat.

Ethan looked at him. "Want to talk about this?"

Brody shook his head. "I'm never going back there, and you can't make me."

 Three

S O HOW WAS SCHOOL TODAY?" MELINDA PASSED a basket of dinner rolls to Tisha. Sadie ducked her chin, her long hair drooping. Tisha looked at Melinda and shook her head, then gently corralled Sadie's hair into a ponytail, letting it swirl down her back. If she could just get through the meal without talking about the disastrous meeting at the school, then maybe she could figure out what to do next.

"Uh-oh." Tom's brows scrunched together as he ladled beef stew into his bowl. "What happened, pumpkin?"

Tisha's stomach growled. Melinda's savory beef stew and homemade dinner rolls smelled incredible. The classical music streaming from a speaker on the kitchen counter, the vanilla candle flickering in the center of the table, and the fire crackling in the woodstove made her feel, well, made her feel at home. Almost. The cozy vibes nearly blotted out her unfortunate interaction with Ethan and Brody—and Mr. Price.

"Here, you have to try one." Tisha took a roll and set it on Sadie's plate. "They are scrumptious."

Frowning, Sadie rested her cheek against Ollie's back. He didn't usually make an appearance at meals, but Tisha let it slide. The poor kid needed a little grace today.

"I see you have some bandages on your hands there," Melinda said. "Want to tell me about what happened?"

"That dumb Brody can't get my name right," Sadie huffed, setting Ollie aside.

"Whoa, whoa, whoa. He is not dumb. And also, there's more to the story." Tisha slathered the dinner roll with butter, which melted and dripped down the edge of the crusty surface. She couldn't resist; she dunked it in her beef-stew broth and quickly took a bite. So good. Warm and buttery, with a little salt from the broth.

How nice to be able to enjoy her mother-in-law's cooking again. She could hold her own when it came to baking, but fixing satisfying meals proved to be a challenge. Chase had always been so patient and complimentary about her cooking. His kindness was one of the many things she missed about him.

Sadie chased a chunk of beef around in her bowl with her fork. "Because of him, I had to go to the principal's office."

"You know, your dad was no stranger to the principal's office, although a different principal." Melinda squeezed a slice of lemon into her iced tea. "We had a few meetings about behavior-modification strategies, didn't we, Tom?"

Tom nodded. "We sure did. Sadie, pass the butter when you're finished, please?"

Tisha dabbed at her mouth with her napkin and helped Sadie butter her roll. "He never told us that."

Tom chuckled. "No, I'm sure he didn't, but he and those McGuire boys kept things interesting."

Tisha paused. "Really? Chase and Luke got into trouble?"

"Oh, yes." Melinda added a few apple slices to the edge of Sadie's plate. "They were always up to something, and Chase, believe it or not, would often take the blame for things that Luke had done."

"No way." Sadie glanced up at Tisha, a questioning look in her eyes, then pinched off a little corner of her roll.

Tisha gave her a helpless shrug. They'd have to talk about that later. "What—um—what do you know about Luke's older brother, Ethan?"

Oh, she had to tread carefully here. She avoided Tom's inquisitive gaze and focused on her stew. Ethan had been so nice and sweet and charming at the café but turned into a jerk an hour later.

"Let's see, Ethan has been away for several years. Coast Guard helicopter pilot, I believe. He and Brody moved back to town right before Christmas."

"Yeah, we know." Sadie blew out an exasperated breath. "Brody is the boy who pushed me, knocked me right down, and then said it was my fault."

"Brody is also the boy who has a nasty bruise on his leg because you kicked him, right?"

Tisha could see Tom trying not to smile.

"Oh dear, that sounds messy." Melinda reached for the basket of rolls. "Are you and Brody having trouble getting to know each other?"

"He called me Daisy."

"Sadie, we've talked about this," Tisha said. "I don't think he did it on purpose, honey. It sounds like he really thought that was your name."

"It's spelled out everywhere, Mama. S-A-D-I-E. How did he mess that up?"

"Maybe he's having a hard time with his letters," Melinda said.

"Everyone in my grade should be able to read by now, Grandma." Sadie stacked two small slices of carrot from her stew and popped them into her mouth.

"That's not necessarily true. Everybody learns at their own pace. It's an honest mistake. I know it really bugs you," Tisha added, "but that's no reason to kick him."

"He just makes me so mad."

"Well, I can relate to that," Tisha said, her mind drifting back to the heated exchange with Ethan. "When people treat us poorly, it's very upsetting."

"Oh no." Melinda set her fork down. "Was someone rude to you at the café?"

"No, the café was fine." She tamped down more thoughts about Ethan's smile and the way he'd teased her about signing a waiver. "I didn't care for the way Brody's dad reacted today in the principal's office."

She didn't miss the glance that Melinda and Tom exchanged.

Tom leaned forward, concern etched in his expression. "I didn't realize you and Ethan had to see Mr. Price as well."

"Oh yeah, all four of us got called in. We're supposed to participate in restorative practices. It's the latest thing. Keeps kids from being suspended unnecessarily, I guess. Anyway, Sadie and I are more than happy to participate."

"What? I'm not happy." Sadie reached for Ollie and clutched him to her chest. "I'll only go because you tell me that I have to. Can I be homeschooled? That was so much easier."

True. Sighing, Tisha balanced her fork on the edge of her bowl. "Sweet pea, homeschooling worked well in North Carolina when we lived on the farm, but now that we're here, this is a great school."

"It doesn't feel great. It's kind of a disaster," Sadie said.

Melinda couldn't stifle her laugh.

Tisha shot her a warning look. "Work with me here."

"I'm sorry." Melinda held up her hand. "It is a great school. Your daddy went there; Brody's daddy went there. I'm sure you have an excellent teacher, and we've known the principal, Mr. Price, for ages. He grew up here, played basketball with Luke and Ethan in high school. We love his family."

Sadie was not having it. "All I know is that homeschooling was easy. I learned a lot. I'm a great reader. I can write. Math is fun for me. And there was way more time to play and see my friends."

"Well, we're making a fresh start here." This was a hill Tisha would die on if she had to. She stabbed a bite of meat with her fork. "I want to work at the café, and you need to go to school. It's going to be fine. You and Brody will work this out."

"Well, not if Brody's daddy isn't gonna obey."

That got Tom and Melinda's attention.

Melinda reached for her iced tea. "What do you mean?"

"He walked out of the meeting," Tisha said. "He's pretty miffed. I don't think he's into the principal's plans." The set of that angular jaw, the way his stunning eyes flashed, his insistence that he speak to Sadie's dad—it had gotten under her skin for sure. But then she'd taken a look at Brody's shin and her heart had given a little bit. She'd probably be upset too if her kid had the bruise that Brody had. Sadie must've kicked him hard.

"Sadie, as soon as you finish your dinner, I'll take you into the other room and show you some old family videos of some things that your daddy and those McGuire boys got up to," Tom said. He shook his head, though she could see the grief still clinging to the edges of his expression.

"Chase and Luke were the best of friends, weren't they?" Tisha asked.

Melinda nodded and gave her husband's arm a gentle squeeze. "They had a lot of good times together, got themselves into a few scrapes, but the McGuires truly are wonderful people, and they've worked so hard to make that resort a successful business. We're thankful for the tourists it draws to town, and they're passionate about making sure Redemption is the kind of place where people want to raise their families."

Who could argue with that? Tisha kept her snarky commentary about Ethan to herself.

After the meal was finished and Tom took Sadie into the other room as promised, Tisha helped Melinda clear the table.

"That's nice of him to watch those videos with her. I bet this is hard."

"Well, it's good for him. Helps him work through his grief. And if you don't mind my saying so, I think it's good for Sadie to know that her dad made mistakes. If she sees Brody's dad and his uncle in our videos, maybe she'll understand that our families have been connected for decades."

That was the part that made her nervous. Tisha turned away and cleared some more plates from the table.

"You know, Tisha, I really believe that God brought you here for a reason. Your pies are going to be a huge hit."

"Yeah, about that." Tisha winced. "I probably shouldn't have served Ethan something that I made here in my own kitchen."

"Oh"—Melinda waved her off—"don't worry about it. I think your next batch of pies probably should be made in a kitchen that's been inspected by the health department, but you're already bringing new ideas and fresh recipes. And if pie helps you connect with Ethan McGuire, then I'm all for it."

She nearly dropped the plate and bowl in her hands. "Excuse me?"

"Your stories are similar. He lost his wife; you lost your husband. You both are here trying to raise your kids. And Sadie and Brody will have to work this out. All I'm saying is God brought you here for a reason. Don't be surprised by how He uses pie and a kid who thinks your daughter's name is Daisy to work out His good plans. You know, the ones that are for our good and for His glory."

Tisha scraped the plates off into the trash, then faced Melinda. "What are you saying?"

"Chase isn't with us anymore. You've come to Redemption for a second chance, and we love that you're here. But maybe it's time to let your heart open a little too."

A butter knife slipped from her hand, then clattered on the floor. "I—I don't want anyone else but Chase."

"I understand that." Melinda retrieved the knife and tucked it into the dishwasher. "But that little girl in there might need a daddy. As much as you're trying to keep Chase alive, he's not here anymore."

Tisha stared at her. "Are you suggesting—"

Melinda held up her hand. "All I'm saying is that God's in charge, and it's okay for you to move on."

"No, I'm not going to do that. I love Chase and there will never be anyone else." Tisha turned back to the table to clear the rest of the plates, but part of her didn't want to admit that she'd been tempted to flirt with Ethan. Their banter, her determination to find his ideal pie flavor—it was kind of embarrassing knowing that she'd been enjoying her time with him while their kids were duking it out on the playground.

She hadn't come here to fall in love. Stories about Chase, old family photos, videos—so what if there were McGuires in the background? She wanted Sadie to know that this town had meant everything to Chase, and she had promised her husband that Sadie would have the childhood he'd intended for her. And now, more than ever, she had to double down on her determination. No matter how handsome Ethan McGuire looked when he took his seat in the café.

Wow, okay. So that meeting with Aaron had not been his finest moment. Ethan bounced the basketball on the floor in the shed, savoring the familiar sound of the parquet floor squeaking under his sneakers. He launched the ball, loving the feel of the worn nubs as it brushed his fingertips. It sailed through the air, clanged off the rim. Man, he couldn't make a basket for anything tonight.

Thoughts of Tisha's piercing blue eyes and her proud smile as she set a slice of jumbleberry pie in front of him contrasted sharply with her anger as she stood in the doorway of Aaron's office. Shame had flickered in Brody's eyes when he dipped his head, embarrassed that he had messed up saying Sadie's name. It didn't matter what had happened between himself and Tisha. What mattered was his son and getting to the bottom of his issues at school.

The ball rolled to a stop beside Brody, who was sitting against the wall, absentmindedly rolling his skateboard back and forth with one hand while he watched a video on Ethan's iPad.

"Hey, bud. Wanna come play ball?"

"In a minute." Brody didn't even look up from the screen. Ethan sighed. Okay, yeah, he wasn't proud of how he'd walked out of the school today, except part of him was. Tisha might have disagreed with his old-school ideas, but extra chores were the things that he and Luke and Chase had to do when they got in trouble back in the day. Sitting around talking about their big feelings? Blech. No, thanks. He crossed the court and scooped up the basketball, peeking at the screen. "What are you watching?"

"I want to build a skateboard ramp."

Ethan opened his mouth to protest.

"Check it out. This video makes it look easy."

Ethan wiped at the sweat on his forehead with the hem of his faded Redemption High School T-shirt. "Uh-huh, and where do you want to build that?"

"In here, obviously. There's too much snow and ice outside."

"Right." He scooped up the ball. "Come on, come shoot with me."

"Dad, I don't really like basketball."

"I know, but I do, and I'm trying to spend some time with you. Would you rather play badminton? Or I can go find Grandpa. He'll play Sorry! with us, but I promise we'll lose. Grandpa's the Sorry! champion around here."

Brody shook his head. "I don't feel like losing. I had enough of that today."

"Yeah, you and me both." Ethan walked back onto the court, stepped inside the key, then put up an easy shot. The ball swished through the net. Finally.

When he grabbed the ball and turned around, Brody had joined him. He gently sent the ball to Brody in a bounce pass. Brody caught it, dribbled a few times. Huh. So he did know what to do with a basketball. Brody stared up at the rim, his little brow furrowed, paused, bent his knees slightly, and launched a shot.

"Whoa!" Ethan stared. The kid had perfect form. The ball arced through the air, bounced off the center of the square on the backboard, and dropped effortlessly through the net.

"Nice shot, kiddo. That didn't look like somebody who doesn't like basketball."

Brody shrugged. "When you were away working, Mom would take me down to the park. Sometimes the skateboard half-pipe was too crowded, or if the kids there were mean to me, she'd grab a basketball instead."

"Kids were mean to you?" Ethan picked up the ball and wedged it against his hip as Brody shrugged.

"Lots of times. Don't worry, I didn't push anybody or get in any fights."

"No, I'm sure you didn't." Adeline would've told him about that, right?

"So Mom would—she always had a basketball in her trunk. She'd take me over to the courts and we'd shoot around. It was fun. She was good at it."

"Huh." Ethan retrieved his water bottle from the spot where he'd tucked it behind the basketball stand.

"Hey, Dad, watch this. I'm gonna take another shot."

"All right." Ethan passed him the ball, then took a long sip of his water.

Brody snatched it, then launched another easy shot from inside the key. He was very close to the basket, but it was a full regulation-height rim. The ball slid through the hoop with a *swish*.

Not bad for an eight-year-old.

"So, what do you like about skateboarding?"

"It's fun, and kind of dangerous." Brody collected the ball, dribbled a couple of times, and then handed it back to Ethan.

"And basketball's . . . what?"

"It's fine, I guess." He glanced down, squeaking the toe of his shoe on the court a few times.

"But what do you not want to say?"

"I don't really get the strategy. Being on a team looks fun, but I don't know. I'm just not into it."

"I get it." Ethan tossed up an easy shot. Thankfully, it went in. The ball bounced away. Brody moved to go get it for him.

"Wait, hold up, son. Is there anything you want to say about what happened today?"

Brody shook his head. "Anything *you* want to say?"

Ethan sighed. "I, uh, feel like I set a bad example walking out like that."

"Yeah, Mr. Price is probably gonna tell you that was disrespectful."

"You're right. He probably will. So, what happened with Sadie? I mean, does her side of the story match up with yours? Why did you call her the wrong name? Were you trying to tease her?"

"No," Brody said, looking horrified. "I didn't know that was her name. And what's wrong with Daisy? I've met people named Daisy before."

"Well, her name's Sadie, and I guess she doesn't like it when people get it wrong."

"It happens though. I do it a lot, actually." Brody stuffed his hands into the front pocket of his hoodie.

The hair on the back of Ethan's neck prickled. "You do what?"

"Mix up my letters." Brody looked away.

Ethan moved closer and sank down on his heels. "Brody, are you having a tough time at school?"

Brody wouldn't look at him. Ethan reached out and gently placed his hand on his shoulder, panic arcing through him. Adeline had tried to talk to him about this more than once, and Ethan had always conveniently left it up to her to handle. His heart hammered in his chest. "Brody, can you read?"

Brody's chin wobbled. He shook his head slowly, and a tear tracked down his cheek. He angrily swiped it away.

"Oh, bud, come here." He opened his arms, and Brody ran into his embrace, his body trembling. Shame washed over him—a rogue wave of embarrassment and regret. What kind of a dad didn't know that his eight-year-old couldn't read?

"It's all right. I love you, bud." He just held him tight and let him cry. "We're going to get this figured out. I promise. I'm going to fix this."

Brody pulled away, wiping away the tears. "You can't fix it. That's the thing. You just can't."

He turned and kicked the ball away. Ethan stood, finding Luke and Aaron Price standing in the doorway. When did they come in?

"Hey. How about you come over to the woodshop with me and we, uh, take a look at what's stashed in there?" Luke said. "I bet I've got pretty much everything we need to build you a ramp."

"A ramp? Really, Luke?" Ethan braced his hands on his hips. "How'd you know he wanted one?"

"Because he's been talking about it for a week," Luke said.

"Do you mean it?" Brody sniffed and looked at Ethan. "You said no skateboarding in here."

Ethan hesitated. "Why don't you go with Uncle Luke? If anybody can build you a skateboard ramp, it's him. Let me talk to Mr. Price, okay?"

Brody gave Aaron a sidelong glance. "Am I in trouble?"

Aaron smiled. "No. You're not the McGuire I came to speak to about their behavior."

"Good. See you later, Mr. Price."

Aaron held out his hand, and Brody slapped it, then followed his uncle out of the shed. Aaron walked across the court, retrieved the ball, and dribbled it slowly as he moved toward the basket. When he got to Ethan, he picked up the ball.

"How about a quick game of H-O-R-S-E? You first."

"I'm a little tired for H-O-R-S-E, but I'll take you on in a game of P-I-G." Ethan shrugged, went to the top of the key, took a shot, swished. "So, what brings you by?"

"Seriously, man? I knew you were too stubborn to come back to the school, so I came to you." Aaron draped his jacket over the base of the hoop. He wore a long-sleeve shirt under a fleece vest, paired with black joggers and trendy basketball shoes.

Ethan scooped up the ball. "Yeah. That's fair."

"What happened?"

"What do you mean, what happened? Dude, my kid can't read."

Aaron's jaw dropped. "What?"

"That's why he called her the wrong name. He can't read."

"All right. Pieces are starting to fall into place, but hold up. That doesn't mean you two can get out of this."

"Why not? We didn't do anything wrong."

Aaron made the shot and passed him the ball. "We have to think big picture, friend. These kids have to learn to work out their conflict instead of getting suspended. And you and Mrs. Binford can be adults about this and show each other that you can resolve your differences too."

Ethan rolled his eyes.

"Yeah. The eye-rolling tells me that you need some work."

He bit back a snide comment, then launched a jump shot from the top of the key. The ball clanged off the front of the rim. Bummer.

Aaron chased down the ball, then sank an effortless shot. He grinned. "Show me what you've got, Clutch."

Ethan mimicked Aaron's position on the court, then shot the ball. It clanged off the rim again. Aaron lunged and grabbed it before it rolled across the room.

"You've got a P and an I there, my guy," Aaron said. "I know you don't like to lose. Lost your touch?"

Ethan glared at him. "Hardly."

Aaron took the ball to the hoop for an easy layup. "If you don't mind my asking, how did you figure out that Brody couldn't read?"

"I asked him."

"You didn't have any idea?" Aaron frowned. "You strike me as a hands-on dad."

"Because I have to be." Ethan grabbed the rebound and made a layup.

Finally.

"To be honest I wasn't around much until I retired from the Coast Guard. My wife's been gone a little over a year. She handled everything, and I do mean everything, when it came to Brody."

"Yeah. I'm sorry about your wife. What was her name?"

"Adeline."

Aaron held the ball in both hands, then nodded. "I bet she was a great mom."

"Yeah, she was."

"Well." Aaron bounced the ball once. "You're here, you've got a whole community around you and your incredible family, so we need to work together—not only to get Brody back on track but to get you to work through your big feelings."

Um, no thank you.

"What do you say, Clutch? You in? You willing to make this right? Show your son what it means to restore a broken relationship?"

Ethan sighed. "All right, I'm in. I'm sorry for how I walked out of your office today. That wasn't right, and I set a bad example for Brody."

"Apology accepted." Aaron grinned, then stepped back and launched the basketball from behind the three-point line. The ball sailed through the air, then swished through the net. "Now, if you want to win, you'll need to make this next one."

"Why'd you have to nail a three?" Ethan groaned. He hadn't hit one of those all night.

"Game's on the line." Aaron retrieved the ball that had just swished through the net. Again.

"Yeah, well, that's not all that's on the line."

Ethan stepped into the spot Aaron had just vacated, double-checked to make sure his toes were behind the line, and shot the ball toward the rim like he'd done thousands of times. It hit the front of the rim and bounced off.

"Yes!" Aaron pumped his fist in the air, then taunted Ethan with a ridiculous victory dance. "That's P-I-G for you, my friend."

"Your lame dance is a bit much, don't you think?"

"Sorry, I know it's not right to gloat. I'm glad Brody wasn't here to see that."

"Facts." Ethan took a bottle of water from the cooler he'd loaded earlier and handed it to Aaron.

"Clutch, would now be a good time to ask you if you're interested in coaching basketball?"

"What? No. Why would you ask me that?"

Aaron twisted the cap off the bottle. "Because you're a legend around here. Or have you forgotten?"

"Some legend." Ethan scoffed. "I missed a basket at the worst possible time."

The plastic crinkled in Aaron's hand as he took a sip. "We learn our best lessons when we have the courage to bounce back from our failures."

"I feel like that should be a poster on the wall behind your desk."

"Have you always been this mouthy?" Aaron gave him a playful shove. "The reason I'm recruiting you to coach is the winter rec league for basketball starts up soon. I saw Brody nail that shot, so—"

"Breaking news. He told me he doesn't like basketball."

"Well, it'd be a great way for you both to do something together."

"Here's the thing. I don't want to force him to do something he doesn't want to do. If he's struggling in school, mandatory after-school activities aren't the way to go."

Aaron shrugged. "But maybe he'll come around. You'd be coaching a co-ed team—boys and girls. One practice session plus one game a week—low commitment. It's about sportsmanship and working on basic skills."

"How about our big feelings?" Ethan teased. "Will we work on those too?"

Aaron gave him a look. "Don't mock me. This is a serious offer."

Ethan ran his hand through his hair. "I'll think about it, because I certainly owe you one."

"No, you don't owe me anything." Aaron shook his head. "You're an incredible athlete, Ethan. You've had a fantastic career. I know how much Redemption meant to you. I'm just here as your friend and former teammate, offering you a second chance to make things right."

Except that coaching a sport Brody didn't want to play seemed like the worst way to right any of his past wrongs. What if this backfired and drove them even further apart?

Four

H I THERE, I'M NINA STROM, ONE OF THE COUNselors here." A young woman, she probably wasn't even thirty yet, breezed into the room carrying a puzzle. Tisha eyed the box with a picture of puppies frolicking in a flower garden. The woman wore her brown hair twisted into a bun. She had on leggings, ballet flats, and a V-neck T-shirt under a worn cardigan.

"Hello." Tisha smiled, draping her hand over Sadie's shoulder, which Sadie promptly shrugged off. "I'm Tisha Binford, and this is my daughter, Sadie."

"I've met Sadie, Mrs. Binford, but hello. I'm pleased to officially meet you as well," Ms. Strom said.

Tisha glanced at Ethan, sitting across the table beside Brody.

"Mr. McGuire, it's nice to see you again. My brother is a huge fan of yours."

Ethan gave a tight smile. "Thanks. Trent, right? How is he doing?"

"Great. He lives in Nebraska and works for his in-laws on a farm. Seems to be living his best life."

"Glad to hear it. Please tell him I said hello."

Tisha sat back. A huge fan? Of what? She sat up straighter and pasted on a smile. "Sadie and I are ready to do whatever we can to make this work."

Nina's dark eyebrows sailed upward. "Today's session is quite simple. Our goal is to focus on teamwork. Collaboration, I'm sure Mr. Price explained to you, is one of our core values. So you're going to work together on a puzzle. It's only three hundred pieces, and it's brand new, so you're the first ones to try it."

"Oh, I like to be first." Sadie clapped her hands.

Ms. Strom set the box down in front of Brody and Ethan on their side of the table. "Here, Brody, why don't you unbox it? And if there aren't any questions, I'll let you all get to it. I'll be back in an hour to see how things went. In the meantime, if you need me, just poke your head out the door. I'm right down the hall."

"Great, thanks," Ethan said.

Brody lifted the lid and pushed it aside. Then he turned the box over and dumped it out.

"Wow." Ethan frowned. "Those pieces are smaller than I expected."

"Dad, I've done puzzles like a million times." Brody pushed his sleeves up. "It's no big deal."

"I'm glad you're feeling confident." Ethan patted Brody's shoulder. "Why don't we start by finding all the pieces that go around the edge?"

"Or we could let them do the puzzle however they want," Tisha said. Why did he have to be such a taskmaster?

Ethan scrunched his brows together. "It's just a suggestion, Tisha. I like to do the border first. It makes me feel like I've accomplished something."

"Oh, and is that the goal here? To accomplish something?"

He paused, his hand hovering over another piece. "Yes. If I've been assigned a task, I like to complete it."

"See, I like to enjoy the experience and allow my daughter to have a little fun along the way. Do you have something against fun?"

Sadie gave her a strange look.

"What? No, I don't have anything against fun. But we only have an hour, so why don't we work together to finish this puzzle?" He picked up the lid and studied the image. "Puppies. Cute. I like them."

Tisha sagged in her chair. This wasn't going at all how she'd planned. She thought she and Sadie would show up and demonstrate that they were here to be part of the solution. Because, to be honest, she was still a little concerned about how Sadie had overreacted and kicked Brody in the shin. Especially since she wasn't a hundred percent certain that Brody had meant to be mean. Maybe he'd made an honest mistake. She did not want her little girl labeled a troublemaker, that was for sure.

Come on. Focus.

Tisha twisted her wedding rings in a slow circle around her finger. She was spiraling. She had to get out of her own head. Sadie and Brody were turning all the pieces over and chatting about something they'd done in science today that they'd both enjoyed. Well, that was progress. Tisha tried to meet Ethan's gaze and smile, but he was not paying any attention.

She found a couple of pieces that went together to form the border. It looked like grass. Ethan took a piece, reached across, and popped it right into the gap in front of her.

"There." He grinned.

"Um, you could have just handed me the piece."

"Except I could already see where it belonged from here. You're welcome."

She narrowed her gaze. Was he trying to aggravate her? Tom's mention of Ethan's past work filtered through her head. "So, my father-in-law says you had a career in the Coast Guard?"

"Twenty years as a rescue swimmer and then an aviator."

"My dad's an awesome pilot," Brody declared, making a pile of pink and red pieces.

"My dad was a pilot too," Sadie said.

"Well, my dad flies helicopters and rescues people."

"I *used* to rescue people." Ethan added another piece to the sky-blue border on the table in front of him. "Right now, I fly people up to the top of the mountain so they can ski down to the bottom."

"Oh, my dad liked to help people too," Sadie said. "Here, Brody, here's another red piece."

Ethan's phone rang. He plucked it from his pocket, glanced at the screen, then sighed. "I need to take this. Excuse me, please." He left the room.

How about that? He got to leave the meeting to take a phone call. Did she get to take a break and step out if she wanted? Ms. Strom probably made special exceptions for her brother's heroes.

Relax. You're being unreasonable.

She glanced down at her purse sitting by her feet, then noticed she had flour on her jeans. She tried to wipe it off, but it clung to the denim.

"So, Brody, what did your mom do?" The question was out of her mouth before she could snatch it back. Brody looked at her, shock flashing across his face.

"My mom's gone. She's in heaven."

"Yeah, my dad's in heaven too," Sadie said quietly, glancing down at the table.

Oh no. Tisha's stomach sank. How had she squashed all the joy that quickly? "I'm so sorry, Brody. You must really miss her."

Nodding, Brody glanced toward the door. "When's my dad coming back?"

"I'm sure he'll be off the phone in just a minute."

"Good. I don't—we don't—talk about my mom. Hardly ever."

"That's too bad," Sadie said. "We talk about my dad all the time. At the cabin, our new place, there are pictures of him everywhere."

"True," Tisha said. "No shortage of pictures of your daddy. Brody, do you have a favorite picture of your mom?"

Brody shrugged.

Ethan strode back into the room. His eyes flashed and two mottled splashes of red stained his neck. "What are you doing?"

"Excuse me?"

"I heard you asking him personal questions. The kinds of things I'd prefer you not mention because you're going to upset him."

"Dad, it's fine," Brody said. "I'm not upset."

Seriously? She reached for another puzzle piece. "We were just talking, Ethan."

"Yes, about my late wife, whom you've never met. And you barely know my son."

"You were being kind of nosy, Mama," Sadie said.

Whose side was she on? "I'm sorry, Brody."

Brody squirmed in his chair. "I said it was fine. Can we do the puzzle now?"

"Absolutely," Ethan said. "Let's stay on task."

"Completing a task doesn't have to be just about getting the job done," Tisha insisted. "Sometimes conversation can be helpful. Some people feel it's a nice icebreaker."

He stared at her, his expression unreadable.

"What?"

"You have something on your face."

She dug around in her bag for a mirrored compact, then flipped it open and checked her reflection. Oh. So he wasn't messing with her. Flour and a smudge of dried pie-crust dough clung to her cheekbone. She scraped it off with her fingernail, then tucked her compact back in her bag. "You know what?" she said. "I've been thinking, and I'm determined to find the right flavor of pie for you."

"Really? You're asking me about pie right now?"

"Yep." She flashed him a smile. "Because I think a slice of rum raisin would be right up your alley."

"Rum raisin?" Brody said. "Ew, gross. Raisins don't go in pie."

"Sometimes they do. I think we should make your dad a rum-raisin pie."

Ethan shook his head. "I don't want pie. I want us to finish this so we can get out of here."

"On second thought, maybe you need something with prunes or lemons to match your sour mood."

He narrowed his gaze. The tension in the room thickened.

"At this point, it's probably best if you find a new taste tester," he said.

Ouch. She hadn't meant to upset Brody or Ethan. And her attempts at lightening the mood had clearly backfired. She glanced at Sadie, who watched the exchange with a furrowed brow.

Before she could think of a response, Mr. Price entered the room, breaking the uncomfortable silence. Tisha straightened in her seat, grateful for the interruption.

"Hey, how's it going?" Mr. Price craned his neck to see the puzzle. "Looks like you're making progress."

Ethan gave a curt nod in response, focusing on the puzzle pieces in front of him.

Brody beamed up at Mr. Price. "This is fun," he said. "I like it."

Tisha managed a small smile, relieved that the attention had shifted away from her awkward conversation with Ethan. She glanced over at Sadie, who was already connecting more pieces to the puzzle with renewed interest.

Mr. Price gave a nod of approval. "Glad to hear things are going well. Great job, everybody," he said. "I'll check in again before I leave for the day."

"There sure is a lot of checking in," Ethan muttered under his breath.

Tisha shot him a warning look before turning back to the

puzzle. She noticed a piece that seemed to belong near the center and reached for it, only to have Ethan grab it just before her hand landed on it.

"Let me," he said, smoothly fitting the piece into place.

So much for not letting him get under her skin. Tisha suppressed a frustrated sigh and forced herself to keep her composure. She couldn't let Ethan's dismissive attitude ruin the progress they had made with Brody and Sadie. But did he have to be so arrogant?

Man, he could not get out of this school fast enough, especially with his conversation with Kaylee still echoing in his head.

"See you, Sadie," Brody waved.

"Bye, Brody." Sadie pushed her arms into her coat sleeves.

Wow, that was easy. Ethan stared in disbelief as the kids parted ways in the elementary-school conference room. Maybe they didn't need all three sessions? They both acted like they'd forgotten their conflict already. He and Tisha, on the other hand, needed an intervention.

"See you around," Ethan said, waving to Tisha.

"Have a good weekend." Her thin smile sort of implied that she hoped he would find a nail in his tire later. Whatever.

Okay, so maybe he shouldn't have been so snippy with her. But she'd only added to his annoyance with people for prying into his past. Why couldn't Kaylee and Tisha and everyone else just leave him alone?

"How was it?" Aaron stood in the hallway as they all filed out of the room.

"Awesome." Brody slapped Aaron's outstretched palm.

"That's what I like to see. I appreciate the good attitude, my man." Aaron turned toward Sadie and Tisha. "Sadie, what'd you think?"

"It was a fun puzzle, Mr. Price." Sadie smiled. "I love puppies."

"Same." Aaron smiled. "Mrs. Binford? Everything okay?"

"We're just fine, thank you. See you next time." Tisha took Sadie's hand and walked toward the exit.

Ethan stared after her until she left the building. She had an odd definition of *just fine.*

"You good?"

Ethan met Aaron's questioning gaze. "Splendid. Never better."

Aaron hesitated, then gestured toward the gym at the end of the corridor. "Glad to hear that. Walk with me. Basketball tryouts have started. No pressure. Just thought you might want to see what the local seven- and eight-year-old talent pool is like."

"Aaron," Ethan said, tipping his head toward Brody, "he's not a fan, if you catch my drift."

"Understood," Aaron said. "Maybe it's worth having him at least check it out."

"But—"

Before Ethan could finish, Aaron turned to Brody. "Hey, Brody, come on down to the gym. Kids your age are trying out for basketball. It's just for fun. You'll only practice once a week, and then you'll get to play a game. It'll be over in a couple of months."

"That's quite a sales pitch," Ethan said. "Parks and Rec department would be thrilled."

"I'm pretty good with kids, despite what you might have heard."

Brody tugged on Ethan's jacket. "Dad, I don't really want to stay."

"I know." Ethan clapped Brody on the shoulder. "Me neither. But Mr. Price asked us to peek in, so it'll just be a minute."

They stepped into the gym, where boys and girls had been divided up into four groups, one at each of the baskets.

"Wow." Ethan looked around. "New gym?"

"Yep. Had to knock down the old one. Wasn't up to code." Aaron leaned against the wall inside the double doors and tucked his hands into the pockets of his gray slacks. "This is great. Two full courts, bleachers, space nearby for concessions. When the high school teams host a big regional tournament, we can run games over here as well."

"Oh my. Ethan McGuire, is that you?" A woman he sort of recognized stopped in front of him. "I can't believe it. I'd heard you were back. Are you going to coach?"

"Hey, Tammy." Aaron smiled. "I'm just bringing him by, giving him a little behind-the-scenes tour of the league."

"Looks like you've got a great turnout," Ethan said.

"This is our largest group for the seven- and eight-year-olds ever," Tammy said. "At least since I've been volunteering."

"Dad, come on." Brody tugged his arm. "I'm ready to eat."

"Just a few more minutes, I promise. Then we'll go. I know you're hungry."

"Hey, Clutch. I thought that was you." A man Ethan vaguely recognized jogged over. He offered a wide smile and a strong handshake.

"Ethan, you remember my husband, Derek. You probably played against each other in high school. He grew up in Delta."

He couldn't come up with a last name but recalled playing against a kid named Derek from Delta who never missed a free throw. "Nice to see you both."

Derek slid his arm around Tammy's waist. "We're going to coach our son's team. He's seven."

"Good for you." Ethan smiled, but he couldn't ignore the twinge of jealousy that snaked through him.

"Hey, man. Hop in on this drill." Derek motioned for Ethan to join the group of kids on the court. "We're just doing layups. You'll give these kids a great example to model."

"This isn't the best time," Ethan said. Brody sighed and flopped on the floor.

"Can I play with your phone, Dad?"

"Sure." Ethan unlocked his device and handed it over.

Aaron gave him a look that dripped with disapproval.

"Hey, he doesn't like basketball, plus he's hungry and doesn't want to be here. What do you want me to do?"

"I'll hang with him," Aaron said. "Go on. Hop into that drill real quick."

Ethan took off his jacket, left it on the floor beside Brody, then stepped into the end of the line. All the kids stared up at him.

"Hey everybody, this is Ethan McGuire," Derek said. "He played basketball at the high school a few years ago."

Ethan laughed, feeling every bit of his thirty-eight years standing in a gym full of seven- and eight-year-olds.

"He's going to show us how to do a layup." Tammy smiled, then motioned for him to move to the front of the line.

Ethan took the ball Derek passed him, dribbled it a few times, then jogged toward the hoop. He tried to remember his form, laid the ball up onto the backboard, and thankfully it fell through the net.

The kids clapped. It felt good to have somebody cheering him on after his puzzle-building session followed by a tense conversation with Adeline's bestie. He'd needed a little confidence booster.

He went through the line again, shot another layup on the left side of the basket this time, and then gave Derek a polite wave.

"Thanks for looping me in. I appreciate it. I need to get my son home."

"No problem. And your son is welcome to join the league. I'm sure he's a natural," Derek said.

"Yeah. Thanks." He walked off the court.

Grinning, Aaron gave him a high five. "That's how it's done. You ready to coach? With forty-eight kids signed up, they're definitely in need of more parent volunteers."

"I can't commit to that, Aaron. Besides, Brody's not interested."

"Brody," Aaron said, glancing down at him. "You want to try out for basketball?"

"No."

"I saw you last night. Nailed that shot. You look like you were made for hoops."

"Nope." Brody went back to playing a bubble-popping game on Ethan's phone.

"Give him time," Aaron said. "I'm sure you're all still getting situated."

"Yeah, right." Ethan bit back a terse response. For someone who claimed to be good with kids and spent a lot of time with them, he didn't seem to be picking up on Brody's vibe. Or maybe he didn't want to accept that Brody didn't like basketball.

Aaron palmed the top of his head and studied Ethan. "You okay?"

Ethan shrugged back into his coat. "There are some loose ends back in Florida that I still need to tie up. I had kind of a tough phone call a few minutes ago. Guess I'm not in the best headspace for a meaningful conversation."

"I get that," Aaron said. "Hope everything works out, and I'll follow up next week. Ms. Strom and I will compare notes, then let you all know what we have planned for your next session."

"Good. Keep us posted." Ethan motioned for Brody to stand up. "Come on, pal. Let's go."

The warmth of curious stares heated his skin as he and Brody left the building. Man, he'd love to coach. He kind of hated that he was leaving so soon, to be honest, but he'd put Brody through a lot. He couldn't expect him to play a sport he didn't like.

Could he?

His internal frustration over Brody's refusal to join the basketball team mixed with guilt from his phone call with Kaylee. Stubborn didn't even begin to describe Adeline's bestie. She'd assured him she'd come to Alaska if she had to because she wasn't going to let the story fade.

The conversation hadn't ended well. Tisha had aggravated him with her comments about his being a taskmaster over that silly puzzle, so he'd already been irritated when he took the phone call. His tone and word choice had been blunt. Probably a little too blunt, frankly. But the facts hadn't changed. Adeline had been lovely and beautiful and an exceptional human. But why did he and Brody have to share her story now? Why couldn't Kaylee leave them alone?

Brody got in the car and slammed the door. "I'm not playing basketball, Dad. Just so you know."

Ethan gripped the steering wheel with both hands and stared at his son, with his sullen expression and arms linked across his chest. Clearly Ethan wasn't making progress with anybody today.

SMALL GROUP DEVOTED TO GRIEF RECOVERY? *Hard pass. Tried that. Didn't help.*

Tisha crumpled the flyer she'd found tucked inside the church bulletin and tossed it into the trash can on her way out of the sanctuary. She couldn't bear to be surrounded by strangers trying to heal from their losses.

Besides, she'd agreed to spread Chase's ashes soon. Wasn't that a giant leap forward in her grieving process? So a small group was hardly necessary. Sighing, she turned back toward the crowded foyer.

Melinda's gaze pinged between her and the trash can. "Are you all right, honey?"

Tisha nodded. "Not interested in group therapy, that's all."

Pain flashed in Melinda's eyes.

"I mean, I think it's great that the church offers a support group for people going through loss. It's . . . I'm . . . I don't need it."

"I understand. If you change your mind, please know that there are people here who can help you heal." Melinda slipped her purse strap over her shoulder. "Do you have a few minutes to stay for coffee? I'll get Sadie from children's church so you can visit with folks."

Tisha hesitated. Tom and Melinda had been so welcoming, inviting her to church today and helping her get Sadie plugged into the proper class. She scanned the people mingling near the coffee station. It wouldn't hurt to say hello to a few faces she already recognized from their visits to the café.

Except weariness clung to her. Tempted to sleep in this morning, she'd almost skipped the service. But sitting in the sanctuary, where the music washed over her like a soothing balm for her weary soul, she'd leaned over and whispered her humble thanks to Melinda for bringing her along. She'd even dug a pen and highlighter out of her bag and made notes about Job's suffering in her Bible. But now all she wanted was a quiet afternoon spent by the fireplace in their cabin, watching a movie with Sadie.

As she scanned the crowded room, she spotted Luke McGuire walking toward her. Her breath caught in her throat. Memories of him and Chase standing together on the dock, their laughter echoing across the lake, flooded her mind and threatened to bring tears to her eyes.

"Oh, wow." She blinked quickly and tried to smile. "I wasn't quite prepared for the way seeing Luke would stir up thoughts of Chase."

"I'm sure Luke will want to chat and catch up. I'll get Sadie." Melinda squeezed her arm and headed down the corridor, leaving Tisha alone. She locked eyes with Luke. He hesitated, his brow furrowed, then he worked his way toward her, pausing to speak with people as he passed them. When he finally stood in front of her with open arms and a wide grin on his face, she couldn't help but smile back. But as they hugged, more memories rushed in.

Luke had spoken at Chase's memorial service and been by her side throughout that whole nightmare. She'd never be able to thank him enough for all he'd done for her and Sadie. Despite the warmth of their reunion, she couldn't shake off the sadness.

"McDowell, what's up?"

She leaned back and looked into his familiar face, trying to read any hint of the pain she had seen before. But all she saw was the same carefree, adventurous Luke she remembered from their last Christmas visit with Chase. He seemed genuinely happy to see her.

"Hey, Luke. It's so good to see you."

"It's great to see you too, Tisha. Welcome back to Redemption."

"Thanks."

His smile faltered. "Sorry it's taken me a whole week to say hello. I popped into the café a couple of times, but you weren't there."

"No problem. I hit the ground running as soon as I got here. I'm sure you're busy too."

"Yeah, we've been slammed with new clients this month, which is a huge blessing. It's great for business, but Ethan and I have been flying skiers and snowboarders into the backcountry almost every day." Luke tucked his hands into the front pockets of his vest. "Have you had a chance to meet my older brother yet?"

She nodded, hiding her frustration behind a forced smile.

"Oh, right." Luke's mouth twitched. "Brody and Sadie."

"Hey, why are you trying not to laugh?" She playfully nudged his shoulder. "What's so funny?"

"I heard about the . . . scuffle," Luke said. "Don't stress. My brother's got a lot on his mind. He'll settle down."

"Tisha Binford?" A young woman with an edgy pixie cut and a buffalo-plaid scarf wrapped around her neck interrupted. She wore a gray sweater, jeans, and short black boots. Tisha didn't recognize her, but her friendly smile and bright green eyes put her at ease.

Thankfully, Luke stepped in. "Tisha, have you met Chloe Sullivan yet? She chairs the committee planning our Love Is in the Air festival."

"Which is coming up in less than a month," Chloe said. "I

overheard someone in the coffee shop talking about your pies, Tisha, so that's why I wanted to speak with you."

"Uh-oh." Tisha pulled a face at Luke.

"Only good things, I'm sure," he said, smiling reassuringly.

"Instead of our usual cake walk, we're thinking of doing a pie walk during the festival. It's actually a fundraiser for the church. We're raising money for new playground equipment for the preschool." Chloe pulled her phone from her oversized berry-red handbag. "What do you think?"

Tisha rubbed at the tightness in her chest. "What do I think about the church preschool?"

Chloe's manicured nails glistened as she tapped against her phone's screen. "No, about baking pies for the fundraiser. We'd only need a dozen or so."

Oh boy. The last thing Tisha needed was another commitment. "I just moved here a week ago, plus I'm a single mom with a part-time job. So I'm afraid I can't serve on a committee right now."

But Chloe didn't even bother looking up from her phone. "We don't need you to join the committee. We just need your pies. Twelve will work, but twenty-four would be even better."

Tisha's breath hitched. "Twenty-four?"

Luke leaned in, his voice lowered to a conspiratorial whisper. "You should know that Chloe doesn't take no for an answer."

"Sure don't." Chloe grinned, then waved her phone in the air. "If you give me your number, I'll send you all the details."

Tisha hesitated. It was hard to say no to a church fundraiser. Especially one that raised money for playground equipment. Besides, what were twelve more pies on top of what she already baked for the café? "I—I suppose I could help out. Pies are my superpower. But I'm afraid twelve is my limit, and I'll have to double-check with the Binfords first. It's their café and their ingredients."

"Understood." Chloe's dangly earrings sparkled in the overhead light as she tipped her head to one side. "So what's the best email address and number to reach you?"

Tisha sighed, then reluctantly gave up her contact information.

"Excellent." Chloe dropped her phone into her bag. "Great to see you both. Have a wonderful day."

"Oof." Tisha shook her head as Chloe weaved through the crowd, then left the church. "She's good."

"Sure is," Luke said. "We wouldn't have a festival without her. My folks think she'll be running for mayor before long."

Before she could comment, Brody and Sadie came racing around the corner, both laughing, each with a paper in one hand and a coat in the other.

"Uncle Luke, look!" Brody thrust a piece of artwork in his face. "I made this."

"Hey, big guy." Luke sank to his knees and took the paper from Brody. "What do you have there?"

"Hey, you're Mr. Luke!" Sadie stopped, smiling up at him. "My daddy's friend."

Tisha's heart pinched.

"You're right." Luke patted her on the head, then offered Tisha a bittersweet smile. "It's nice to see you again, Sadie. Welcome back to Redemption."

"Thanks! Look, Mama. Me and Brody made these." She held up her drawing, her eyes shining.

"Wow. Very nice," Tisha said, studying the colorful picture. "Were y'all in the same class?"

"Uh-huh." Sadie nodded. "And we both knew the Bible story our teacher taught us."

"Well, that's good." Luke stood and looked around. "Brody, how'd you, um . . . how'd you get out of children's church?"

"My dad's here." Brody pointed behind him. "See?"

Sure enough, Ethan stood in the hallway, chatting with someone.

Tisha eyed the exit. Did he have to be everywhere she went? She wasn't in the mood to engage with Ethan right now.

Before she could guide Sadie toward the door, Ethan walked over and joined their group. "Good morning."

"Hey." Tisha's hands grew clammy. She couldn't help but stare at Ethan's sharp jawline and the dimple that appeared in his cheek as he flashed a charming grin at his brother. Ugh. A guy that arrogant didn't deserve to look that good. Their eyes met and she quickly looked away, pretending to be engrossed in the artwork Sadie had thrust into her hands. She couldn't let herself get distracted. She'd moved here to focus on building a new life for herself and her daughter, not to get involved with someone new. But it was hard when Ethan's piercing green eyes seemed to bore right through her walls and elicit a feeling she couldn't quite name. Curiosity? Annoyance? Or maybe something in between?

"We were just telling Tisha here about the Love Is in the Air festival. Sounds like she'll be contributing her pie-baking skills. What are you going to contribute, Big Brother?" Luke asked Ethan, a teasing lilt to his voice.

"Good question. I'll have to get back to you on that." Ethan's gaze found hers again. Softer this time. "Tisha, I'd like to apologize for my behavior during our meeting at the school. I was rude, and I'm sorry."

Oh. Her mouth drifted open. "I appreciate that, Ethan. Thank you." She offered a bright smile. "Apology accepted."

"Great. Thanks." He reached down and ruffled Brody's hair. "Ready for lunch, pal?"

"Yep." Brody trotted toward the door. "Let's go."

"See you later," Ethan said.

"See you." Tisha breathed a sigh of relief as Ethan jogged to catch up with Brody. "Wow, that was unexpected."

Nodding, Luke palmed the back of his neck as he stared after his brother.

She caught another glimpse of Ethan's strong profile as he stopped under the portico outside. Then he turned and met her gaze through the glass front doors.

Yikes. She quickly averted her eyes and gave Sadie's art a closer look. She'd used crayons to draw an airplane flying in the sky with a rainbow overhead and a blue lake below. Chase would've loved it. Tisha swallowed back the lump in her throat. Oh, how she missed her husband. Missed being a complete family. Pushing those thoughts aside, she smiled at Sadie.

"This is beautiful, sweet pea. You're quite the artist."

Sadie beamed up at her, clearly proud of her creation. "Thank you, Mama. I love drawing."

Tisha turned her attention back to Luke, who watched her with a knowing expression.

"You okay?" he asked, his voice gentle.

"Yeah. This move is a much bigger adjustment than I expected, I guess."

"We're glad you're back. Redemption missed having you around."

"I appreciate the warm welcome," Tisha said. "It's going to take some time to settle in, but I'm hopeful things will work out here."

"Mama, I'm hungry," Sadie said. "Can we go soon?"

"In a minute." Tisha threaded her fingers through Sadie's. "I'm almost finished speaking with Mr. Luke."

Luke's phone rang. He pulled it from his pocket and dismissed the call. "Change is never easy, especially with everything you've been through. But you and Sadie will find your place here. And who knows? Maybe getting involved with the festival will help you settle in quicker."

"Hope so." Still, her lingering sorrow over losing Chase collided with her encounter with Ethan. Guilt washed over her. How could she miss her husband so much but then get caught staring at some guy's jawline?

Luke's phone rang again, and he excused himself to take the call. Yeah, okay, so she couldn't pretend the pull toward Ethan didn't exist. But that didn't mean she had to act on it. Because the very last thing she needed was to fall in love with somebody else. And hello—definitely not a pilot.

Maybe getting involved in the festival would be a good distraction, a way to channel her energy into something positive. Maybe it could be a chance to connect with the community and find a sense of belonging in Redemption.

Ethan dug his keys out of his pocket and unlocked the car door. Did he just catch Tisha checking him out? Or was it all in his head? Not that it mattered. Because Brody and Sadie mixed about as well as oil and water. Minus the rare moment of peace when they'd collaborated on the puzzle. Plus, he didn't have the emotional capacity to handle someone who was so cheerful. Though he had to admit, her homemade pie was quite tasty, with its flaky crust and golden topping bursting with—jambleberries? Was that what she'd called them? Were those even a thing? His stomach growled, and he pushed thoughts of Tisha and pie aside.

He had to put Brody first. Had to stay focused on being a great dad and making up for years of working so much. Because he'd let Adeline shoulder far more than her fair share of the parenting responsibilities. Now was not the time to let someone new—like a pretty blonde with a gorgeous smile—distract him.

Thick wet flakes fell from a gray sky and clung to Brody's eyelashes. "Dad, look." He pointed toward a bunch of kids at the edge of the church parking lot, yelling and laughing as they launched snowballs at each other. "Can I play?"

Ethan hesitated. "Are you sure? How many snowball fights have you been in before?"

"None, but it looks fun." Brody handed him his art and two other papers from his church class. Ethan took them and quickly slid them onto the Suburban's dashboard.

"Can I? Please?" Brody hopped up and down. "Promise I won't cry if I get hurt."

Oof. That stung. Since when did Brody think it wasn't okay to cry? Add that to his long list of things he'd mismanaged as a parent.

The metallic smell of winter mixed with the pungent odor of exhaust from cars idling wafted toward them, a far cry from the coconut-scented sunscreen and salty humid air they'd left behind in Florida.

Ethan surveyed the group of kids again. They were probably close to Brody's age. But they'd all bundled up in thick winter coats, hats, and gloves. Brody had put his coat on before they'd left the church, but he had forgotten his hat back at the resort.

Shoot. A deep ache spread through his chest, squeezing like a vise. Adeline would have made sure they had everything they needed. But she wasn't here anymore, and Ethan had to figure things out on his own.

"Okay," he said. "But you have to wear your gloves, and you have to keep them on the whole time."

"I will. They're right here." Brody's face lit up as he tugged his gloves from his coat pockets, then shoved them onto his hands.

"And remember, Grandma and Grandpa are making lunch, so we can't stay long."

"Okay! Tell me when it's time to go!" Brody yelled over his shoulder, then raced toward one of the other boys.

Shaking his head, Ethan laughed, then found his own gray knit hat on the front seat and pulled it on. The art Brody had drawn caught his attention. Ethan peeked at the paper. Brody had drawn the ocean, vibrant waves crashing around stick figures surfing. A family of three stood on the beach next to a chair, and as Ethan squinted, he could make out an umbrella, bright against the otherwise muted colors of sand Brody had scribbled. Wow. He must really miss Florida. And being a family.

He swallowed hard, then pushed the drawing back onto the dash and slammed the door. They'd have to talk about that. Later. Shivering, he tugged his hat down around his ears. There wasn't any point in standing here in the snow, getting cold, and feeling sorry for himself though. He walked toward the building, where he'd be sheltered by the church's portico but could still keep an eye on the snowball fight. Ethan glanced back over his shoulder. Brody had no trouble joining in; he scooped up some snow, formed it into a ball, and launched it at the kids, who'd divided into two teams.

"Boy, he has a good arm, doesn't he?"

Ethan turned to see a familiar face from the basketball rec-league tryouts. *Grant? Greg?* He'd been one of the guys helping out with the kids.

"I'm Grant Stephens, by the way. I have a seven-year-old son who's probably in school with yours. You sure he doesn't want to play basketball?"

"Nice to see you again, Grant." Ethan looked back toward Brody, who'd taken a snowball to the shoulder but still had a smile on his face. "I would love for him to play basketball, but he's made it pretty clear he's not interested."

"How about you? You sure you don't want to coach?"

Ethan stuffed his cold hands into his coat pockets, frustration bubbling beneath the surface. "I do want to coach, actually. Something I always hoped I'd be able to do after I retired from active duty. But that's off the table now that I'm a single dad."

"Well, we've got a roster full of kids who need a coach." Grant smiled. "You'd be a huge asset to the league."

"Here's the thing: I would need space for Brody on my team, even if he doesn't want to play. I can't just foist him off on my parents or my siblings every time I need to be at the gym."

He'd already done way too much of that. Brody's struggles at school might only get worse if Ethan didn't do something. Soon.

Grant nodded. "Makes sense. We automatically put kids on the same team their parents are coaching. So you can bring him to practice with you, even if he just sits on the sidelines and does his homework."

"Appreciate it." A flicker of hope ignited. "This is low-key, right? We focus on fundamentals and teamwork?"

Laughing, Grant clapped him on the shoulder. "C'mon, Clutch. This is a basketball town, remember? When has it ever been low-key?"

Ethan's stomach clenched and he looked over at Brody. He pegged an older boy in the shoulder with a snowball, then high-fived the kid next to him. Three seconds later, they all stood in the snow, the battle delayed. Brody tipped his head back and caught a snowflake on his tongue. So maybe he needed to spend more time around kids his own age.

"All right. I'll coach," Ethan said. "Should I reach out to Derek and Tammy?"

"Nope, I'll take care of it." Grant pulled out his phone. "Let me get your number and email address."

As they exchanged contact information, Ethan felt a swell of anticipation. It would be great to be back on the court, teaching little kids about the sport he'd loved for nearly his whole life.

"Oh, wait, one more thing," Grant continued, pulling Ethan from his thoughts. "The all-alumni scrimmage is coming up. We've timed it with the festival since there'll be more people back in town. What do you say? You wanna play?"

"Sure." Ethan opened the calendar app on his phone. "Remind me of the date again?"

"February sixteenth. I'll send you everything you need to coach in the rec league. Game schedule, waiver, how to complete your background check," he said. "And if you think of anybody else who wants to play in the alumni scrimmage, let me know."

"Yep. Got it." Ethan put his phone away. "See you later."

Just then, the church door opened again and Luke stepped out. "Hey, man. I didn't know you were still here."

Ethan pointed to Brody.

"Ah." Luke nodded. "Kid's pretty good for someone who didn't grow up playing in the snow."

"Yeah. That's what Grant just said. Sometimes he just latches on to things, you know? Wish he'd show the same enthusiasm for basketball."

"Keep trying. You'll find something in common. We didn't like everything Mom and Dad introduced us to. Remember debate club?"

Ethan grimaced. "Don't remind me."

"After I finished catching up with Tisha, I took two back-to-back calls from new clients," Luke said. "I'll give you the updates when we get home. We're booked solid for the next few weeks."

"Sweet," Ethan said. "Hey, can I ask you something?"

"Sure. Make it quick because Mom's going to have lunch ready soon."

"Yeah, I know. I'll give Brody a couple more minutes." Ethan's pulse sped. Luke would probably give him a hard time about this, but he had to know. "Why do you think Tisha's back in town?"

"Same reasons you are, probably. Family, small town, fresh start. Coping with grief. Why?"

Ethan avoided his brother's curious gaze. "I know that you and Chase were close. Thought you might have some insight into why she came all the way to Alaska."

"Oh boy." Luke kicked at a small chunk of ice and sent it skittering across the ground. "You'd have to ask her about all that. It's complicated."

Complicated? Ethan frowned. Not the answer he'd hoped for.

"Not that you asked for my opinion, but if I were you, I'd tread carefully," Luke said quietly. "She's been through a lot."

Ethan pinned him with a look. "I don't know what you're implying, but there's nothing to worry about on my end. Brody and Sadie sometimes struggle with getting along, that's all."

"Looked like they were getting along fine to me."

"For now, they are. It's just . . . I don't know. Things felt different today."

"Different how?" Luke's brow furrowed, concern creeping into his voice.

Ethan shifted from one foot to the other. Maybe he'd misinterpreted the way Tisha had looked his way. Probably best to keep that thought to himself. "They clashed at school, but in their church class, evidently, they got along fine. Can't figure out why."

"Huh." Luke watched the kids throwing snowballs. "Different teacher with different expectations?"

"Maybe." Ethan shrugged. "I guess we'll have to see how our next meeting with the school counselor goes."

"That was nice of you to apologize this morning," Luke said. "Was your last meeting a little rough?"

Ethan huffed out a laugh. "More than a little."

"Tisha puts up a cheerful front, but I bet she's struggling to find her footing here. With the festival coming up, she's got a lot to do working for the Binfords and getting Sadie back on track. Don't be too hard on her, man. You two are really not as different as you think."

Except she was all sunshine and happiness and sugary sweetness. No thank you. Ethan scrubbed his palm over his face. "Well, I just agreed to coach a team of seven- and eight-year-olds, plus you said we're booked out, and Brody's giving me a run for my money. So I'll slog through this restorative-practices thing and try to be on my best behavior." He cupped his hands around his mouth to amplify his voice. "Brody, let's go. Time for lunch."

Brody waved goodbye to the other kids, then trotted toward them and tossed a snowball at Luke's feet.

"Hey, pal, don't you start anything!" Luke lunged for him, and Brody spun out of reach, laughing.

"Wow," Ethan said, "you're brave. You know what happens to kids who throw snowballs at their uncles, right?"

"No," Brody squealed, his eyes wide with feigned horror.

Then Luke picked the boy up and flung him over his shoulder and pretended to toss Brody into the snowbank nearby.

"No, it's cold—don't do it!"

Laughing, Luke settled Brody gently on his feet. "All right, big guy, I'll see you back at the resort. Grandma's got lunch waiting."

"That was fun, Dad! After lunch, can we have a snowball fight with our family?"

Ethan laughed, feeling warmth spread through him at his son's excitement. "We'll see." Was now a good time to tell Brody he wanted to sit down and get some extra practice reading? Brody would probably hate that more than he'd hate shooting baskets in the shed.

They walked toward the Suburban together. Brody kept up a running commentary about his epic battle with the other kids. Ethan tried to pay attention, but thoughts of Tisha's bright blue eyes and her engaging smile clashed with Luke's insight. Although now that he thought about it, when he'd apologized, she had relaxed a little. And that smile had impacted him more than he cared to admit.

As much as he hated to acknowledge his younger brother's wisdom, Luke had been spot-on. He and Tisha had both been through a lot, and they had huge responsibilities. So what if they'd both flirted? That was normal. But it needed to stop. Because he had no business thinking about Tisha when Brody needed all his attention. He couldn't afford to let messy emotions surface now, especially not with Tisha around. She clearly had a ton of baggage.

He had to stick with fixing his own family because he was not going to fail again.

Six

TISHA DONNED HER OVEN MITTS AND OPENED the oven. As she slid the rack out, the rich aroma of golden-baked crust, tart apples, and cinnamon filled the air, making her mouth water.

"Oh my goodness, see? You've got this," she whispered, carefully lifting the pie and setting it on the metal cooling rack.

"Well look at you," Charlie said, coming in from her break and retying her apron. "Wow, that's gorgeous. You really have a knack for this, pie lady."

"Ha, thanks." Tisha grinned, pulling off the mitts and hanging them on the peg on the wall. Steam curled up from the pie. Pulling her phone from her back pocket, she opened the camera app and took a quick photo. She and Melinda had discussed updating the café's social-media accounts—another task Jennifer had managed until she'd left for Wyoming.

Owen gestured toward the fridge. "There's sliced cheese in there if you want to put some on top."

"What?" Charlie made a gagging face. "That's a great way to ruin a good piece of pie."

Grinning, Owen leaned against the counter. "What? You don't put cheese on your pie, Miss North Carolina?"

Tisha wrinkled her nose. "Nope, sure don't."

She headed back out to the café, a flicker of annoyance crossing her mind. Owen's teasing nickname had dampened her mood with thoughts of her complicated beauty-pageant history.

The door swung open, bringing in a gust of cold air. Outside, the wind rattled the building, picking up snow and blowing it across the street. It was howling so fiercely that she could barely see the yellow caution light blinking at the intersection.

"Oh my." She pulled her pen and pad of paper from her apron. "It looks intense out there."

A middle-aged blonde woman sat down at the counter, shrugging off her coat. "They just canceled the evening flight out," she said, resting her elbow on the counter and propping her chin on her hand.

The man beside her unzipped his coat and settled in. "This calls for pie," he said, his brown eyes crinkling at the corners as he smiled. "What are you serving, young lady? I hear you have some new options."

Tisha fumbled her pen, and it slid from her fingers. "I'm Tisha. My late husband was Tom and Melinda's son—oh golly, why did I lead with that?"

Recognition flashed in the woman's eyes.

"I'm Amanda, and this is my husband, Reese. I think we went sea kayaking with you years ago!"

"Yeah, that might have been me." Tisha retrieved her pen from the floor. "I used to come in summers and work as a guide."

"Right, right. That was a fun trip. Not nearly as fun as Hawaii though," Amanda said, her smile fading.

"Oh, are you headed to Hawaii?"

"We were." Amanda frowned. "Since we can't get our flight out of here, we're going to have to rework our plans."

"But not your whole trip, right?" Tisha pressed. "You can't miss Hawaii!"

"We were just going to go to Anchorage a day early and stop at Costco to see the eye doctor. You know, boring grown-up stuff," Reese said.

"Oh yeah, I get that." Tisha drummed her nails on the Formica countertop. "I can't make up for a canceled flight, but nothing says tropical vacation like coconut custard."

"Ooh! You know, I'm normally not into coconut, but you've piqued my interest," Amanda said, her hazel eyes lighting up. "Besides, I heard someone at church talking about how you're going to make the pies for the festival next month, and well, I'm just nosy enough to come over here and see what you've got."

Tisha laughed. "Amanda, I value your honesty. A slice of coconut custard coming right up."

"You know, I'm in the mood for chocolate," Reese said. "What do you have?"

"Well, back in North Carolina, we make something called chess pie."

"I don't like chess," Reese said, frowning.

"Not like that. It's more of a funny expression. Instead of saying, 'It's just pie,' over time it was shortened into chess pie. It's basically just chocolate. And I made my own whipped cream. How about a little dollop of that along with two coffees?"

"Absolutely." Amanda rubbed her palms together. "Sounds delicious."

"Perfect. Be right back." Tisha quickly jotted down the order and tucked her notepad back into her apron.

"I've got the coffee," Charlie chimed in, grinning as she approached. "You've got this, girl. I'm so impressed."

"Thanks," Tisha said, squeezing by her.

The bell on the café's door jingled. A delicious jolt zipped through her. Tisha glanced over her shoulder, hoping for Ethan, but Mrs. Dawkins stepped inside. Oy. She clenched her jaw and headed for the back to fill the order. She hated the ridiculous anticipation. The way her stomach flipped against her will. Why did she care if he came by, anyway? He'd already said she'd have to find a new taste tester. But then he'd thrown her for a loop when he'd apologized after church on Sunday, so now here she was, acting like a giddy teenager.

Get. A. Grip.

Reese and Amanda seemed pretty free with their opinions, so she'd ask them what they thought about these flavors. She hadn't made coconut custard in a long time, but chocolate chess pie? She could whip that up in her sleep. The fresh whipped cream would surely make it a crowd-pleasing favorite.

Finding her pie server, Tisha grabbed the coconut custard and the chess pie, leaving the apple pie to cool a bit longer. The plastic handle felt cool against her warm fingers as she plated the desserts, then retrieved the whipped cream from the walk-in fridge. After adding a generous dollop to the chess pie, she carried both plates out to her new customers.

"All right, y'all, here you go," Tisha announced, placing the plates in front of Amanda and Reese.

"Oh, you said 'y'all.'" Amanda smiled. "That is so cute."

"Thanks." Tisha sighed, a little embarrassed. "I try to eliminate it from my vocabulary, but it creeps back in."

"Why?" Amanda reached for her fork. "There's nothing wrong with the way you speak."

"Well, I feel like most people around here say 'you guys.' Not a lot of 'y'alls.'"

"We're glad you're here," Amanda said warmly. "I'm sure Tom and Melinda appreciate the help."

"I heard you have a daughter," Reese said. "In Miss Johnson's class?"

"Yeah. Oh my gosh—yes—oh no!" Tisha glanced at the clock, panic surging through her. "I'm late for a meeting."

"No worries." Charlie patted her shoulder. "Owen and I will hold down the fort."

"Tisha, this is excellent," Reese said, his mouth full. "What'd you call it?"

"Chess pie," Tisha said, tugging at the knotted strings on her apron. "Chocolate chess pie. The topping is super easy—just whip up some heavy cream and add a little sugar."

"Oh, it's so good," Amanda said, swiping a bite from her husband's plate. "And this coconut custard with this flaky crust? Incredible! I know you have to go," Amanda added, "but man, ten out of ten."

"You should take a picture of this and post it online." Reese nudged Amanda's shoulder with his own. "Spread the word about what's up at the Homestead Café."

"You know what? You're right, sweetie." Amanda dug through her purse until she found her phone. "It's not a Hawaii picture, but I don't care. I'm telling everybody about this! You are the pie whisperer!"

"Thanks, I think," Tisha said. "Charlie, I'm so sorry. I've got to run." She left Reese and Amanda's check beside the napkin holder on the counter.

"It's fine. Sadie needs you. Get to your meeting." Charlie tipped her head toward the back. "See you tomorrow."

"Oh, Tisha, I'm glad you're here." Mrs. Dawkins waved at her from the last stool at the counter. "I want to speak with you about these new flavors you're offering. Have you considered—"

"I'd love to chat, but I'm running late. We'll talk soon." Tisha raced out the back door, sucking in a breath as blustery snow swirled around her. High winds and air so cold it stung her cheeks would take some getting used to.

She hurried to her car, then turned it on to let the engine warm up. She pulled her phone out of her bag. Sure enough, a text message from Aaron Price flashed on her screen.

"Oh no," she groaned. Was he even still at the school? She was half an hour late for the restorative-practices session. Buckling up, she flipped on her headlights. The dwindling daylight and high winds made it hard to see, but thankfully, she didn't have to go far.

As she eased onto Main Street, one of her favorite '90s country songs came on the radio, but she didn't feel like singing along. She turned down the volume, her thoughts drifting back to Sadie. The little girl had been so upset this morning, crying and not wanting to go to school. Tisha had worried that Brody had messed with her again, but no—it was a girl who'd teased Sadie for wearing leggings under her dress. Today, though, Sadie had opted for jeans, sneakers, a T-shirt layered with long sleeves, and a basic ponytail. It broke Tisha's heart that her daughter was already learning to change her appearance to please someone else.

"Oof, a lot to unpack there," she whispered.

Minutes later, she pulled into the nearly empty school parking lot. When she got out of the car, the force of the wind slammed the door shut.

"I'm not built for this," she whispered, tucking her chin deep into the collar of her jacket as she trudged toward the school's entrance. How was she supposed to get in at four fifteen? She buzzed the intercom. *Please, please answer.*

"Hi, may I help you?" A man's voice greeted her.

"Hi, this is Tisha Binford. I missed a meeting, but I still need to pick up my daughter, Sadie."

"No problem, Mrs. Binford. Come on in," he said, and the door unlocked. Tisha stepped inside, taking a moment to look around. She could hear shoes squeaking on the gym floor, basketballs bouncing, and the sound of someone blowing a whistle.

Mr. Price emerged from his office. "Hi there. Everything okay, Mrs. Binford?"

"I am so sorry." Tisha peeked into the room where they were supposed to meet. "I lost track of time."

"Hey, I get that." Mr. Price smiled. "It's great to see you."

"Please forgive me. I got really involved serving pie and chatting with customers."

Oh brother. Could she sound any more scatterbrained? Ms. Strom moved around the room, sliding chairs under the table and collecting a stray marker from the floor.

"What can I do to help?" Tisha eyed the stack of construction paper and container of markers alongside Sadie's backpack slouched against the wall. "Oh, that's Sadie's bag. Where is she?"

"I think she went down to the gym. Brody's dad offered to keep an eye on her until you got here," Ms. Strom said.

"Oh no."

The woman's eyes widened. "Is that a problem?"

"It's fine. Brody's dad is okay. I just…" Tisha hesitated, her heart racing. "He already has doubts about me and—"

"Oh." Ms. Strom offered a knowing smile. "That's all right. I think you'll survive. We'll see you next week, right?"

"Sure. Again, I apologize."

"It's okay. We all make mistakes."

Tisha hurried down to the gym, stepping inside. Her daughter didn't see her, so she leaned against the doorframe. Mr. Price followed her in. "I'm so sorry."

"Really, it's okay." He stood beside her, scanning the activity inside the gym. "Like Ms. Strom said, we all make mistakes. You all right? Weather's nasty out there. We were worried about you."

"Everything's fine. I just got caught up at the café and spaced on the meeting."

"I'm sure Brody and his dad can fill you in."

Was he trying to matchmake? She gave him the side-eye. No, couldn't be.

"Mom, look!" Sadie spotted her and awkwardly bounced a

basketball. Tisha waved. Hold on. Where were her shoes? Why was she in her socks?

Ethan looked up and smiled.

Her pulse quickened.

What? No. Stop it. She willed her heart to return to its normal grieving-widow pace.

"Here, Sadie," Ethan said, motioning for Sadie to come closer. He helped her balance the ball on her palm, her elbow forming a sharp ninety-degree angle. "Bend at your knees, and then—boom!"

The ball kissed the backboard before dropping through the net. Sadie thrust both hands high in the air, a triumphant grin lighting up her face. "Perfect!"

"Nice shot!" Ethan high-fived her, and Tisha felt a rush of warmth.

Brody sat on the sidelines, scribbling in a notebook, trying to look nonchalant while clearly watching.

"Hey." Ethan approached with Sadie trotting along beside him, slipping and sliding in her socks.

"Honey, where are your shoes?"

"Oh, they got wet at recess, so I took them off."

"Is it okay that she's in here in her socks?" Tisha asked.

"Of course," Ethan said. "Missed you at the meeting. Are you all right?"

"Yeah, I just got caught up in something at the café. I'm so sorry."

"No worries. We have a homework assignment." He gave her a knowing look. "Teamwork, collaboration—you know the deal."

"Great." Tisha forced a smile. "Looking forward to that."

Mr. Price stood by, watching the whole exchange with a curious expression.

"Hey, Mr. Ethan," Sadie piped up. "Can I join your basketball team?"

"You'll have to ask your mom if that's okay," he said, passing the ball back and forth from one hand to the other.

"Are you having tryouts?" Tisha asked.

"Uh, no. I think tryouts happened already," Ethan said.

"But now that we have enough coaches, we don't have to turn anyone away." Mr. Price nudged Ethan in the side with his elbow. "Thanks for stepping up, Clutch."

"Appreciate the offer, but I think we'll pass for now," Tisha said. "Is Brody on your team?"

"No, not yet." Ethan glanced over his shoulder at his son, then frowned.

"But I'm trying to talk him into it," Mr. Price said. "The kid's a great shot. You've taught him well."

A muscle in Ethan's jaw twitched, but he didn't say anything.

Tisha glanced between them. Yeah, okay, so passing on an opportunity for Sadie to get some exercise and make new friends might not be ideal. But letting Ethan coach Sadie in a sport she'd never played might be a bridge too far. Because the less time she spent around him, the better.

———

"Dad, is it time for pizza yet?" Brody hovered beside Ethan's elbow, twirling his new red fidget spinner in a circle.

Ethan glanced at the clock on the gym wall. "Almost. We have about fifteen minutes to get to the restaurant."

"Pizza? That sounds yummy!" Sadie bounced the ball, slapping at it with both hands. He resisted the urge to correct her and instead offered Tisha an awkward smile. Part of him wanted to invite Tisha and Sadie to dinner, but it didn't feel appropriate, especially after all of their ups and downs over the past few days. Besides, she hadn't been receptive to joining the basketball league, so why would she say yes to a McGuire family gathering?

"You can come," Brody said. "We can do our homework."

"Oh, I don't know if tonight's the best night for that," Ethan said.

"But me and Sadie can play air hockey!" Brody insisted, his eyes shining with excitement.

"It's okay," Tisha said, a knowing look in her eyes. "Sadie and I should probably head home anyway."

"But when are we going to do our assignment?" Brody asked, his brows scrunched together.

"Brody loves Dockside Pizza Company because they have an air-hockey table." Ethan plucked Brody's coat off the floor and handed it to him. "And my sister, Megan, is in town with her new boyfriend, and they're bringing a dog that just had puppies by the resort."

"Puppies?" Sadie squealed, her face lighting up.

"Oh, fun." Tisha smiled. "I remember your sister Megan. Wow, she was a teenaged barista the last time I saw her."

"Yeah, a few things have changed in her life. She's dating somebody who's about to be deployed. His family has been dogsledding for ages. Anyway, she wants us to meet him."

"That sounds complicated," Tisha said. "Sadie and I are not going to interrupt that."

"It's not an interruption, it's . . ." He trailed off. Man, he was really messing this up. "Look, I'll tell you what. On Saturday, we're having a resort-only activity. It's not open to the whole community. How about if you and Sadie come by? I'll make arrangements with Megan and her boyfriend. You can hang out with the puppies, and there's a snowshoe-softball tournament if you're interested in that."

"Thank you for the invitation, but don't you have clients to fly up into the mountains?" Tisha asked.

"I will make sure I'm available. How about Saturday at ten o'clock? Will that work? We can come up with something for Brody and Sadie to do that's collaborative."

"All right." Tisha shrugged. "Sounds good. We'll be there."

"Dad, come on. I'm starving," Brody whined, bouncing on his toes.

"Bye, Brody!" Sadie yelled as Tisha led her out of the gym.

"Come on, pal. Let's get your backpack," Ethan said.

Aaron gave him a high five. "Way to go, man. Really proud of both of you, and I'm glad to have you back, Clutch."

"Thanks." Ethan smiled, buoyed by his old friend's encouragement.

As they stepped outside the school, the wind had died down, but bitter-cold temperatures enveloped them.

"Brody, where's your hat?"

"I forgot it again," Brody said, trudging along beside him.

"Come on, let's hurry," Ethan urged, quickening his pace. They walked briskly to the Suburban, where he started the engine before hopping back out to dust off the snow that had blown across the windshield.

A few minutes later, he found a parking spot facing the boat harbor and across the street from Dockside Pizza. Several boats bobbed gently in their slips. He stared over the railing. Snow had stacked up on the roofs of the houseboats, and the water looked unbelievably cold.

"Wait, why isn't it frozen?" Brody asked, craning his neck to look over the railing.

"The ocean doesn't freeze here," Ethan explained. "Fun fact, Redemption is the northernmost ice-free port."

"Cool. Let's get some pizza."

Ethan looked both ways before crossing the street, guiding his son to the entrance.

As Ethan and Brody stepped into Dockside Pizza Company, they were immediately enveloped in a warm, inviting atmosphere. The air was thick with the rich aroma of freshly baked pizza mingling with notes of garlic and herbs. The walls, adorned with dark wooden paneling, were decorated with nautical-themed memorabilia—old fishing nets, vintage photographs of the local harbor—and colorful hand-painted signs advertising classic sodas.

Soft, ambient lighting cast a golden glow across the room. An old jukebox in the corner played a mix of classic rock and upbeat pop tunes, adding to the lively vibe. Clattering plates and the cheerful laughter of families gathered around booths and tables created a comforting din that made the restaurant feel alive.

In one corner, an air-hockey table gleamed under the warm lights. Nearby, a Pac-Man arcade machine flickered with neon colors. The bar was lined with stools, where locals gathered for a quick bite or a few drinks, their conversations punctuated by hearty laughter.

The staff, clad in matching red aprons, moved swiftly between tables, balancing trays laden with steaming pizzas and frosty mugs of soda. Ethan paused and soaked it all in. He hadn't been here in years. What a relief to see that some things hadn't changed at all.

"Ethan, hey! We're over here."

Ethan turned in the direction of the familiar voice. His youngest brother, Tate, stood at the end of a crowded table, waving them over.

Brody dodged a server carrying a loaded tray and raced toward the table. "Uncle Tate, what are you doing here?"

"I came for the pizza, just like you." Tate grinned, then pulled Brody in for a hug. "What's new? How's school?"

"Fine, I guess. We stayed late because Dad wanted to play basketball," Brody said, peeling off his coat and flinging it onto the closest empty chair.

Ethan shook Tate's hand, then gave him a back slap. "Good to see you, man."

"You too." His brother raised an eyebrow. "Basketball?"

Ethan jumped in. "Brody and I had a meeting with the counselor and another student, but the other parent was late, so we were just hanging out in the gym, shooting some baskets. Somehow, I was persuaded to coach a team of seven- and eight-year-olds."

"Cool. That sounds fun." Tate reclaimed his seat.

Ethan sat down beside him and opened the laminated trifold menu with the same red cover and Dockside Pizza logo that had been around forever.

"Dad, no one's playing air hockey. Let's go!" Brody urged.

"Hang on, hang on. Let's say hello to everybody," Ethan said, scanning the table. Heaving a sigh, Brody flopped down in a chair at the far end of the table.

Megan shoved back her chair and squealed. Her blonde ponytail bobbed against her shoulders as she hurried toward Ethan.

"Oh my gosh, I can't believe it." She flung her arms around his neck. "I'm so glad you're back."

"It's good to see you too, squirt," he said, patting her arm. "Where's your boyfriend?"

"Over there." She pointed to the far side of the table. "Hey, Lance. Come say hello to my oldest brother."

A tall, athletic man with dark brown hair, clear blue eyes, and a broad smile approached.

"Hey, I'm Lance Thomas. Good to meet you," the man said, extending his hand.

"And you as well. I'm Ethan. First time in Redemption?"

"We've conducted drills in the area. I've never been here just for fun though." Lance draped his arm around Megan's shoulders and kissed the top of her head.

"I see. Heard you got your orders?"

The man's expression sobered. "Yes, sir."

"We appreciate your service."

"And yours as well," Lance said. "Megan tells me you just got out?"

"I did," Ethan said, nodding.

"Miss it?"

"Uh . . . sort of. But it's time for me to be a dad full-time. I still get to fly here but it's different," Ethan said, glancing toward Tate, who had given in to Brody's pleas for a game of air hockey. "Thanks for bringing the puppies. I think they're going to be a huge hit."

Lance grinned. "Yeah. Happy to do it. Anything to keep Megan happy, you know?"

Megan stared up at the guy with a dreamy look in her wide-set blue eyes, and Ethan turned away, feeling a prickle on the back of his neck. Something about that whole interaction felt off. He had been away for most of Megan's teenage years, and their father often said her ability to pick a good man was broken. And she seemed to be having some challenges as a single parent; Ethan could relate.

"Hey, look! Isn't that Tisha?" Megan asked, her eyes lighting up.

Ethan's breath caught in his chest. He glanced toward the door. Tisha stood at the hostess stand, fishing her wallet out of her purse. All of a sudden the air in the room felt a little too warm.

"Huh. That's interesting timing, isn't it?" Luke winked. "Want to say hello, Meg?"

"Absolutely," Megan said, trailing after Luke.

Great. He scrubbed his hand across his jaw. Now he'd have to pretend not to care that she'd walked in. Like he wasn't hyperaware of her presence. Like his heart hadn't kicked against his ribs just now when Tisha recognized his sister and flashed that stunning smile.

Oh boy. He turned away as the air-hockey puck pinged off the edge of the table, then sailed into the goal Tate had left wide open.

"Yay!" Brody cheered as the digital screen awarded him a point.

"Wow." Tate shook his head. "Never saw that coming."

"Great shot, kiddo. Well done!" Ethan praised, warmth blooming in his chest.

Brody beamed. "Thanks, Dad. I'm pretty good at this."

"Yeah, you sure are."

Brody stood taller, held his chin higher, and had a light in his eyes that Ethan hadn't seen enough of lately. He'd have to remember to praise Brody more often. Tate retrieved the puck, set it back on the table, and it glided across the surface. Tate tapped it gently.

"Don't go easy on me, Uncle Tate. Play me as hard as you would play my dad or Uncle Luke," Brody challenged.

"I don't know that you need to go quite that hard," Ethan said, shooting Tate a pleading glance.

"No need to worry, Bro," Tate said, defending his goal from another one of Brody's shots. "This boy's got skills."

Just then, Luke joined them, and Dad rolled up beside him in his wheelchair. Ethan tried to focus on Brody and Tate's game, but he couldn't shake the nagging distraction of Tisha standing there, waiting to pick up her order.

Brody scored again, and Ethan leaned over to give him a high five. Then, almost against his will, he glanced toward the door again. Tisha slipped out, the brown paper takeout bag bumping against her hip. She didn't look back.

He blew out a breath and shook his head, a quiet laugh rumbling in his chest. Like it would have mattered if she had stayed. But for some ridiculous reason, a part of him wished she had.

Seven

S HE WAS NOT GOING TO LET SADIE TALK HER into getting a puppy.

"Mama, these puppies are so cute!" Sadie pressed her cheek against the wiggly husky puppy cradled in her arms. "You have to hold one."

"Be careful, Sadie," Brody cautioned, using a tone Tisha had never heard him use before. "They're babies. You have to be gentle."

"I know that, Brody. Don't be bossy," Sadie shot back.

Tisha suppressed a smile as she glanced at Ethan, crouched next to his son. He offered a knowing smile. It caught her off guard, that fleeting connection, and she looked away.

"You guys are both doing a great job," Tisha said, standing between Sadie and Brody near the tailgate of Lance's pickup truck outside the resort.

Megan and Lance had gone inside to grab drinks and popcorn for all of them. Nearby, the excitement of the snowshoe-softball game echoed through the crisp, cold air. Laughter and cheers mingled with the crunch of snow underfoot, creating a festive atmosphere.

"I didn't know people could play softball in snowshoes," Brody said, his eyes wide with wonder. "I want to try."

"Whoa, whoa. Focus on the puppy, big guy," Ethan replied, kneeling beside him.

Brody frowned. "I can watch the game and hold a puppy, Dad."

"I'm sure you can." A muscle in Ethan's jaw twitched. "But the puppies' mother is here in the back of the truck, and she might not want us carrying her babies away."

"Is this an annual thing? Snowshoe softball?" Tisha asked, taking in the scene where players stumbled and laughed, their snowshoes flopping comically as they ran.

Ethan nodded. "Somebody in town puts on a tournament every year. My parents thought it would draw more traffic to the resort if they hosted a game."

"Is it working?"

"Sort of, but it's a little hectic. We have people who want to ski and snowboard as well, so I think we've got a bit more than we can handle. Especially since . . ." His gaze shifted, and something she couldn't quite decipher flashed in his eyes. "Well, since Megan showed up with Lance and a truck bed full of puppies."

"I'm glad she came over and said hello at the pizza place last night."

The words left her before she could stop them. She hadn't meant to bring it up. Really, she hadn't. Megan had been so thrilled to see her, crossing the crowded restaurant with Luke in tow. She'd tried to tell herself that it didn't matter that Ethan didn't join them. But it did. Probably more than she cared to admit.

"Yeah, Megan's our social butterfly." Ethan stood and brushed snow off his jeans. "She's always been someone who makes people feel welcome."

Tisha nodded, gently scratching the puppy in Sadie's arms under the chin. So soft. Not to mention adorable. No wonder Sadie was enamored. "Melinda asked me to run by and pick up our order. I didn't want to intrude, so that's why I didn't come over and speak to y'all."

He frowned. "You wouldn't have been intruding."

His simple objection tugged at her heart. "Well, you looked like you were super into that air-hockey game."

To be honest, she hadn't trusted herself to cross the restaurant. Not with Ethan standing there looking all handsome and broody. Besides, even though Megan and Luke had been so kind, she'd seen the high fives and the laughter. Where did she fit into that cozy picture of a big family sharing pizza and cheering around the air-hockey table?

Ethan studied her, something unspoken lingering in those piercing eyes. "I'm sorry if it seemed like I didn't want to talk to you."

Oh. She blinked. "It's fine." She shrugged, then pasted on a bright smile. "I think it's great that Megan is here."

"Yeah, we're glad she's here," Ethan said, pushing to his feet. "I don't think she plans to stay long though. Lance is about to ship out."

"Oh?" Tisha felt a pang of sympathy. "Where's he going?"

"He's in the Army, but I'm not sure he can say exactly where he'll be."

"So what will Megan do?"

"She has a job at an apartment complex and works at a bank in Fairbanks."

"Got it." Tisha nodded, uncertain how to ask about Megan's baby in front of Sadie and Brody. Megan had caused quite a stir when she'd come home from college in Washington single and expecting. That child would be in fifth or sixth grade by now, probably.

"And your sister Caroline? I haven't seen her yet," Tisha said. "Where's she living now?"

"She's in Colorado," Ethan said. "Finishing up her last rotation in—"

"Wait. If Mr. Lance is leaving with the Army, what will happen to the puppies?" Sadie looked up at Ethan, her blue eyes wide with curiosity.

"Sadie," Tisha said. "Please don't interrupt."

"It's fine." Ethan gave Tisha a reassuring smile, then turned to Sadie. "We can ask him when he comes back outside. I'm pretty sure his parents will take care of the puppies and teach them how to be great sled dogs."

"Oh, sled dogs." Sadie squealed so loud that the puppy in her arms whined. "Can we ride in a sled?"

"Sadie, easy." Tisha patted her back and lowered her voice to a soothing tone. "You startled the puppy."

"Sorry." Sadie switched to a loud whisper. "Can we ride a dog-sled though?"

"Or try snowshoe softball?" Brody added. "I want to play!"

"It's kind of dangerous, Brody," Ethan said. "We'd probably get hurt."

"You don't know!" Brody argued, his cheeks flushed. "We haven't even tried yet."

"Mama, here." Sadie thrust the puppy at Tisha. "You have to hold it. This is the cutest one."

"Oh, okay. Um, hold on." Tisha took the blue-eyed animal, feeling its warmth begin to radiate against her chest. *Stay strong. Don't cave. Puppies are cute, but so much work.* Between her shifts at the café, baking pies for the festival, and making sure Sadie had a handle on things at school, there was no way she could add a pet to their busy lives.

"You have to hold it close to you, right by your heart." Sadie patted her own chest.

"Like this." Brody tucked a puppy under his chin and closed his eyes, a content smile spreading across his face.

"Thanks for the tips, kids," Ethan said, a low, throaty laugh escaping him.

Tisha couldn't help but smile. She liked the sound of it. "Does this count as their collaborative assignment?"

"Maybe. I'll have to ask Mr. Price about that," Ethan said. "If you guys want to try snowshoeing, we could probably find time."

"Let's go today." Brody tugged on Ethan's sleeve. "As soon as we're done here."

"Actually, I have a flight this afternoon. You're gonna stay here and hang out with our family." Ethan pulled out his phone and scrolled. "How about tomorrow after church?"

Tisha ran her hands over the puppy's soft, fluffy fur. "We could do that. Sadie, do you want to try snowshoeing?"

"Um, I'll have to think about it. Do you have kid sizes?" Sadie pointed to the players in the distance. "Because those ones are way too big."

"Yes, we have kid sizes. Plenty for you and Brody."

"Where will we go?" Brody asked, his excitement palpable. "We can't just go around here. Bor-ing!"

"Well, lucky for you, your grandpa and your uncle Tate made sure there's a trail through the woods."

"Are there bears?" Sadie asked, her eyes darting toward the forest. "I don't think I want to see any bears."

"If there are, they're sleeping. We'll be fine," Ethan said. "What do you think? How about two o'clock tomorrow?"

Tisha hesitated, and her thoughts drifted back to the pizza place. So maybe it wasn't a big deal that he hadn't spoken to her. His silence had stung a bit though. Would a brief hello have been too much for him? And yet, here he was now, inviting her and Sadie to join them again tomorrow for snowshoeing. Maybe she'd misjudged him. Or maybe this was all part of the collaborative assignment with the school. Maybe he just wanted Brody and Sadie to learn to get along.

"Tisha?" Ethan's eyebrows raised. "Will that work for you and Sadie?"

"Two o'clock tomorrow sounds great. Thanks! What should we bring?"

"Just dress in layers of warm clothes. Hats, gloves. The whole nine yards." Ethan smiled as he put his phone away. "Wear your regular snow boots too—they'll fit right into our snowshoes. It'll be fun."

"Fun, right." Tisha thought of the cold air, the crunch of snow beneath her feet, and the chill that seeped into her bones. She'd rather bake a pie or hold this puppy for a whole day than traipse around in the forest in the snow. But he was being kind and gracious, and she and Sadie could use the fresh air and exercise.

"Sorry to keep you waiting," Megan said, her snow pants swishing together as she and Lance joined them. They'd brought red-and-white-striped plastic containers full of popcorn and mini cans of soda for everyone.

"Oh my," Tisha said. "Thank you so much."

"Mom just cranked out a whole batch of fresh popcorn. I couldn't resist. And Lance here says you need soda with your popcorn."

"A little salty to go with the sweet," Tisha said, laughing as the puppy licked her cheek.

"Yeah, that's what my mama always said." Lance grinned. "I've never heard anyone in Alaska use that expression before."

"Where did you grow up?"

"I moved around a lot. Can't really say that I'm from any one place. But my family settled in Fairbanks, and they're pretty busy with their dog kennels now."

"Huh, interesting." Tisha returned the puppy to the bed Lance had arranged in the covered cab of his truck. The mama dog received her puppy and licked it protectively. Meanwhile, Brody and Sadie were arguing about which puppy was cuter.

"Here, maybe it's snack time." Ethan produced a squirt bottle of hand sanitizer. Megan set some napkins on the tailgate of the truck, weighting them down with a can of soda, and slid the box with the cartons of popcorn beside them.

Tisha cleaned her hands, then reached for a carton of popcorn for Sadie and cracked open a can of diet soda. What a fun little gathering. The bat cracked against the ball, and the crowd cheered as a woman stomped through the snow in her giant, teardrop-shaped shoes, laughing as she hurried toward first base.

"What's the matter?" Tisha glanced at Sadie. "Don't you want any popcorn or Sprite?"

Sadie quirked her lip to one side, then looked away. "I actually have to use the restroom," she said in a hushed whisper, her cheeks flushing slightly.

"No problem, honey." Tisha took the popcorn and the unopened can of soda, setting them back on the truck's tailgate. "I'm glad you said something." She brushed a stray lock of Sadie's hair from the collar of her jacket, smiling reassuringly.

"I'll show you where it is," Brody offered, puffing out his chest. "I know the way."

Tisha offered Ethan a questioning glance.

"He can handle it," he assured her with a nod. "Be a gentleman, Brody. Show her where it is and wait outside the door."

"I got it, Dad." Brody held up his palm like a stop sign, clearly eager to prove himself.

"All right. Come right back," Tisha instructed, watching as Brody motioned for Sadie to follow him inside the resort.

Megan's eyes sparkled with amusement. "Brody's got his father's leadership skills."

Ethan grimaced. "Is that a good thing?"

"Of course," Lance said, pouring some water into a portable bowl for the mama dog.

"You McGuire boys are being awfully attentive today." Megan gently nudged Ethan's shoulder, a playful challenge in her voice. "What gives?"

"What's that supposed to mean?" Ethan frowned. "I'm always attentive."

Megan pinched her lips together and gave him a doubtful look.

"We really appreciate you inviting us out here." Tisha said, determined to intervene before Megan provoked him into a grumpy mood. "Sadie will be talking about these puppies for days."

One side of his mouth hitched up in a playful smile. "What kind of pie am I today, then, if you think I'm being sweet?"

"I didn't say you were being sweet. Don't get carried away." She tapped her chin thoughtfully. "But since you asked, I'd say . . . hmm, strawberry rhubarb."

"Strawberry rhubarb? Those do not go together."

"Hey, they sure do! I'll make you a strawberry-rhubarb pie. You'll see."

"Take your time. I think I can wait." He leaned back against the tailgate, crossing his arms with a smirk.

"By the way, where have you been? I never accepted your resignation as my official taste tester. I had to rely on the commoners for feedback this week."

Something flashed in his eyes, and his expression turned serious. "So you're saying you missed me?"

"Hmm. I wouldn't go that far."

"Interesting. Well, I guess I'll have to come back again. What's been your biggest hit so far?"

"I served some coconut custard to a lady who missed her flight on her way to her Hawaiian vacation. She said it was good, and then I served her husband chocolate chess pie."

"Chocolate what?"

"I know. It's a Southern thing. Long story short, it's just a chocolate pie with whipped cream that I made myself. He loved it."

"Sweet. Whipped cream is always a good idea."

"Noted."

His arm brushed against hers as he reached for a carton of

popcorn. "You know, all kidding aside," he said, popping a few kernels into his mouth, "I do think you're up to something good with your pie. We have to find small victories where we can get them this time of year, right?"

"Thank you. That means a lot." Warmth stirred in her chest. "I really am just taking it one day at a time, trying to find my way."

"That's relatable," he nodded, his gaze steady.

Tisha glanced at Megan and her boyfriend, who were too absorbed with each other to pay attention to their conversation. Lowering her voice, she added, "I really want Sadie to have a great life, you know? She's heard a dozen stories—probably more—about how much I loved living in Alaska after I graduated from college. North Carolina has a lot to offer, but my family sort of scattered after my dad passed. Only one of my sisters is married with a family, and things just weren't the same once we sold the farm. I want her to carry a piece of her dad with her."

"I get that," Ethan said, cracking open a soda. "Sometimes we have to do the hard, scary things because we know it's going to be what's best in the long run. But I think you're very brave, moving here. Not a lot of single moms would start over close to their in-laws, you know? I really admire what you're doing."

"Uh-huh. Is that a compliment, Ethan McGuire?"

"Indeed, it is." His gaze met hers, then held for a beat longer than necessary. "Don't get used to it. I don't hand them out very often."

"Wow. Banner day." She wasn't about to admit how much his compliments about her pie and her parenting skills meant to her.

She took a long drink of her soda, grounding herself in the truth. They were here for Brody and Sadie, and for the puppies, but mostly to ensure that their kids learned to get along. Well-adjusted kids—that was their shared goal, but nothing more.

And yet, as Ethan laughed at something Brody said, an unexpected warmth blossomed in her chest. Not entirely unwelcome either. Until she glanced at Sadie, whispering softly to the puppy cradled in her arms. Falling for Ethan was one thing. But letting her daughter see a new relationship unfold? That probably wouldn't end well.

Wow, he had really mismanaged this.

Ethan pulled off his knit hat, swiped the back of his hand across his forehead, then put his hat back on, feeling the chill of the Alaska air pierce through his layers. The snow crunched underfoot, and the cold nipped at his cheeks, reminding him of how far he was from the warmth of Florida's coastline.

"Mama, I'm freezing! Can we go back?" Sadie trembled, her little face scrunched up with displeasure, and her breath visible in the frosty air.

"Yeah, Dad, this isn't any fun." Brody had found a stick, likely a branch that had fallen from a tree. Now, he was whacking the broad base of a healthy spruce tree, sending snow cascading down onto Sadie.

"Brody, stop! That's cold!" Sadie squealed, her eyes wide as the snow showered down on her.

"What? What did I do?" Brody turned and looked up at Ethan, confusion etched on his face.

"When you hit the tree, you knocked snow off the branches, bud," Ethan said.

"And it went down my coat," Sadie said, her eyes shimmering with impending tears.

"Oh no! Oh no, please don't cry. Brody, what do you say?" Ethan urged, a knot tightening in his stomach.

"Sorry. I didn't know," Brody mumbled and tossed the stick aside, glancing apologetically at Sadie. Ethan turned toward Tisha, who stood beside him, cheeks flushed from the cold. The light that normally sparkled in her beautiful eyes had dimmed, replaced by a look of shared concern.

So she looked totally annoyed too. Super. Ethan blew out a long breath.

Brody gasped, suddenly distracted by the whine of an engine through the trees. "What's that sound?"

"Uncle Luke has a snow machine out," Ethan said.

"Do you think he'll tow us?" Brody tromped in a semicircle in his snowshoes, clearly ready to head for the resort.

"We're not broken down," Sadie said, her voice rising.

Brody rolled his eyes. "We tie a rope to this thing. It looks like a giant cereal bowl, and we climb inside. Then he tows us back and forth around the parking lot. It's super fun! You have to try it, Sadie."

Tisha glanced at Ethan, skepticism written all over her face. "Do tell. What's the story there?"

"Years ago, when the utility company installed fiberglass balls on the power lines to warn pilots about the overhead obstructions, they had a couple left over. So they asked my parents if they wanted them. Brody's right. It is kind of like a cereal bowl, and we run a rope through a bolt hole, tie the other end to the back of a snow machine, and pull each other around."

"What's a snow machine?" Sadie asked, breathing hard as she plodded along on her snowshoes. Probably wanted to keep up with Brody, who'd picked up the pace.

Ethan stayed beside Sadie. "A snowmobile or a snow machine. It runs on a track and handles like an ATV."

"Oh." Her breath left little white clouds in the air. "I don't know what any of that means."

"You've never ridden on the back of a snow machine?" Ethan asked, glancing at Tisha.

"Nope."

"Oh, we've got to change that," Ethan said.

"Dad, I'm thirsty." Brody stopped and called back over his shoulder. "Did you bring any water?"

"No. Let's go back to the resort," Ethan said, resisting the urge to sigh. Strike two. No snacks or beverages. He tried not to rush ahead, but now that he had failed at this outdoor adventure, he wanted to get back and forget about it as quickly as possible.

"Ladies, you go first," he said, gesturing for Tisha and Sadie to go ahead of him.

Note to self: Don't take kids accustomed to playing outdoors in the South on a snowshoe adventure, no matter how much they say they want to try new things.

An agonizing twenty minutes later, punctuated with lots of whining, they emerged from the trees. The resort came into view, a warm beacon against the cold backdrop. Ethan slowed his pace, and the tension eased from his jaw.

"Thank You, Lord," he whispered, his shoulders dipping as the weight of the last thirty minutes loosened its grip.

"Yeah, a hundred percent." Tisha reached over and high-fived his gloved hand. The warmth of her smile ignited something inside him that he couldn't quite name.

"Sorry," he said, shaking his head. "I feel like I really screwed this up."

"Why do you think that?"

"People are whining. I didn't bring any beverages or snacks. Snowshoeing evidently isn't as fun as I thought it was." Just then, the pungent smell of exhaust from the snow machine filled the air, and Luke zipped by, Megan squealing in delight as she held on to the edge of the bright-red cereal-bowl sled.

"Oh my." Tisha tracked her movements, her eyebrows raised. "That does look fun, but also sort of terrifying."

"Yeah, it only hurts if you fall out." Ethan laughed, but there was a nervous edge to it, a reminder of how quickly joy could turn to chaos. "I'm just kidding. I mean, yes, it is bad if you fall out, but Luke is a perfectly safe driver. I'm going to stop talking now."

Tisha frowned. "I'm not really sure I want to put my kid on that."

"I'll go," Brody said, eager. "I'll show you how it's done."

"Let's take off our snowshoes first and put them away."

"Aw, man," Brody said, frowning. "Can't I just leave them here?"

"No, you may not. We have to pick up after ourselves, bud."

They took off their snowshoes. Ethan helped Brody and then Sadie. Tisha tried, but then she looked at him and blew out a long breath.

"Here." He knelt beside her in the snow and undid the bindings. The feel of her hand on his back made his pulse thrum—a stark reminder of how long he'd been alone.

"There. You're all set." He glanced at her, and their eyes locked.

"Thanks." She smiled, and for a moment the world around them faded.

"You're welcome."

"Please don't worry about this." She stepped out of the bindings, then picked up the snowshoes. "It's good for us to try new things."

"That's really sweet of you to say, but I can tell you all are miserable."

"Miserable is kind of a strong word. It's just . . . it was hard. It was challenging. Good exercise though. Kept the kids off their devices, and we got outside. It's a beautiful day so—"

"Tisha, relax. You don't have to sugarcoat this for me. I get it. Snowshoeing is not your thing."

Her expression grew serious, her smile fading. "I appreciate you getting us outdoors. Really, I do. Brody and Sadie tried something new, and my daughter experienced the joy of having cold, wet snow fall down the inside of her jacket."

"Ha. Yeah. Brody taught her an important life lesson there." He turned and waved his hands in the air to get Luke's attention. The snowmobile slowed to a stop in front of them, the sound fading as he eased up on the throttle.

"Hey, everybody." Luke flipped up the visor on his helmet. "How was your adventure in the woods?"

"Terrible," said Brody. "They don't like snowshoeing." He jerked his thumb over his shoulder. "Can we go sledding instead?"

"If you can talk your aunt Megan out of giving up her turn."

"Yeah, I'm good. That was fun. But I'm more than happy to let you guys have a try." Megan climbed out of the bowl. "Thanks, Luke."

"I'm going first," Brody said. "Sadie's too scared. And Miss Tisha said no thank you."

"I'm not scared. I just want to see you do it first," Sadie said, her chin lifted defiantly.

"Okay." Brody shrugged. "Watch this."

Megan held on to the edge of the fiberglass bowl, giving Brody a hand climbing inside. "Okay, sit on your bottom, keep your hands and feet inside. Remember?"

"Yep, got it. Let's go, Uncle Luke."

"All right." Luke grinned, then flipped his visor down.

Ethan saw his own image in his brother's reflective lens, lines of worry etched deep. His phone hummed in his pocket. He pulled it out.

"Ugh. Not again." He thumbed the call away, but the weight of it lingered.

"You know, you do that a lot. Who's calling you so much that you don't want to talk to?" Tisha asked, her brow furrowing.

"Hey, Sadie, want to make some snow angels?" Megan offered, her voice bright and inviting.

"I guess," Sadie said, hesitating. "What's a snow angel again?"

"Come here." Megan guided Sadie a few feet away, leaving Ethan and Tisha alone, an electric tension hanging between them.

"So, my late wife, Adeline, she was amazing. She did a lot of great things for our community, no matter where we lived. She was the lady who helped the other Coastie wives feel welcome and get settled and plugged in. She did some philanthropic work, and her best friend wants to do a story—kind of like a long-form interview, I guess. I don't really know what to call it, but she wants me to answer several questions, and I keep telling her no, but she is not taking no for an answer."

"Why don't you want to do it? Sounds really cool."

"Probably for the same reason you would resist if someone wanted to write an article about Chase. It's hard. I don't really want to talk about her. I'm trying to put all of that behind me. She was a really incredible mom, and I'm focused on Brody because right now I'm a mediocre dad."

"Oh, that's not true," she said, her tone earnest. "You're a great dad."

"I don't feel like a great dad. Evidently, my kid has a learning issue that I didn't know anything about."

Tisha's mouth formed an O. "Really?"

"Yeah, he can't read."

"You know, Sadie mentioned that he might be having a tough time. She struggled at first too. But I just read to her a lot and made sure she knew her letters and her sounds, and she's pretty much back on track."

If only it were that simple. He hesitated, biting back the sarcastic comment. "He literally cannot read. I think he has some substantial issues, and Adeline would have just handled it, figured it out, given me the update when I was home."

"Listen, I'm sorry that you lost your wife, and I hate that Brody has to grow up without his mom, but you are a good dad. I'm certain you'll figure this out and get Brody the help he needs."

"How do you know?"

"Because I've watched you with him, and I can see by the way you act with your family. You protect your people. You care about them, Ethan. That matters. You're a person of character."

"Aw, stop. You're making me blush." He tipped his head, trying to deflect the sincerity of her words, but they struck a chord deep within him.

"It's true."

"Well, thank you," he said, his voice softening. "By the way, I hope I wasn't out of line saying you wouldn't want a story written about Chase, because if anybody was going to write about a great pilot who made a difference in the world, it would be about Chase Binford."

She stared at him, pinching her lips to a thin line.

"Oh no. What? What'd I say?"

She cleared her throat and blinked hard. "Nothing. Thank you. That was really nice of you to say. I guess I just assumed you never knew Chase."

"No, I did. He and Luke have been friends forever, and even though I haven't lived in Redemption for the past twenty years, Chase has an incredible reputation as an aviator, and he was just an all-around good guy. I'm sorry that he left us far too soon."

"Thank you, Ethan. That means a lot."

They stood there staring at each other, and Ethan felt a rush of emotions swirling—attraction, fear, longing, and the heavy weight of loss.

Wow. She was beautiful, and so kind.

"Mom, come here! Come make a snow angel with me!" Sadie's voice broke the moment.

"All right, I will." Tisha jogged over, her snow pants swishing with each step, and Ethan couldn't help but smile. His sister gave him a knowing look, and he gave the slightest of head shakes. He didn't know what Megan was up to, but clearly she thought she was clever for initiating this snow-angel situation.

He turned to check on Brody and Luke. Luke had driven the

snow machine as far as he could on the edge of their property and then made a slow U-turn back. Brody swung out wide, obviously having the time of his life.

Sadie popped up. "Mom, look!"

Megan and Tisha turned to admire her. "Oh, sweetie, that's beautiful! Let me get my phone out—I'll take a picture."

"Thanks! That's fun, Miss Megan!" Sadie exclaimed, glowing with delight.

Tisha took a picture and then held the phone up. "Hey, let's take a selfie, just you and me, kiddo." They grinned at the camera. "Say 'snow angel'!"

"You want me to take the picture?" Ethan asked, stepping forward.

"That's okay. We got a cute selfie." She looked at the screen, shielding it with her hand.

His phone hummed again, this time with a text. He checked the screen, feeling the weight of it pull at him.

"Hey, when we're all done playing out here, my mom says she's got the hot-cocoa stand up and we're welcome to come in and try it out."

"Oh, a hot-cocoa stand? What does that mean?" Sadie asked, her excitement bubbling over.

"Oh, girlfriend, you don't even know," Megan said, her eyes sparkling. "She has the most delicious homemade hot cocoa. Plus whipped cream, sprinkles, and these amazing marshmallows."

"Oh, forget sledding," Sadie said. "Let's go do that!"

He and Tisha shared another smile, but as their eyes met, fear unfurled in his gut like a signal flag snapping in the wind. When she looked at him like that, he felt like he could do anything—and that scared him. He was still grappling with his grief, with the remnants of a love that had once filled his life. The idea of moving forward, of letting someone new into his heart, made him want to sprint in the opposite direction.

But as he watched Tisha laugh with Sadie, the warmth of the moment seeped into his bones, and for the first time in a long while, he wondered if perhaps it was time to let go of the past and embrace the possibilities of the future.

Eight

SHE COULD DO THIS, RIGHT? TWENTY-FOUR pies—how hard could it be? She'd made a dozen last year for the county fair. Doubling her output? Certainly doable.

Melinda piled another five pounds of flour and ten pounds of sugar onto the counter, along with a large jar of vanilla extract and a bottle of Karo Syrup. She added two containers of cocoa powder, her movements brisk and efficient.

"There you go, sweet pea. Have at it." Melinda squeezed Tisha's shoulder, her smile warm. "I'm so glad you're doing this. A pie walk? What a great idea!"

"I hope so," Tisha said. "I might've overcommitted."

"You're going to pull this off," Melinda said. "And Tom and I are happy to donate the ingredients. Feel free to commit to making more than twelve pies if you'd like."

Tisha gave her a look. "Did Chloe put you up to that?"

Melinda shrugged, her eyes gleaming. "Maybe."

"Then I'm going to tell Chloe that I—that we—will donate twenty-four pies."

"Perfect." Melinda clapped her hands. "I'll be right back with eggs and butter."

Just then, Charlie walked in, twisting her hair into a bun. "Is all that for you?"

"Sure is." Tisha tied her apron around her waist, then fished her phone out of her back pocket. "I committed to baking twelve pies, but Chloe seems to think twenty-four would be even better."

"Wow. Somebody is going to be busy," Charlie said.

Tisha quickly swiped through her social-media notifications. Cami, her youngest sister, had commented on the photos Tisha had posted—her first post in ages. The first photo featured her snow-angel selfie with Sadie outside the resort, smiling, and the second one was of her and Sadie's mugs of cocoa, topped with giant dollops of whipped cream and chocolate sprinkles.

"You sure are smiling this morning for a girl who has to make eleventy billion pies." Charlie plated the last slice of coconut custard.

"Not eleventy billion," Tisha said, her fingers tapping on the screen. She felt a flutter of guilt—was she really enjoying this too much? She added a comment to Cami's.

WE SNOWSHOED FOR THE FIRST TIME. SEVEN OUT OF TEN STARS. BUT THE HOT COCOA? FOR SURE A TEN OUT OF TEN.

Cami must've read her comment in real time, because she quickly replied.

I'M SO GLAD YOU'RE GETTING SETTLED AND HAVING FUN. LOVE YOU!

Tisha's heart warmed, and she typed, "Love you too," and added a pink heart emoji before putting her phone away.

"Why are you extra happy these days?" Charlie asked, a teasing lilt in her voice. "I mean, I have nothing against happiness, of course."

"Well, I guess because I'm feeling a little more settled here." Tisha pulled out her phone and showed Charlie the pictures. "Not that everything's perfect, by any means. Sadie and her classmate Brody are supposed to collaborate, demonstrate some team-building skills, and work on communicating their feelings instead of getting angry. So far, we've tried puzzles, snowshoeing, snuggled with some puppies, and enjoyed hot cocoa."

Charlie flashed her an amused look. "And how are you and the pilot getting along?"

"Fine. Why?"

"Well, he's here." Charlie gestured toward the counter. "I'm sure he'd appreciate it if you took his order and not me."

"Oh!" She tucked her phone away, clearing her throat. She glanced at her purse hanging on the peg by the back door. Why did she suddenly feel the urge to refresh her lipstick?

Easy, there. Don't get in over your head.

"Hey." Charlie blocked her path, studying her face. "You look beautiful. He's already so into you. I see you eyeing your purse. Don't." She gently turned Tisha back around. "Go be you. You're awesome at it."

"Aw. Thanks." Tisha managed a smile, then brushed past Charlie and went out the swinging doors into the café.

Ethan sat at the counter, shrugging off his coat. Oh man. Suddenly, she realized she had a thing for waffle-print Henleys. Today's version was slate blue, and he hadn't shaved. The scruff along his jawline made her heart skip.

"Good morning," she said, forcing her tone to be light.

"Hi." Ethan leaned his elbows on the counter, his eyes searching her face. Warmth heated her skin.

He's so into you.

Charlie's comment echoed in her head as she reached for her pen and order pad. "What can I get you?"

"Well, I've got a quick trip up into the backcountry ahead of me, so why don't we start this day with pie?" he replied, a playful glint in his eyes.

She peeked out the window. Snowflakes danced in the air, swirling in a soft white blanket. "You're going to fly?" She pointed her pen toward the storm brewing outside, her mind racing with worry. "In this?"

He glanced over his shoulder, then back at her, his expression quizzical. "I've got to. We have clients up there. I'm scheduled to pick them up in an hour. Flying through snow is nothing new in Alaska."

His mouth twitched, and he added, "You're not worried about me, are you?"

She rolled her eyes. "No. Not at all." But inside, doubt gnawed at her. "Tell me what you wanted to order again."

"I need pie."

"For breakfast?" She angled her head, trying to maintain her composure.

"You of all people should not be discouraging me from trying pie."

"I'm just pleasantly surprised, is all."

His gaze shifted to the wall over her shoulder, probably checking out the chalkboard menu. "What would you recommend?"

She tapped her pen against her cheek. "You know what? I've got just the thing. But it goes best with a glass of cold milk."

"Really?" His tone was teasing, and she didn't quite know what to do when his eyes lingered on her face a second too long.

"Trust me." She turned and headed back into the kitchen, her thoughts a whirlwind.

Owen stepped away from the refrigerator, the door squeaking

as he pushed it shut. "Lot of eggs in there, pie lady. What are you up to?"

"I have a lot of pies to make and bake, Owen. But there's more than enough eggs to go around."

"Indeed. Let me know if I can help."

"I think I'm going to bake the crusts and freeze them ahead of time. It's the only way. So if it's all right with you, I'll need some freezer space."

"You got it. Plenty of room in there."

"Thanks." She felt the tension ease just a bit.

On the cooling rack sat her latest concoction, a funny cake. Flaky pie crust, a chocolate fudge layer, with yellow cake on top and a swirl of chocolate mixed in. Hopefully Ethan would love it. She poured a glass of milk, plated the pie-shaped cake while it was still warm, and carried the order out to him.

"Ta-da! Funny cake with a side of milk." She set them both on the Formica countertop, her hands trembling slightly.

"Funny cake, huh? Never heard of it. And I thought I ordered pie."

"My roommate at a pageant once was from Pennsylvania. Her mom had packed funny cakes for us—they're a fairly common treat, I guess. Anyway, carbs are so not allowed during a competition, but the other girls heard we had this dessert and flocked to our room. It was amazing! Of course, when my mama found out, she was irate and told me McDowells didn't do things like this..."

Wincing, she trailed off. "Sorry, I'm oversharing, aren't I?"

Lines at the corners of Ethan's eyes crinkled as he smiled. "I don't mind if you overshare. Tell me what's funny about this pie-slash-cake combo."

"Funny in the sense that it's odd. As opposed to humorous. It's a pie with a crust, obviously, but there's also a cake in the middle. And the best part? There's a layer of gooey chocolate on the bottom."

"Whoa, I'm in."

She handed him a fork and a napkin, her heart racing as he took a bite. She stared, arms crossed, waiting. He closed his eyes, and as he chewed slowly, a smile spread across his face.

"That's good stuff right there, pie lady."

"Thank you." She longed to stand there and chat longer, but more customers filed into the café.

A man sitting a few stools down from Ethan gave a polite wave. "Excuse me, can we place an order?"

"I'll be right back," she said, grabbing her notepad and the coffee carafe and scooting down the counter where a couple who'd only been in once waited to be served.

"I was gonna ask if you had any cinnamon rolls or coffee cake, but I think I'd like to try what he's having."

"Absolutely!" Tisha made a note on her pad. "And for you, ma'am?"

"I'll have the same, please, but we both like coffee—extra cream and sugar."

"You got it."

After she brought them their servings of funny cake and poured two cups of coffee, she conveniently wandered back to where Ethan sat scrolling through his phone.

"Have you heard any more from your friend in Florida?" she asked, trying to keep her voice steady.

"No, not yet, and she's gone radio silent. I'm sure she's aggravated that I keep ignoring her calls." He checked the time. "Thanks for the funny cake. It was awesome, and the milk as well. I've got to meet Luke in a few minutes."

"Okay," she said, her heart sinking. "Stay safe out there."

"You bet." He shrugged into his coat, his casual demeanor making her heart race. "And hey," he added. "Don't worry. I know we have a meeting today. I won't miss it."

"All right, see you then."

He took his order slip to the cash register, paid, and with a wave, he was gone.

Charlie sidled up beside her. "Don't know how to tell you this, but you're staring."

"Oh, I'm not—I'm not!" Tisha blurted, her cheeks heating. Again.

She turned and went back to the kitchen and measured out ingredients to start her next pie. But thoughts of Ethan kept intruding. That smile could really make a girl think hard about her future, but that scared her to death. Sure, they'd ended up having a good time together on Sunday, but a couple of outings in the snow did not a future make.

"Everything all right back here?" Charlie came in carrying a brown rubber bin loaded with dirty dishes. "You're making your worried face again. Hope I didn't irritate you by mentioning you were staring."

Sighing, Tisha tucked her phone back in her pocket. "I like him, but I'm not sure if this is the right thing to do—to move on. I mean, my mother-in-law says it's okay, and maybe it is, but . . ." She shook her head. "I'm worried about Sadie and how this might affect her."

Charlie lugged the bin over to the dishwasher. "That's understandable. But is Sadie worried? Or is this just you second-guessing yourself?"

"Maybe both." Tisha glanced toward the window, where the snow fell harder and blew sideways. "He's handsome and he's kind, but he's also been through a lot. Losing a wife, raising a son. What if this is just our loneliness reaching out to each other?"

Charlie gave her a knowing look. "Tisha, loneliness might be what makes two people notice each other, but it's not what keeps them coming back. You're allowed to want more than just surviving. And so is he."

"I know. It's just . . . too soon. For me and for Sadie."

For the rest of the morning, she kept busy planning her pie-baking strategy, waiting on customers, and chatting with Charlie. When her shift was over, she hung up her apron, tucked her phone into her purse, and headed outside, ducking her head against the snow that still fell. They had to have received at least another foot today.

She found the ice scraper that Tom had stowed in her car, tugged her hat lower, put on her gloves, and made short work of clearing off her car. She was getting better at it, seeing as how she had to do it almost every day.

She hurried over to the school. The administrative assistant buzzed her in, and she strode down the hall to the conference room, stepping inside. Mr. Price, Ms. Strom, Brody, and Sadie sat around the table.

"Hi. How's it going? How are y'all?" She kept her voice upbeat despite the tightness in her chest. Where was Ethan?

"We're good." Aaron frowned, angling his head toward the empty chair. "Just waiting on one more."

"Yeah. I saw him this morning. He came into the café. Said he had a flight but he'd be back."

She could still hear the teasing lilt in his voice, the way his eyes crinkled when he laughed. *You're not worried about me, are you?*

At the time, she'd rolled her eyes, brushing it off. But now? Now he was late. Missing. And she was definitely worried.

Her grip tightened around her phone as she checked for messages. Nothing.

Maybe this was exactly why she should put the brakes on whatever feelings were starting to take root. Because Ethan wasn't just a man who made her smile. He was a pilot. And she knew better than anyone what it felt like to fall for a man who was made to fly.

"Where is he?" Brody asked, a hint of frustration in his voice. "Can you text him?"

"Sure. We can try." Tisha quickly tapped out a message.

Tisha

Hey. Just checking in. We're
starting our meeting in a few
minutes. Is everything all right?

There. Not too bossy, not too whiny—just a concerned friend.

But as the minutes ticked on and the kids grew restless, Aaron's brow furrowed. An icy ball planted itself in Tisha's gut, its tentacles squeezing her insides. Where was he?

"How about you each take turns telling me the top five things you loved about your adventures together?" Ms. Strom said, folding her hands on top of her iPad.

Brody slouched lower in his chair, stared down, and kicked the table leg. Sadie tugged at her lower lip with her thumb and index finger, glancing at Tisha. Poor kids. Was her worry over Ethan that obvious?

"You know what, if you don't mind, may I make a suggestion?"

The counselor's smile faltered. "Absolutely. What would you like to say, Mrs. Binford?"

"I think it might be best if we saved this conversation for another time, when Ethan could contribute. He played a big role in fostering collaboration and getting us outdoors, encouraging us to try new things."

"And his mama gave us hot cocoa, and it was so yummy," Sadie said. "Right, Brody?"

Brody nodded. Tisha caught the flash of amusement in Aaron's eyes.

"If that's what you think is best, I'm happy to reschedule." Ms. Strom made a note on the sticky-note pad beside her. "Mr. Price, how do you feel about that?"

"That's an excellent suggestion, Mrs. Binford."

"Perfect. Thanks for understanding." Tisha shoved back her chair. "Brody, Sadie, come on. Let's go over to the resort. I'm sure your dad's just running late, Brody, and he'll probably meet us there."

The kid was out of that chair fast, tugging his coat on. "I'm ready!"

"We'll be in touch when we know Ethan's availability." She ushered the kids out to the car. They settled side by side in the back seat and buckled up without being prompted.

Tisha gripped the steering wheel tightly as she drove toward the resort. Snow lashed the windshield in a relentless blur. The wipers struggled to keep up, smearing more than clearing. Darkness pressed in, and her headlights carved out two narrow tunnels ahead. The wind funneled through the trees and around the car, an ominous whistle that made the silence inside feel even heavier.

"Are we almost there?" Brody peered through the window and scrubbed at the condensation on the glass with his coat sleeve.

"Almost," Tisha said. She forced a smile, but it felt more like a grimace. She glanced in the rearview mirror. Sadie fiddled with the zipper on her jacket.

She swallowed the bile climbing up her throat. One wrong move and they'd end up upside down in the ditch. Every nerve in Tisha's body buzzed with the need to *not* think about Ethan in this storm, up in the sky somewhere, flying through whiteout conditions. The thought clawed at the edge of her mind, but she shoved it back. Not now.

As she turned into the resort and drove up the freshly plowed driveway, she couldn't help but crane her neck toward the helicopter landing pad, hoping to see the bright-red machine and its rotors still.

The pad sat empty.

Her stomach plummeted.

"He's not here," Brody said.

Poor kid. He sounded as worried as she felt. She had to be brave though. For all of them. "Let's go inside. Maybe your grandparents have some more information."

They stepped inside, flames crackling in the fireplace, guests gathered around it on the worn leather sofas, and Megan serving hot cocoa from the hot-cocoa bar. Ethan's parents hovered beside the check-in desk. The concern etched on their faces sent a shiver down her spine.

How long were they supposed to let Ethan and Luke remain lost in the storm? What would the guys do if they couldn't get back? Were they prepared to ride out bad weather on some backcountry mountaintop?

"Oh, I'm so glad to see the three of you." Mrs. McGuire hurried over and pulled both kids in for quick hugs. Her gaze slid to meet Tisha's. "Have you heard anything?"

"Not yet. When Ethan didn't show up for our after-school meeting, the kids and I thought we should come over here."

"What's wrong, Grandpa?" Brody's chin wobbled. "Why haven't they landed yet?"

Unease hung in the air. Thick and suffocating. Ethan's dad sagged back in his wheelchair, his knuckles turning white as he clutched the armrests. He hesitated, then cleared his throat. "Your dad is an excellent pilot. Don't worry. They'll be back soon."

But how could they not worry? Her stomach tightened. What if—

No.

"They'll be back," she said, her voice brittle as she parroted Mr. McGuire's words. But doubt still gnawed at her, sharp and relentless.

Her phone buzzed in her pocket, and she pulled it out, her fingers trembling. *Please, please let it be Ethan.* Nope. Just a text from her sister Cami with a silly meme. The edges of her vision blurred.

"Let's go get some hot cocoa," she said, trying to sound upbeat. But her voice wavered as they crossed the lobby toward Megan and the counter. She glanced out the window. Lights in the yard illuminated the thick fat snowflakes still falling. The storm wasn't letting up.

She wasn't stressed just about Ethan and Luke and their clients, who were out in this terrible storm. Of course she wanted them all to come inside, safe and accounted for. But her own irrational emotions, billowing like a tempest inside her, sent her reaching for another hot cocoa loaded with whipped cream. Because how could she be this worked up over a man she'd met two weeks ago?

Mrs. McGuire joined her at the window. "Are you all right?"

Still clutching her mug of hot cocoa, Tisha shook her head. "No."

"What can I do?" Mrs. McGuire pressed her hand to Tisha's arm. "Do you want to sit by the fire?"

"I waited and I waited for Chase to come home." Tisha stared out at the empty helicopter pad. "And now here I am, doing it all over again, waiting for a man who flies." She blinked back the hot tears pressing against her eyes. "This is why I can't fall for him," she whispered.

"I understand. I do. And I'd be lying if I said I didn't worry every time Ethan's up in the air. A mother never stops worrying." She paused, her gaze following Tisha's to the empty helicopter pad. "But Ethan's strong, like his father. He's careful. And if there's one thing I've learned after all these years, it's that love can be the thing that helps us heal. If we let it. It's not easy, but . . ." She smiled, a hint of sadness in her eyes. "Sometimes the people who scare us the most are the ones worth holding on to."

<hr>

Yeah, he still had it. Mission accomplished.

Ethan pulled off his headset, hung it up, then powered down the helicopter. Outside, the wind howled, whipping snow in every direction. Thick flakes swirled in the glow of the resort's floodlights. The chopper rocked in the gusts, but they were on solid ground. A safe landing despite the near-whiteout conditions.

"That was awesome. Nicely done." Luke reached over and shook his hand. "Proud of you. I haven't flown in a storm like this in ages. Thanks for getting us back on the ground."

"Not a problem," Ethan said, tugging his hat down over his ears. "I've flown in far worse."

"I'm sure you have." Luke pushed open the door. The wind shoved it back against him. "I'll help these guys unload, then meet you inside. Mom and Dad are probably anxious to see us."

"Really? You think they're worried?"

His brother shot him a look, then hopped to the ground.

Huh. Ethan hesitated. What was he missing here? Okay, so visibility had dropped significantly, and the winds had picked up halfway through the trip. But he wasn't about to leave these guys stranded on a mountain in January. Especially when one of them had just found out his father had suffered a heart attack back home. He got out, his boots crunching in the fresh snow. The cold smacked him, seeping through his jacket.

Both of the men who'd flown with them had already climbed out of the helicopter and waited as Luke unlatched the cage to get their ski gear.

"Hey, guys." Ethan raised his voice to be heard above the wind and the whine of the rotors still slowing. "Appreciate you choosing to ski in Redemption. Come see us again sometime."

The man standing closest to him shook Ethan's outstretched hand. "Thanks for the lift. Nice job up there, sir."

"Yeah, a little hairy on top, but we made it." Ethan grinned. "Have a safe trip home, and we hope everything works out with your family."

His expression sobered. "Yeah, me too. Thanks. Take care."

As both men slung their backpacks over their shoulders, Luke grabbed their skis. He turned to Ethan and tipped his head toward the parking lot. "I'm guessing there's at least one other person who was worried about you too."

Ethan squinted, trying to see through the thick wet snowflakes still falling from the dark sky. "Who?"

Luke pointed. "Isn't that Tisha's car?"

Ethan frowned. "Oh, right. Yeah, I missed my meeting with Brody, Sadie, and Tisha."

"Now you'll get to apologize in person." Luke motioned for their clients to lead the way. "I'll help you guys load up so you can get out of here."

Hunching his shoulders against the wind, Ethan strode toward the resort. Man, he hated that he'd missed the meeting. Somehow he'd forgotten his phone at the resort, so he hadn't been able to send an update. Even though he had told Tisha where he'd be, it probably didn't help that he hadn't kept his word and shown up on time.

Yeah, okay, so Luke was right. He'd definitely have to apologize for that. He stepped inside the resort. Warm air carrying the slightest hint of soup or something savory greeted him. His stomach growled.

"Oh, thank You, Lord." His mom rushed toward him, pulling him into a warm hug. "I was so worried." She leaned back and craned her neck to see past him. "Where's Luke?"

"He's walking our clients to their rental and helping them load their stuff." Ethan surveyed his mom's face. The pinched lines between her brows and the tightness around her mouth made him gently squeeze her shoulders with his hands. "Mom, what's up? I haven't seen you look this worried in a long time."

"When Tisha showed up with Brody and Sadie, and then they said you missed your meeting, we all got worried." Mom slid a gentle smile his way. "Glad you're all back on the ground safely."

"Dad!"

Brody raced across the room and cannonballed into his knees. Ethan leaned over, then wrapped his arms around Brody's shoulders and held him tight. "Hey. Wow. I appreciate the warm welcome, everybody. What happened? Why all the fuss?"

He looked around for Tisha. She'd set her mug down on the coffee table by the fire, then slowly crossed the lobby. Now she stood a few feet away, arms linked across her chest and one hip jutted out. "You're back."

Uh-oh. Ethan straightened, then pulled off his gloves. "Yeah. Sorry I missed the meeting."

"Where were you?" Sadie frowned up at him. "Ms. Strom couldn't do her part because you weren't there to say *your* parts."

Oh. He palmed the back of his neck. "I'm so sorry. I didn't plan to miss our meeting. We had to sit for a few minutes on top of the mountain and wait until visibility improved. I really had to get those men off the mountain because they need to fly back home to Idaho. They've got a family emergency. I wanted to make sure I did everything I could to get them home safe. Tomorrow I'll call Mr. Price and Ms. Strom and reschedule that meeting as soon as we can, okay?"

Sadie sighed. "I guess that will work. Right, Mama?"

Tisha nodded.

Ethan glanced down at Brody again. "You okay, bud?"

Brody hesitated. "Yeah, but can I say something important?"

Ethan's stomach clenched. "Sure."

"I—I was praying like they taught us at kids' church, and it worked." His eyes lit up. "God heard me."

Oh wow. An unexpected lump formed in Ethan's throat. He patted Brody awkwardly on the back. "That's, um, that's awesome. Thanks for telling us."

Brody beamed. "I can't believe He answered."

That earned a soft laugh from the grown-ups standing in a circle around him.

"Sometimes I'm surprised when God answers my prayers too." Ethan turned to Tisha and Sadie. "Ladies, I'm truly sorry I kept you waiting. Thank you for being concerned and looking out for Brody."

"It's fine," Sadie said. "But you'll have to go first next time when Ms. Strom calls on us to answer her questions."

"Deal," Ethan said. He extended his fist. "Did you have a good day at school?"

She bumped her fist against his. "Yeah, it was okay. We got to play kickball in PE. This one boy, he kicked the ball so hard that it hit the wall on the opposite side."

Ethan eyed Brody. "Anybody we know?"

"It wasn't me," Brody said. "It was Christopher. He can kick super hard. It went so far. Next time we play kickball, I want to kick it and see if I can make a basket. But Mr. Wilkerson says he puts the baskets up so that doesn't happen."

"That would be pretty sweet," Ethan said. "I wish I could kick a kickball hard enough to make a basket."

"You totally can, Dad. I know it. Can we go watch some skateboarding on YouTube before dinner?"

"Yep. Just give me a minute to say goodbye to our friends."

"Come on, Sadie," Tisha said. "Grab your coat. Time to go."

"Thanks for bringing Brody back to the resort." Ethan followed them back to the couch in front of the fire, where they'd left their coats. The warmth from the crackling flames heated his back. "Hopefully we can reschedule for early next week."

"I'm glad you're safe." Avoiding his gaze, she put on her coat, then guided Sadie toward the door. Ethan watched them leave, a helpless feeling needling him. Was she mad?

Luke stepped inside, blocking their exit. "Hey, girls, what's up?" He high-fived Sadie and gave Tisha a quick hug. "Nice to see you. On your way home for dinner?"

"We are. Gotta run. See you around." She brushed past Luke and ushered Sadie outside.

Ethan didn't need Luke's pointed look to tell him he'd screwed up.

Luke unzipped his coat. "Seriously? You're just going to let her go like that?"

"She's got it." But even as the words left his mouth, they felt wrong.

Luke's brow furrowed. "Are you sure? She came all the way over here and brought you your kid. The least you can do is—"

"You're right. I'll go." Ethan rushed back out into the snow and hurried after Tisha. "Hey," he said, as he approached. "Let me help you clean off your car."

She stiffened, barely glancing at him as she took out the scraper. "Come on, Sadie, get in. Buckle up, please." She slammed the door, then skirted around him. "I can do it."

He followed her around to the driver's side. "I know you can. I still want to help you though."

A muscle in her cheek twitched. "You don't have to take care of me. I might be a Southern girl, but I know how to handle snow."

He reached for the scraper, but she held tight. "Tisha, why are you so upset?"

"I'm not."

"Yes, you are." He moved closer. "Is this about me missing that meeting?"

Her chin wobbled. "You really don't get it, do you?"

"Help me understand. Please."

Snow fell around them, landing on her hair, her eyelashes, and the shoulders of her jacket. "I waited for Chase to come home, and he didn't. And today I stood here, watching this storm, knowing you were in it, and all I could think was that I might lose someone else. I—I can't do that again."

His chest tightened. He reached for her, his fingers grazing hers as she gripped the scraper. "I'm so sorry."

She didn't pull away. But then somehow her diamond ring caught on the cuff of his jacket sleeve, tangling them together. Her breath hitched and she jerked her hand back, severing their connection.

"Tisha—"

"I can do this alone." She spun away, her hand trembling as she brushed the snow from her windshield. "I need to do this alone, because I don't want to depend on anyone."

"Why not?"

Her throat bobbed as she swallowed hard. "Because if I do, and they die . . . I can't survive that."

"Just because you lost Chase doesn't mean you have to shut me out." He gently pried the scraper from her grip. "So let's start small. Get in the car and warm up. I've got this."

She blinked at him, her lips parted and her breath coming in uneven puffs in the cold air.

"Please," he added, his voice soft.

She hesitated, then stepped back. "All right."

It wasn't much, but for now it was enough. She slid behind the wheel, then started the engine as he cleaned off the windshield. When he'd finished, she rolled down the window.

"Thank you." She offered a tight smile.

"You're welcome." He handed her the scraper. "Have a good night."

He stood in the parking lot until her taillights disappeared around the corner. His pulse still hadn't settled. Tonight confirmed what he'd sort of suspected—this thing between them wasn't just attraction. It was something deeper. Something real. And it terrified her.

To be honest, maybe it scared him a little too.

He turned and jogged back to the resort, her words still echoing in his head. *I don't want to depend on anyone.*

Yeah, well. Funny thing—he could totally relate. Because losing Adeline had wrecked him. But pushing people away? Maybe that wasn't the answer either.

Inside, his mom stood behind the check-in desk. "I'm booking one more reservation, and then I'll fix dinner. Brody's sitting at the table with Luke."

"Sounds good." He walked past the desk and went into the family's living area. Brody sat beside Luke at the farmhouse-style table, munching on cheese and crackers. They'd propped up an iPad on a stack of books.

"Dad, you've got to see this guy. His tricks are sick," Brody said through a mouthful of crackers.

Ethan washed his hands at the sink. "I'll watch in a few minutes. Right now I should probably help Mom with dinner."

"I'm just going to reheat the leftover chili and make some cornbread." Mom came into the kitchen. "Your dad is out with Hank because the hot tub is acting up."

Luke groaned. "Not again. That's the second time Hank's been out here this month."

Drying his hands on a paper towel, Ethan leaned against the counter. He didn't want to get in the middle of a discussion about the ongoing issues with the hot tub. Besides, if Brody had reading homework to do, they'd need to get on it. Soon. "Brody and I can set the table or mix the batter."

"Perfect." She handed him the cornbread box mix. "You know where to find the eggs and milk. I'll get you the oil."

"I'm really sorry about today, Mom. I didn't mean to worry you guys."

"It's all right, honey." She patted his shoulder. "Luke says you've flown in worse."

"That is a hundred percent true. I'll spare you the details."

Frowning, he unboxed the cornbread mix. Good thing he hadn't shared any stories of his Coast Guard days with Tisha. She would be shocked if she knew how many close calls he'd had over the years.

His mom set a glass measuring cup and a bottle of cooking oil on the counter beside him. "Everything all right?"

"Yeah, just, you know, second-guessing my decisions," he said, keeping his voice low. "Tisha was upset."

"Her concern for you was quite touching." Mom handed him a mixing bowl. "We're all relieved that you and Luke are here, and that you were able to get those men off the mountain. I'm sure their families will be happy to know they're on their way home."

"Minus the weather, we had a good outing. I think I even spotted more of Trevor's plane wreckage."

Behind him, a metal pan lid clattered on the floor.

Ethan spun around. "What? What'd I say?"

Mom straightened, a pan and the lid in her hands. "I did not expect you to mention Trevor. Or his plane. People have been looking for him for months."

"That's what I hear. We've flown over the same area twice, and I didn't want to take any unnecessary risks, but it sure looked like remnants of fiberglass from a plane."

"Wow. That would be so healing for his mom if you could find something. Anything."

"I'm going to keep trying," Ethan said. "Weather permitting, of course."

"Of course."

While Ethan whisked the milk, eggs, and oil into the dry ingredients, the weight of guilt pressed in. The memory of Trevor's brother MJ and his father's final moments still haunted him. A relentless reminder of his failures. What if he could finally bring closure to the family that had already lost so much? He glanced at his mother. Empathy filled her eyes, and she offered another reassuring smile.

"I have to find him," he said quietly. Because this wasn't just about Trevor and his family anymore—it was about making wrong things right. And he wouldn't stop until he achieved what he'd set out to do, no matter the cost. Because he had to put the past behind him. Especially if he wanted to start something new.

Nine

THIS WAS RIDICULOUS. *HE* WAS RIDICULOUS.

Why did she have to care so much?

Tisha sniffed, then dragged the back of her hand under her nose.

"Wouldn't that be sooo super fun?" Sadie bunny-hopped from the car toward Tom and Melinda's porch. "Then we could go sledding again, and Brody could do his skateboarding, and you and I could—Mama?" Sadie stopped hopping and swung one backpack strap onto her shoulder. "Are you crying?"

"I'm fine." Tisha shoved her hands into her coat pockets. "Everything's fine. Let's go inside."

"You don't look very fine," Sadie said.

Blinking back more tears, Tisha clicked the key fob to lock the car. Sadie trudged up the steps. Tisha followed, her insides twisted in knots.

Pull. It. Together.

She swallowed hard and mentally ran through a list of ingredients she'd need to make her next pie. Because she couldn't fall apart. Not now. And certainly not in front of Tom and Melinda.

"We're here," Sadie called out, pushing the front door open. "Grandma? Grandpa?"

The smell of tomato sauce and garlic wafted toward her. Melinda came into the hallway to greet them.

"Oh good, you're just in time. We're about to have lasagna and salad and French bread—oh dear." Melinda's eyes widened. "What's wrong?"

"Lasagna," Tisha sobbed. "It was Chase's favorite, and I could never make it taste as good as yours."

"Oh dear. Hey, Tom." Melinda turned back toward the family room. "Hon, could you take Sadie out into the garage, show her that new project you're working on?"

The recliner creaked as Tom put down the footrest and stood, shoved his feet into his slippers, and came closer. "Um, sure. Isn't it almost time for dinner though?"

"We'll call you guys when it's ready."

"Come on, sugar, keep your coat on." Tom patted Sadie on the head. "Wait until you see what I'm up to out here."

"Aw man, I'm hungry," Sadie said.

"I know. Me too. This will only take a couple of minutes." Concern etched his features, and he squeezed Tisha's arm. "You're going to get through this."

Tisha sniffed and tried to smile. "Thank you, that's sweet of you."

"Mama, what's the matter?" Sadie tugged on Tisha's coat sleeve. "Why are you crying about lasagna?"

"I'll be all right, sweat pea. I just need a few minutes with Grandma, okay?"

She swiped her fingertips across her cheeks. Sadie hesitated, her blue eyes swimming with concern.

"Come on. This way, Sadie."

She took her grandfather's hand, and they went out toward the door leading to the garage.

As soon as they were out of sight and the door clicked shut, Tisha fell into Melinda's arms, sobbing.

"Oh, sweet girl." Melinda stroked her hair. "This is a lot of tears over a lasagna recipe. I'm sure yours was delicious."

"It's not really about the lasagna," Tisha said, her whole body shaking.

"Then tell me what else is going on. Come in here and have a seat." Melinda guided her into the living room and sank down on the cozy sofa. The news played on television, and Melinda reached over and grabbed the remote, turning it off.

She pulled a box of tissues off the end table and set them beside Tisha.

Pulling her knees up under her chin and hugging them to her chest, Tisha took the Kleenex and blew her nose.

"I do wish I could replicate your lasagna recipe, but the real reason I'm crying is because Ethan McGuire came into the café today and he's been tasting my pie. I served him some, and he loved it, and then we were supposed to have this meeting after school for Sadie and Brody, right?"

"Right. You told me about that." Melinda nodded. "Sounded like those meetings were going well so far."

"They were, until he didn't show up."

"Uh-oh."

"But evidently he was off doing his job rescuing some people."

"A rescue?"

"Not really a rescue." Tisha wound the Kleenex around her fingertips and drew a shuddering breath. "They were on a routine trip, but they needed to come back down, and this weather is atrocious."

Melinda glanced toward the windows. "Well, there's a lot of snow and some wind, but we've had more severe conditions."

"So you'd call this a normal storm?"

"Yeah, pretty ordinary."

Sighing, Tisha shook her head. "Super."

"Why? What's the matter?"

"I was worried about him flying." More tears welled up. "And then I told him I was worried. And then he didn't come to the meeting, and we all freaked out. Even his mom was concerned. So I took the kids over to the resort to wait, and we had way too much sugar, which is why Sadie will not stop talking a mile a minute."

Melinda's mouth twitched, and she pressed her lips together.

"What? What's so funny? There's nothing funny about this."

"You were worried about Ethan McGuire flying a helicopter in a snowstorm?"

"Yes." Tisha threw up her hands, dropping the crumpled tissue in her lap. "Why is that so surprising?"

"Can you say more about that?"

"It scares me how much I cared, okay?" There. She said it. "I—I don't like caring about him. He's hardheaded and handsome and hardly ever likes the pie."

This time, Melinda couldn't stop her laugh, and she pressed her fingers over her mouth.

"Why is that funny?"

"Listen." Melinda's expression grew serious, and she covered Tisha's hand with hers. "Chase loved you. A thousand percent. You were the one for him. And he loved Sadie so very much, and I hate that he's gone. What I wouldn't give to hear him crack a lame joke or to make him lasagna one more time."

Another lump formed in Tisha's throat. She squeezed Melinda's hand.

"I know you miss him," Tisha whispered.

"But here's the thing. I don't think that he would want you to stuff all these feelings."

Tisha squirmed. "But I'm not ready."

"You're not ready to do what? Think about moving on? Go on a first date? Or be friends with a man? I need you to name what it is you think you're not ready for."

Tisha waved her hand in the air. "All of it."

"Well, it seems like maybe part of your heart is turning toward moving on. Why don't you take some baby steps?"

"I'm already serving him pie, and our kids are fighting but then acting like they're best friends the next minute. I don't know." She tipped her head back on the couch. "Ugh, this is exasperating."

"Can I make a suggestion?"

"Sure."

"Why don't you start by taking off your wedding rings?"

Tisha sat straight up. "No."

"Why not?"

"Because . . ." She looked down at the band and diamond combination that she had worn for almost a decade.

"Why don't you try taking them off and just getting used to not wearing rings while you're at work? You can always put them both right back on when you come home."

"I take my rings off sometimes."

"You do? When?"

"Like right now, when I'm helping you get ready for dinner."

She stood and crossed to the kitchen. Melinda had a gorgeous crystal ring holder beside her sink. She took off the band and the diamond solitaire and set them on the post, then squirted soap onto her hands and rubbed them together.

"See?"

Melinda stood and joined her in the kitchen. She donned her oven mitts, then pulled the oven door open and peeked inside. "Taking your rings off is the first step, honey. But it's the first of many."

"Oh no." Tisha crossed to the refrigerator and pulled out the salad. "What else do I need to brace myself for?"

Melinda teared up, then tipped her head toward the urn of Chase's ashes sitting on the table nearby.

"Oh. Well, I moved his ashes from the cabin to here the other day while you were both at the café, thinking maybe it was a small step in the right direction." Tisha blinked back more tears. "But I'm definitely not ready to spread them yet."

"I know," Melinda whispered, then drew a ragged breath. "But someday you will be. Like I've already told you, God called you here for a reason. And I know grief is hard. Believe me, I know. But He will equip you. And if you're meant to have a second chance at love, by all means, grab it with both hands."

Tisha turned away from Chase's urn. She reached for the salad tongs as Melinda's words spooled through her head. She tossed the salad and avoided looking at her ring sparkling from its parking space on the counter. Outside, the snow kept falling, soft and relentless. A second chance. A new beginning. A fresh start. Whatever. It didn't matter how she labeled her next chapter. The question was, could she really let herself believe any of that was possible?

⇜

Ethan pulled the metal rolling cart out of the closet that the custodian had just unlocked for him. The wheels squeaked as he pulled it closer to the side of the court.

"Here you go." He handed the basketball to Brody.

"Thanks." Brody dribbled it around a little bit. They were the only two in the elementary-school gym, and the sound echoed off the walls. Ethan draped his whistle on a lanyard around his neck and grabbed a ball, bouncing it a few times. The bright lights and the shine on the parquet floor made the gym feel alive. His shoes squeaked as he crossed to the bench, setting his whiteboard and dry-erase marker on the last chair. He pulled a couple of towels and a water bottle for himself and Brody out of his string bag.

Brody stood under the backboard, staring up.

"You want to take a shot, bud?"

"All right." Brody tossed the ball up toward the backboard, but it bounced off and rolled away.

"Oops. Missed that one." Brody chased after the ball.

Ethan opened his mouth to correct his form but thought better of it. It was game day—their first together. "Nice try though. You'll make the next one, right?"

"Maybe. Dad, did you tell Miss Tisha you were sorry for missing our meeting?"

Ethan paused, wedging the ball on his hip under his arm. "I did. Yes. Why?"

"Just wondered." Brody squeezed the ball between both hands. "She's super nice. I just wanted to make sure you said you were sorry."

"I did. I invited her and Sadie to come to our game today, but they have a lot of pies to make."

"Oh. All right." Brody shrugged. "That's cool."

Laughter in the hallway outside the gym filtered in as parents and kids came in talking, wearing their winter coats and hats and carrying water bottles. The next thirty minutes flew by as Ethan made sure all the kids had their T-shirts with the number screen-printed on the back and the hardware store's logo on the front. Derek and Tammy had done a great job getting local businesses to sponsor the teams.

Ethan scanned the roster on his phone, then did a quick head count. Twelve players, including Brody, was kind of a lot. He'd make it work though. Grant had sent him a PDF with a guide to make sure every kid had close to equal playing time. His assistant coach, Nicholas, rounded the kids up. Brody took his seat on the last folding chair at the end of the row, and Ethan sank down beside him, putting his hand on his shoulder.

"Hey, I know you're not super excited to be here, but I might need you to sub in. We haven't practiced very much, and your teammates will probably get tired."

Brody looked away, quirking his mouth to one side. He nodded finally. "I can do that."

"Great. You want to jump up? Put your hand in the huddle?"

Brody nodded, then followed him toward the players huddled together near the sideline.

"Hello, Ninja Narwhals!" Ethan could hardly say the team name they'd voted on without laughing. "Welcome to your first game. I'm so glad you're here. Remember, pass the ball, look for the open shot, just like we talked about in practice. Everybody hustle and let's have fun."

"Teamwork on three," Nicholas said.

They all piled their hands in. "One, two, three. Teamwork!" they yelled.

Ethan picked out his starting five, and the high school kids who were volunteering as refs got the game started. He was tempted to pace the sideline just like his coach had done in high school, but he sat down instead. Nicholas claimed the seat beside him. They didn't know each other really, but Ethan didn't have anybody else in mind to coach with, and he'd grown up playing ball with the boy's dad.

"Nicholas, what do you think? Man-to-man defense or zone?"

The kids lined up for the jump ball. "We'll be lucky if they dribble without traveling. And let's hope they can score at least one basket."

"Keeping our expectations low, then. That's probably wise." A few minutes into the game, three players had already traveled, dribbled the ball off their feet, and shot two air balls. But the errors were equally spread out across both teams, so Ethan couldn't really complain. They were only going to play four six-minute quarters, which was probably for the best. As the minutes rolled on and they approached the halftime break, the game was still tied two to two.

At halftime, they sat on the floor behind the bench, faces flushed and sweaty. They all looked up at him expectantly. He didn't know what to say; he was used to winning no matter what. Thankfully, Nicholas had a few pointers to share.

"You guys are doing great." He clapped his hands. "We're super proud of you. Right, Coach?"

He pinned Ethan with a long look.

"Absolutely." Ethan cleared his throat. "Super proud."

One little girl was picking at the icon on the side of her sneaker. Her friend was studying the ends of her ponytail. Two boys were poking each other and laughing. Brody sat crisscross style, his chin resting on his folded hands, eyes on Nicholas. At least somebody was paying attention. The ref blew a whistle, summoning the team to come back to the court. Ethan sat on the bench, one knee bouncing up and down. The other team scored one basket in the third quarter, putting the Narwhals down three to two. The kids couldn't seem to remember almost anything they'd practiced, but they sure did like to dribble and dribble and dribble some more.

After the fifth traveling call, Ethan was about to come out of his chair. "What is even happening right now?"

"It's only our first game," Nicholas said. "Plus it's not over yet."

With two minutes on the clock, Ethan leaned down the bench. "Brody, I need you to sub in."

Brody's eyes grew wide. "Okay." He stood and walked slowly toward his dad.

"I want you to go in for Xander." Ethan put his hand on Brody's shoulder. "Time's almost up, so try your best to shoot a basket just one time. Can you do that?"

"I guess so, Dad."

Brody subbed in, and the next time their team had the ball, Sierra dribbled down the court and passed it to Brody. He dribbled twice, his tongue tucked in the corner of his mouth, and stopped. The opposing team waved their hands in the air—a blur of purple.

"Come on. Come on." Brody seemed to take forever. "Come on, shoot the ball!"

With near-perfect form, Brody launched the ball toward the basket. It hit the center of the backboard and dropped through the net. Ethan shot to his feet, jumping up and down. "Brody, that was brilliant!"

Brody mirrored Ethan's pose, both arms thrust in the air.

"Easy, Coach, don't run out on the court." Nicholas tugged on the hem of Ethan's shirt.

While the other team inbounded the ball, Ethan turned around and scanned the crowd. He really wanted to share this moment with Tisha, but she'd stayed true to her word and hadn't come by. He smiled at his mom, and she and his dad waved. Luke, Tate, and Megan were all there too. They each clapped and gave him a thumbs-up.

Okay, so it was only seven- and eight-year-old rec-league basketball, but it was Brody's first basket—at least the first one he'd ever seen in a live game. Sierra ended up scoring a basket with only ten seconds left in the game. After lots of high fives and handshakes, Ethan and Nicholas corralled the kids. A mom handed out apple slices. Brody took the bag but didn't eat them.

After everyone had left, they met their family at the end of the bleachers.

"Great job, buddy." Megan pulled Brody into a tight hug. "That was amazing."

"Thanks." Brody squirmed out of her embrace. "Grandma, did you bring any drinks?"

"You just had a juice box, pal." Luke ruffled Brody's sweaty hair. "Still thirsty?"

Brody nodded. "Hungry too."

"Way to go, Coach." Tate clapped Ethan on the shoulder. "It was touch and go there toward the end."

"Yep. They kept us on the edge of our chairs, didn't they?" Ethan couldn't stop grinning.

"Great job, Brody." Tate bumped Brody's fist. "You and Sierra made a great team."

Brody glowed under everyone's praise as they headed out to the truck.

"Hey, let's go by the café and celebrate with pie," Ethan said.

"All right," Brody said, clicking his seatbelt into place. "Do you think Sadie's there?"

"Probably. She likes to help make pies, right?"

"I don't know. I guess."

Ethan turned on the radio and sang along to a popular song while Brody nibbled on his apple slices and drank the rest of his water. But when they pulled up in front of the café, the Closed sign filled the window.

"Oh man," Brody said. "Why are they closed on a Saturday?"

"I don't know." Ethan pulled out his phone and texted Tisha.

Ethan

Hey, Brody and I won our
first game. We came by to
celebrate with pie. Looks like
you guys are closed?

He sent the message with a *whoosh*. "Let's see if she answers."

Three dots bounced on the screen, stopped, bounced again, and then stopped.

"Oh, come on," he growled.

"What's the matter?"

"The message is taking forever to get here."

The bubble filled the screen.

Tisha

Come to the front door. I'll let you
in. We've got pie.

"Oh, she's going to let us come in."

They climbed out of the truck and bounded toward the front

door. Tisha met them on the other side, and the smell of paint fumes greeted them.

"What's going on?"

"We're closed today. Tom and Melinda wanted to get the ceiling painted before the festival, and today was the day the painters were available." She gestured to a ladder and a tarp in the middle of the dining room. "They took a late lunch break, though, so it's just me and Sadie here."

"Hi, Brody." Sadie came out of the kitchen, flour on her face and sprinkled down the front of her apron.

"Hey. What are you making?"

"Pie. Lots and lots of pie," Sadie said. "Mama, can I take a break?"

"Sure." Tisha pointed to a booth. "Brody, you and Sadie want to hang out there? I'll bring you a snack. She's got some markers and a coloring page."

"All right." Brody followed Sadie. "Sadie, guess what! We won our game."

"Oh good. Was it fun?"

"Yeah, sort of."

While Sadie handed Brody markers and a coloring page, Ethan sat down at the counter.

"Congrats on your win," Tisha said. "Want some water or coffee? I just brewed a pot for myself."

"Water's fine, thanks." He grinned. "Aren't you going to try to guess what kind of pie I need? Or do you have a special flavor for game-day wins?"

Shrugging, she set a glass of water on the counter in front of him. "Whatever flavor you want."

Whoa. That wasn't like her. He ducked his head, trying to meet her eyes. "Hey, what's going on? What's the matter?"

She hesitated, then let out a sigh and looked away. "Here's the thing. Chase loved flying." Her voice lower, she gripped the edge of the counter with both hands. "Sometimes I think he loved it more than me."

Her words were like a fist to his heart. "I don't believe that's true."

"There were so many times he went off on some adventure and I didn't say anything about how scared I was. Especially the last time. I hate that I didn't tell him I didn't want him to take that trip. I was filled with dread the whole time, and of course it ended in the worst possible outcome—exactly what I feared." Her voice caught. "But what was I supposed to say? I mean, he was filling in for someone else who was in a bind. He was doing what he thought God had called him to do. So how selfish am I to complain about . . . ?"

She trailed off, her expression twisting.

Poor thing. She'd really wrestled with this. He glanced at her hands, still gripping the counter. His breath hitched. She'd taken off her rings.

He cleared his throat, then reached for his glass of water. "That's a heavy load to carry. And for what it's worth, I don't expect you to live like that. Thank you for trusting me with the truth. It means a lot."

Her gaze slid to meet his, those stunning blue eyes searching his face. Then she straightened and gestured over her shoulder. "Let me go check and see which flavors we have in the back."

"Tisha, wait. I—"

"I'll just be a minute." Her voice was too bright, too rushed, as she pushed through the swinging doors into the kitchen.

He glanced at the kids sitting in the booth. They were chatting away and looked like they were coloring without any issues.

Tisha wasn't checking on pie.

She was running.

And he wasn't about to let her.

Ten

"J ISHA," ETHAN CALLED AFTER HER.

She kept walking. The kids would be all right coloring together. Thankfully, the painters hadn't come back from their break, and Tom and Melinda weren't here either. She had the kitchen all to herself. Or so she thought.

She barely had time to take a breath before Ethan followed her in. She turned, ready to tell him she had apple or chess pie to offer, but the way he moved toward her, something resolute and determined in his expression, stopped her.

"Talk to me," he said. "Please."

A shiver rippled through her. Wow, she had really blabbed it all, hadn't she? *Don't hold back, girl. Way to keep it real.* Maybe it was best to be authentic and raw. Because it did freak her out how much she'd worried about him. And now he knew that she'd worried, and that kind of made it worse.

"I—I didn't mean to say all of that." She paced the quiet kitchen. The refrigerator hummed. Somewhere, ice dropped into the ice-maker bin.

"Why not?" He moved closer. "You think I don't worry about you?"

"We've been over that already. You don't need to worry about me." She faced the industrial ovens and scraped at a mysterious splash on the console. "I don't take risks like you do."

"Do you think I take risks just to take them? I know what I'm doing, Tisha. I'm careful. I train. Rarely do I work alone. But I've also learned that sometimes life doesn't go the way we expect."

"Exactly." She whirled to face him. "Sometimes the worst thing happens anyway."

His gaze flicked to her left hand. "I noticed you're not wearing your rings. Is that just a today thing or . . ."

Her breath hitched. "I don't know," she whispered, rubbing at the bare spot on her finger. "It was Melinda's idea, so I'm trying."

His eyebrows sailed upward. "Trying what exactly?"

"Trying to accept that holding on isn't making my life easier."

Ethan studied her, his hands tucked into the pockets of his gray joggers. "You're allowed to let go. It doesn't mean you have to forget. Doesn't mean you stop loving him. It just means you keep living."

Her throat tightened. "But what if I don't know how?"

Without saying another word, he pulled her into his arms. No second-guessing. No hesitation. Just warmth and steadiness and the solid strength of him holding her together.

Oh.

She blinked back more tears. How she wanted to fall apart in his strong arms. She let her cheek rest against the broad expanse of his muscular chest. Then her arms found their way around his lower back. She pressed her palms against the strong muscles bracketing his spine. He smoothed her hair down with his hand and rested his chin on top of her head. She could get used to this.

"I hope you don't mind me sharing this, but it's possible for you to honor Chase's memory and still have a very full and vibrant life."

She slowly pulled away and stared up at him, but her eyes, of their own volition, drifted toward his lips.

"Are you sure about that?"

His laugh rumbled in his throat. She kept her hands entwined behind his back and let her eyes move slowly up over the planes of his cheeks. Her fingers itched to trace the curve of his eyebrows.

His eyes landed on her lips. "That's what people keep telling me anyway."

It wouldn't take much for her to close the distance between them, to brush her lips against his. What would happen if she kissed him right now?

"What are you guys doing?"

Tisha jumped away as if Ethan were a hot pan with a grease fire. "Nothing."

Sadie stood with her little fists propped on her hips and glared up at Ethan. "Why are you hugging my mommy? I don't like it."

Tisha dragged her palms over her scorched cheeks. Nothing quite like getting caught by your seven-year-old. She drew in a ragged breath. "Sadie—"

Sadie's face crumpled and she turned on her heel, bolting out of the kitchen. The doors swung shut behind her, leaving the kitchen thick with unspoken words.

Tisha blew out a shaky breath. "I knew this would be hard for her, but I didn't expect—" She stopped and shook her head. "I like you, Ethan. I really do. And I like the idea of seeing where this could go. But the reality is, Sadie might not be ready. Maybe she'll never be ready. I don't know. But she is my priority."

Ethan nodded, his face an unreadable mask. "I understand. Brody and I should probably get going."

"But I didn't give you any pie."

"Yeah, there's always next time." He smiled at her, but it held a tinge of sadness, and he quickly looked away. "Catch you later."

"See you," she whispered.

Through the service window, she watched him pluck his jacket off the back of his stool.

"Brody, time to go."

After they left, Tisha walked out into the café. Sadie sat in the booth where she'd been coloring, slumped against the red vinyl cushion.

Sadie's lower lip trembled. "I don't like you hugging him," she said, her eyes welling with tears.

Tisha's heart cracked wide open again. "Come here, sweet girl."

She dropped to her knees on the cold linoleum and pulled Sadie in for a hug. What could she say? She wasn't about to promise that she'd never hug Ethan again, because honestly, it had felt good. But like she'd sensed all along, Sadie wasn't ready for her to have a new man in her life. And she probably wasn't either. No matter how many times he smiled at her.

⁓

"That's the last splint bag. I already checked the crutches. They're in great shape," Dad said, setting the red duffel bag down on the floor in the shed. Luke sat cross-legged beside Ethan on the floor. They had the splint bags, the automated external defibrillator, first aid kits, and their toolbox out for their monthly maintenance check.

"I need to head to the hardware store. Tate's picking me up in five minutes. You two need anything?" Dad pulled out his phone. "Your mom already gave me a list."

"I'll take another roll of duct tape, please," Luke said.

"I don't have anything to add. Thanks though." Ethan hesitated. Now wasn't the best time to ask, since Dad was on his way out to run an errand, but he couldn't not bring this up. "Wait, Dad. Before you go, I want to ask you about something. When I was flying last week out near Townsend Glacier, this piece of ice calved off the face, and the ripple effect in the water was stunning. Has the city council or the emergency response vessel system . . . Are they ever concerned about that?"

"We've talked about it," Dad said, glancing up from his phone. "You know, son, we've put a lot of precautions in place over the years—the retaining wall, for one. After the oil spill and the '64 earthquake, this town got pretty good at establishing emergency protocols and tsunami evacuation routes. We do drills now and again. You should ask Tate. He might be able to give you more information."

"We talked about this when we flew over a couple weeks ago," Luke said. "Have you noticed something more concerning?"

"I've been doing some research," Ethan said. "Not long ago, downtown Juneau flooded when a dam of ice broke loose and the water poured into town. In 2015, a glacier calved and triggered a massive landslide near Yakutat in Icy Bay. I'm wondering if something like that could happen here in Redemption."

Luke lifted one shoulder. "I suppose it could happen, but let's hope it doesn't."

"I don't think you need to be concerned. But I'm glad you're paying attention. See you boys later." Dad turned his wheelchair around and headed for the door.

Ethan unzipped the bag on the AED and ran through the simulation.

"Dude, it works. You've got it," Luke said. "Why are you so distracted today?"

"Oh man." Ethan rubbed his fingertips along his jaw. "I did something I shouldn't have."

Luke grinned. "You? Mr. Rule-Follower Extraordinaire?"

"Easy there, Little Bro. Believe it or not, sometimes I do make mistakes."

"Can't wait to hear more." Luke rubbed his hands together. "Tell me everything."

"Seriously, I think I need your help."

Luke's expression sobered. "Now I'm really listening. It's not very often that you ask for advice."

"Yeah, savor the moment, would ya? Won't happen again for another decade." Ethan zipped up the AED bag, then set it aside. "So I had no idea Tisha was so upset when we came home late."

Luke counted out a stack of gauze pads, then slid them into a plastic bag. "Is this about you flying in the snowstorm the other day?"

Ethan nodded.

"Pretty sure I tried to tell you that."

"And I got the message. But when I tried to help her, she got upset and told me she had to go it alone because she couldn't rely on anyone."

"Yeah, 'cause you scared her."

"Oh boy." Ethan shook his head. "Whose side are you on?"

"Right now? Hers. Because something tells me you're making questionable choices."

"What? No." Ethan groaned and chucked a shrink-wrapped ACE bandage at him. "That's why I need your help."

Laughing, Luke ducked, then plucked it out of the air. "Say that one more time, please. I like the sound of you asking me to impart wisdom."

"Wait, there's more. After we won the basketball game, I took Brody over to the café for pie, but they were closed. So I texted her and asked if she was in there. She let us in. They were having some painting done so they were closed unexpectedly. Anyway, I thought Brody and Sadie were gonna hang out, color, chat. I planned to taste some pie. Everything was going to be glorious. Given the way she'd left the resort, super upset, I sort of expected she'd be angry. But she wasn't. Instead, she pretty much told me that she couldn't ever date a pilot again because she'd spent so much time worried that something bad would happen to Chase."

Luke stilled. Surprise, and then empathy, rolled across his features. "To be fair, her worst nightmare became her reality. I can't blame her for being concerned, and I'm glad she told you how she felt. But the thing is—"

Ethan stood and started to pace the floor. "My worst fear became reality too."

He looked around for a basketball, but they were all put away for now. His fingers itched to bounce something, launch a ball at the backboard. Instead, he fisted his hands at his side. "Adeline was just about perfect." His voice grew rough, gravelly. "Fantastic mom, all-around great human. She didn't need me."

"Oh, that is not true. I think she needed you very much."

"Well, she adjusted to life as a Coastie's wife and fully supported every mission I went on. If she was worried, she never said anything about it, but I failed her, Luke. I could have gotten her better medical care, and I didn't."

"You can't blame yourself. Really great people get melanoma. Really bad people coast through life with no health issues. That kind of stuff just isn't fair, man."

"I know, I know. You're right." Ethan tipped his head back and stared at the ceiling. "But these feelings, Tisha's reaction—I felt blindsided. Then Sadie walked in."

"Uh-oh."

"I hugged Tisha because I felt bad and I didn't know what else to do. It was sort of impulsive, but she was in the kitchen alone and looked like she was about to come undone, and so I just hugged her, and she . . ."

He trailed off.

"And she what?"

Ethan raked his hand through his hair. "If we had been there much longer, we probably would have kissed."

"Whoa, I did not expect that." Luke grinned. "So what stopped you?"

"Sadie. She walked in, pretty much fussed at us, then looked me right in the eye and told me she did not like me hugging her mama."

"Yikes." Luke grimaced. "What about Brody?"

"I didn't tell him what happened. We made a quick exit, and he didn't ask why."

"Huh. Well, what are you going to do about Sadie?"

"I'm going to let her mom handle it for now. But at some point, I'm going to have to win her over. That's the part where I need your help. What do I do next?"

Luke hesitated. "Listen, you have lived through the unimaginable. So has Tisha. And yet here you are, both standing strong. You both had the courage to move to Alaska, start over as single parents, put your kids in new schools, get jobs, everything—it's all different. And I can tell you from my own experience that letting somebody you care about get away fills you with so much regret. So if you care about each other, I vote you go for it. Sadie will come around. You don't really want to be single forever, do you?"

"No. I just didn't expect to meet somebody so soon."

"Grief doesn't have a timeline, and I think you and Tisha will have to figure this out one step at a time, but don't let a good thing get away. And I can't speak for Chase, but I knew him probably better than anybody, and I don't think he would expect her to stay single forever. He would want his daughter to grow up being raised by a good man." His voice broke off, and he stared at the floor.

Ethan swallowed against the tightness in his own throat. "Thank you for your advice."

Luke tipped his chin up, then sniffed. "You're welcome. Hope it helped."

"It did." Ethan nodded. "I'm not going to be at the whims of a seven-year-old's timeline forever. Somehow, I'll convince Sadie that there's room for me and Brody in her life."

Eleven

ONE HUNDRED AND THIRTY-FOUR BALLOONS. Inflated and wedged into the plastic template. Sure, she could do that, right? She'd tackled far more complex projects helping her sister Natalie at the wedding venue back in North Carolina. Tisha turned and scanned Redemption's spacious community center. What a gorgeous new facility. The bright lights, the laminate floor, and the pale gray-green paint on the walls made the space incredibly inviting. About twenty women worked together, chatting as they decorated tables with festive plastic tablecloths and arranged booths for carnival-style games.

"Good news, Tisha. I rounded up two more volunteers to help with our festival prep." Chloe joined her beside the stage. "My sister and niece will be here shortly. Tying the knots in the balloons can be a little tricky though. My niece might not be able to do that part."

"I'll take all the help I can get," Tisha said. Her fingers ached already just thinking about tying more than a hundred knots in balloons. They might need to make an afternoon coffee run first.

"Mommy, where's Brody? I want to play with him." Sadie tugged the cuff of Tisha's sweater. "There aren't any kids here I know."

Tisha spotted Ethan helping Luke carry long tables in the front door. "There's his dad and his Uncle Luke."

Sadie frowned. "But I don't see Brody. Why isn't he here?"

"I'm not sure, sweetie. Look." Tisha tapped her palm on the stage where she'd carved out a space beside the packages of balloons. "I brought snacks, your water bottle, and see—there's a movie all queued up on my tablet. Why don't you and Ollie get cozy and watch?"

"I can't hear the sound. It's too loud in here." Sadie wrinkled her nose. "Besides, I've already seen that movie twice."

Tisha wanted to scream. "Remember, I asked you to make sure to pack your headphones. You also told me this is the movie you wanted to watch."

"Can I help you with the balloons instead?" Sadie picked up one of the pale-pink balloons her friend had already inflated and batted it around. But it landed on the floor and popped. Sadie screamed and jumped in the air, then flung herself against Tisha's legs. A few people standing nearby laughed. Tisha winced. This was not going well.

"It's okay, I brought extra. Maybe we could just do sort of a half arch. That would be faster and easier." Chloe held up her phone with an image she'd found online. "We could just run it up the wall, stage a little spot for people to take photos. I've already got 'Love Is in the Air' printed out in big letters."

"Oh, that'll be so cute," Tisha said, forcing a smile and awkwardly trying to comfort Sadie. "Sweetheart, I really want to help get ready for the festival. Let's see if we can find a project for you to do."

"Everything is heavy and hard to lift." Sadie frowned. "And there's no one to play with."

"Grandma and Grandpa will be here soon."

"But they'll probably just drag out more tables and chairs like everybody else," Sadie said. "Isn't there anything that kids can do?"

"Come here," Chloe said. "I've got a job you can do. I bet you're great at counting."

Sadie beamed. "I'm awesome at counting."

Tisha smiled, then opened a new package of balloons.

"I want you to help me count and make sure I have enough pink pens. Do you think you can count to a hundred?" Chloe opened the lid on a cardboard box.

"Yes. I could count to a hundred like two years ago."

"Excellent. I want you to take all these pink pens out of this box and put them in this cup." Chloe set a plastic disposable cup on the stage. "Do you think you can handle that?"

Sadie tapped her finger against her chin. "I'm not sure if they'll fit."

"Oh, good point. Maybe you could put them into four groups of twenty-five. How about that?"

"I'm on it," Sadie said, settling cross-legged on the stage not far from Tisha and Chloe.

"Thank you," Tisha said quietly. "Do you really need her to count those pens?"

"No, but I think *you* really need her to count those pens. By the way, if she's busy counting pens, that'll give you time to talk to Ethan."

"No, I don't need to talk to Ethan." A strand of hair slid loose from her ponytail, and she tucked it behind her ear. "Ethan and I are good. We don't . . . We're friends."

"Yeah, okay. You keep telling yourself that," Chloe said. "Come on. We'd better get cracking on these balloons."

Chloe found an empty electrical outlet close by and plugged in the inflator. Charlie joined them and automatically blew up one of the pink balloons. She passed it to Chloe, who tied a knot and then slipped it into the opening on the plastic template.

"When she's finished with the pens, maybe we can get her to count out pink, white, red, and silver balloons," Chloe said.

"That would be perfect. I suggest we keep her away from the ones filled with glitter," Tisha said.

Chloe smiled. "I'll keep that in mind."

"Hey." Ethan's deep voice sent a delicious warmth zipping all the way to her fingertips. She turned and smiled. Man, he looked good in a plaid button-down she hadn't seen before, jeans faded just the perfect amount, and scuffed work boots. The teal lines in his navy-blue shirt made his eyes look even brighter.

"Hi."

"I brought you a latte." He held out a disposable coffee cup with a black plastic lid. "Hope you like it."

"Wow." She took the latte from him. The ribbed edges on the cardboard sleeve had a Copper Kettle logo.

"The barista didn't know your usual order, so we had to guess. It's hazelnut."

"Sounds yummy. Thank you. That's really sweet of you." She wanted to press up on her tiptoes and brush a kiss across his cheek, but the whole room seemed to be watching. And Sadie would flip out. "What are you up to?"

As if she hadn't just seen him haul five tables through the door.

"We're finished with tables. Next we'll bring folding chairs in. You?"

"Um, balloon arch."

"I think I got the easier assignment," he said. "What's Sadie doing?"

"Don't look or breathe her direction, but we put her to work counting pens because she refused to watch the movie I rented for her. She's been asking for Brody."

Ethan gave a slow smile. "Has she? Well, he'll be here in a few minutes. He went with my dad and Tate to pick up something they needed."

He looked around. "Where's the pie walk going to be?"

"I've been given one corner of the community center." She gestured over her shoulder. "What's your family doing?"

"We'll hold a raffle for a weekend stay at the resort. Megan's boyfriend can't come back, so we brought in another dog musher with his team. He'll probably give rides. And there'll be free snowshoeing, cross-country skiing, and the alumni basketball game. Plenty to keep us busy."

"This is a beautiful building. Pretty new, right?"

"Yeah, they just built it about eighteen months ago." Ethan frowned. "Although I don't like how close it is to the water."

"We're at least a few feet above sea level, aren't we? And that new retaining wall is incredible. That wasn't here before."

Before, when she'd visited with Chase. She stopped herself from mentioning that part.

Ethan rubbed his palm across the back of his neck. "This town's been hit with a lot over the years. I would hate for something this beautiful to have to withstand water or wind or storm damage."

"True. That would be a huge loss." She smiled brightly. "Thanks for the latte. I better get to work."

"Yeah, you're welcome. Have fun." He turned and crossed the room, and she forced herself to look away.

"You ready to thank me now for keeping your daughter occupied?" Chloe tied a knot in another inflated balloon. "A latte? He tried to bring your usual order. Girl, you better hang on to him."

She felt her cheeks flush. "You and Charlie are relentless. We're friends. That's it."

Chloe pinned her with a long look. "Really?"

"Yes, really." Tisha checked on Sadie, who was deeply engrossed in her project. Thankfully she hadn't popped over to make any comments about Ethan showing up.

"Yeah, well, I don't have any guy friends that bring me lattes and look at me like that," Charlie said, keeping her voice low. "You guys need to go on a proper date."

"I'm not sure if you've noticed, but we are two exhausted single parents with very busy children who alternate between getting along super well and being each other's worst enemies."

"Huh. So a hot, available guy brings you coffee and you're going to pretend it means nothing?" Charlie smiled and nudged her with her hip. "Come on."

Warmth heated Tisha's cheeks. "It's not that simple. Yes, okay, so he's handsome. And thoughtful. But Sadie's made it clear she's not ready for me to date."

Charlie quirked her lips to one side. "Sadie's a great kid, but she's not the boss of your life."

Tisha picked at the cardboard liner ringing her coffee cup. "I know that. But she's been through so much already, and the last thing I want is to make her feel unsettled. She's still adjusting to losing Chase, and moving—"

Charlie set an uninflated balloon down, then pressed her hand to Tisha's arm. "I get that. But would it hurt to push her a little? I mean, you obviously love your daughter, and you know what's best. I just hate for you to let her fear or her discomfort keep you stuck. Maybe it's time to show her that love doesn't always mean we keep things the same. Because life rarely looks like we plan, right? Maybe God will use this as an opportunity to show you and Sadie that taking a risk can be surprising. Rewarding, even."

"But what if she resents me or the person I'm dating?"

"I'm not saying that won't happen." Charlie leaned back against the stage. "But she can't possibly know what's best for you. She's seven. You're letting her hold you hostage to a life that might not be what God has for you."

Tisha winced. "Ouch."

"I'm not trying to sound harsh. All I'm saying is, don't let Sadie's fear stop something before it even has a chance to get started.

Because surely God has your good in mind. What if He brought you both here to Redemption for a reason?"

Huh. That sounded remarkably similar to what Melinda had said. Tisha massaged her forehead with her fingertips. "You really think Ethan and I would be good together?"

Charlie tilted her head. "How will you know if you don't try?"

She wiped her clammy palms on her jeans, then twisted a balloon into place on the arch. Thoughts of Ethan trying to clean off her car in the snow, and the way his strong arms had pulled her close, and how he'd brought her coffee even after Sadie had thrown a fit at the café last weekend all swirled in her head.

Charlie had a point. Maybe it wasn't right to let Sadie try to control something that wasn't hers to control.

"I see you over there," Charlie said, her brown eyes gleaming. "What are you pondering? Green-eyed aviators who wear Henleys really well?"

Tisha couldn't help but laugh. Shaking her head, she reached for her coffee again. "I'm warming to the idea of a first date."

"Yes!" Charlie pumped her fist in the air. "I knew it."

"Shhh." Tisha pressed her palm over Charlie's hand and gently pushed it down. "Sadie can't get wind of this. Not yet."

Charlie feigned a serious expression. "You're right."

"What did you have in mind?"

"Oh, I bet Mrs. McGuire and I could figure out how to arrange some convenient, inexpensive childcare, and I bet if I dropped a few hints to Ethan, he could come up with something romantic." Charlie winked. "What do you think?"

Tisha sipped her latte to hide her hopeful expression. The espresso and hazelnut and steamed milk were the perfect combination of sweet and rich. "It sounds like you're not gonna take no for an answer. So if you help me get this balloon arch finished and come up with some affordable childcare that Sadie won't hate, then yes, I will follow through with whatever you have planned for me and Ethan."

"Dang, you're not demanding at all." Charlie handed her another balloon. "Here, you keep after this arch while I implement Operation Love Is in the Air."

Tisha groaned. "That is so cheesy."

"And you are so going to thank me later."

Would she though? Harmless flirting over pie didn't mean much. A date with prearranged childcare made the backs of her knees tingle. She still wasn't convinced she was ready. But she wouldn't refuse either.

As a Coast Guard aviator, he'd flown thousands of missions over the ocean in all kinds of conditions: rain, hail, and glorious sunshine. But he had never, not one time, flown a woman to see the northern lights. He also hadn't been on a date with anyone other than Adeline in over twelve years.

He glanced toward Tisha riding beside him, the glow from the control panel granting her features a purplish hue.

"How do you think Brody and Sadie are doing with your parents?" Her voice crackled through his headset.

"Oh, I'm sure it's touch and go. Brody can get a little amped up when there's a change in routine."

"Sadie can get a little bossy when it's too close to her bedtime."

"My parents are seasoned pros when it comes to dealing with kids. Are you worried?"

"No, just so rarely without her at nighttime, you know, and we're in a new place."

"Well, hopefully God's handiwork will distract you, at least for a little while." He pointed through the curved windshield to the sky overhead.

"Oh wow." Neon green and rich emerald swirled through the night sky, curving and undulating. Traces of pink mixed in as the light ebbed and flowed across the velvety black backdrop.

He guided the helicopter down onto a flat space.

"How did you pick this spot?"

"To be honest, I fly over this way a lot."

"Taking people to ski?"

"That and I'm looking for an old friend."

The helicopter shook as he set the skis down on the rocky outcropping. He powered everything off, then they waited for the rotors to stop spinning.

"I packed us a few snacks," he said.

"Perfect. Dinner was a little rushed at our place."

"Yeah, sorry about that. This was kind of a last-minute thing."

"Oh, I wasn't surprised. Charlie was rather adamant that they were going to make this happen."

"Is that right?" He couldn't help but smile. "Hold that thought. I'll be right back."

He grabbed the basket his mom had loaned him, then climbed out of the helicopter and opened her door for her.

"You can hang the headset there." He pointed to a hook. "And grab your hat and scarf; it's chilly out here."

He took her hand in his and helped her down onto the ground. Then he opened the basket, pulled out a heavy insulated picnic blanket, and spread it down on one of the only sort-of-dry spots around.

"Here." He offered her some hand-warming packets, squeezing them until they generated heat. "Tuck these in your pockets."

"Oh, thank you, that's so sweet."

"You're welcome. I brought cheese, crackers, grapes, and Charlie gave me some pointers on hot tea."

He handed her a minithermos. "Here's another blanket if you need it."

"Wow, I'm so impressed." She draped the plaid blanket over her lap, then twisted off the lid and smelled the tea. "This is perfect."

"There's chocolate, and Brody said that I needed to make you chocolate chip cookies, so he did help. Pretty much a team effort because cookies are not my forte."

"Ethan." She angled her head. "This is very thoughtful. Thank you."

"You're welcome." He sat down and patted the blanket beside him. "It's a great spot to view the northern lights."

"Do you bring all your dates here?" she teased, bumping her shoulder against his.

Something about her comment made him want to reassure her.

"I've never brought anyone here, actually. Thanks for saying yes. I wasn't sure if I should ask you out after Sadie's response, but . . . I took a chance."

She offered a shy smile. "Me too."

His pulse sped as their eyes locked.

Easy there.

He cleared his throat, then turned and unpacked the food he'd tucked away in lidded containers. "I've started flying this way because I'm keeping an eye on how quickly the glacier is changing. It's not far from here, and I'm looking for a missing person."

"Is that the friend you mentioned earlier?"

He nodded. "You know, I didn't bring you here to dredge up some of Redemption's saddest stories. Don't you want to see the northern lights? They're putting on quite a show."

"We can do both."

She reached for a cracker, topped it with a square of sharp cheddar, and popped it into her mouth. The lights overhead rippled across the night sky as if God were shaking out His favorite blanket. Shades of pink, purple, and green undulated against the velvety blackness.

"It's amazing that the Creator of the universe came up with His own electric light show, isn't it?"

She smiled. "It sure is. That's one thing I've noticed about being back in Alaska. Everywhere you look, there's something beautiful to enjoy."

He turned and stared at her. "So true."

She held his gaze, then looked down and poured herself a cup of tea. "Do you want some tea?"

"No thanks. I packed some decaf coffee."

"Not a big tea guy, are you?"

"Nope." He reached for his own thermos. "There are packets of honey tucked in the basket's inside pocket, and maybe some wooden stir sticks."

"You've thought of everything, haven't you?"

He shifted, crossing his legs at the ankles. "I tried."

"I'm so impressed." She tore the paper off the stir stick. "Now, about that story. Let's hear it."

He blew out a long breath. "So, a long time ago, when I was around thirteen, I went on a father-son fishing trip with some guys from church, and obviously my dad was there as well. We were out on somebody's fishing boat having the best time telling stories. We had planned to camp out on an island in the sound, but a storm took us by surprise and things got a little hairy. Trevor and MJ, who are brothers, both went overboard. MJ did not have a life jacket on. So his dad, as any dad would do, went into the water after him."

Tisha's eyes grew wide. She cupped her tea between both hands.

"We don't have a Coast Guard air station here, so even though we put out a call for help, the closest people to respond were some fishermen on their own boat nearby. And by the time any help arrived, MJ and his father had completely disappeared. The Coast Guard did arrive and searched through the night. When the word spread, people from Redemption looked and looked, and the Coast Guard scoured miles around where we'd been, but we never found MJ and his dad."

He shivered as memories of that horrific day resurfaced.

She reached over and squeezed his hand. "I'm so sorry. That's awful. Is that why you became a Coast Guard rescue swimmer?"

"That's why I joined the Coast Guard, because I never wanted anybody to feel the way we felt. We were helpless. Looking back, obviously, there are so many things we should have done differently."

"You can't blame yourself."

"True. I'm talking about basic boating-safety protocols. The adults should've made everyone wear a life jacket. It's not a big deal to go fishing and not put one on, but with that many people on one boat, we should have been more cautious."

She kept her fingers entwined with his, and he hoped she wouldn't let go until it was time to leave.

"I had nightmares for months but no plans of becoming a rescue swimmer. It's kind of how it worked out. And then I had an opportunity to go for aviation, and that ended up being exactly the right fit for me."

"So you and MJ were good friends?"

"The best. Prior to losing him, every single childhood memory included MJ. Skiing, sledding, snowshoeing, baseball, basketball . . . We did everything together. And the worst part was, when I got home from the trip, I had this really cool piece of jade sitting on my dresser. He had found it when we'd been messing around outside, but he'd let me have it. So I took it to his house to give to his mom."

"Aww, that's so sweet," Tisha said.

"Now, keep in mind, this woman had lost her husband and one of her two sons in this terrible boating accident, and I thought I would make it better by giving her a rock."

"Don't be too hard on yourself," Tisha said. "It sounds like it wasn't just any rock."

"Well, it was a bad move on my part because she turned me away. She was upset, and it was obvious that I'd completely misread the situation."

"Oh, I don't know about that. She was probably in shock and had no idea what to do. I'm sure it wasn't personal."

"I took it personally, and I've never forgotten how she rejected my effort. And that stuck with me, obviously, because here I am still talking about it twenty-five years later."

Sheesh. He shook his head. How embarrassing. "I don't think I've ever told anybody that story before. So much for coming out here to eat some good snacks and look at a pretty night sky."

Her expression grew serious, and her gaze held his. She squeezed his hand tighter. "Stories can set us free. Did you know that?"

"Is that right?" His eyes dipped to her lips. "And what story do you need to tell so you can be free?"

"Oh boy." Her smooth brow furrowed under the cuff of her knit hat. The adorable pom-pom bobbed on top as she tipped her head back and looked at the sky again. "I'm sure you don't want to hear any more about my adventures as a beauty-pageant contestant."

"Now, see, that's where you're mistaken." He reached over, selected two chocolate heart-shaped truffles from the box, then offered her one. "I want to know everything about you."

She took the candy with a nervous laugh. "I'm definitely going to need some chocolate to delve into this one."

Ethan tapped his truffle against hers. "Go on. I'm all ears."

"My mom signed me up for my first pageant when I was very young. They called it a tap-dance competition, but it was more of a training ground for future pageant queens. At first I was super excited because my friends were going to be there. But . . ."

She trailed off, then took a tiny bite of her chocolate. "Oh wow. That's good."

He popped his into his mouth and chewed slowly. The rich texture was a bit much, although the chocolate–peanut-butter combo was nice. He swallowed it down, then took a quick sip of his coffee. "I'm more of a pie guy than a truffle fella, I think."

Tisha's laughter enveloped him. "Stop. You're just saying that."

"No, I'm not. It's true. Your pie is better than these chocolates. But we're getting offtrack. What happened at your not-tap-dance pageant?"

"So I started to panic as soon as I got on stage. We were all about seven or eight years old. The lights were bright, our shoes were uncomfortable, they'd put a bunch of makeup on our faces. It was a whole scene. Anyway, I started looking around for my mom and waving and saying, 'Hi, Mom.' I just wanted to know that she was there and that she was for me."

Ethan reached for her hand again. "Let me guess—that didn't go like you expected."

Tisha shook her head. "She was not having it. I could see right away she was angry with me. Afterward, backstage, she gave me this lecture about how I had to perform and do my best and she'd set me up for success but she couldn't come onstage and dance for me."

Oh wow. Anger simmered low in his gut toward this woman whom he'd never even met.

"Was that your last pageant?"

"Ha." She gave him the side-eye. "As if. One key fact that I failed to mention is that everything about my mother's life is a performance—even where she sits and how she looks in church on a Sunday morning matter to her. But not for the right reasons. She doesn't want to talk about anything difficult or messy. Instead, she micromanages and controls the messaging so everything makes her look good. It's gross, to be honest. But I didn't know how to not play her games. So I competed in tons of pageants. You may not have heard it yet, but people around here used to jokingly call me Miss North Carolina."

"Were you Miss North Carolina?"

She sipped her tea. "Of course I was. I ended up making a lot of friends on the pageant circuit. Most of the time it was fun, and I was voted Miss Congeniality. I could never win enough or do enough to please Mama though. The part of the funny-cake story that I didn't tell you is that she came unglued and told me that McDowells didn't do what I'd done."

"What did you do other than have fun with your friends?"

"Exactly," Tisha said. "I told her I'd do my best to not be a McDowell for much longer then, which was a low blow. I loved my father very much, and his side of the family was well-respected and so kind. Eventually the tension between us nearly ruined our relationship, and that's one of the big reasons I don't want to live close to her anymore."

"Thank you for sharing that with me," he said softly. "I'm so sorry you've had a rough time with your mother. Please know that you don't have to perform. I like you exactly as you are. You're smart, beautiful, and an amazing person. Sadie's blessed to have you as her mother."

The words hung there between them, packed with meaning and emotion that he hadn't meant to share. But as he looked into her eyes, he saw a quiet strength. And more of that vulnerability she rarely let show. And for once, there was no one to interrupt. No reason to hold back. His pulse sped, and before he could talk himself out of such a bold move, he leaned down and brushed his lips against hers as the sky overhead snapped and crackled.

Twelve

SHE'D BEEN WANTING TO KISS HIM SINCE HE stepped off the helicopter. Definitely when he'd offered her tea. And absolutely when he'd opened up about his past. In fact, she'd nearly kissed him first. So yes. She was all in.

He tasted like coffee and chocolate, and his tender, unhurried exploration stole her breath as much as the rippling lights painting the night sky above them. The kiss was gentle—tentative yet full of promise. Ethan's warmth radiated through her, chasing away the chill of the Alaskan night and, for a fleeting moment, the ache she'd carried for so long.

When his lips pressed more firmly, deepening the kiss, she instinctively leaned into him. Somehow, she had edged closer, her hands lifting to cup his jaw. His skin was smooth beneath her fingers, a stark contrast to his rugged strength. Her pulse thrummed as his fingers threaded through her hair, cradling her like she was something precious. The sensation sent a shiver through her, a soft gasp escaping her lips before she could stop it. For the first time in what felt like forever, she let herself believe in something good. In someone good.

But what would Sadie think about this?

The thought pierced through the haze of warmth left by his kiss. Her daughter's face—stormy and suspicious when she'd caught them hugging in the café kitchen—flashed through her mind, wrenching her back to reality. She pulled away abruptly, chest heaving in the soft glow of the battery-powered lantern Ethan had brought.

"Tisha?" His voice was quiet, unsure. "What happened?"

"I don't know," she said, pushing to her feet. The blanket bunched beneath her as she stumbled slightly, pacing back and forth, her palms pressed to her flushed cheeks. "I don't know, Ethan. I think . . . I think that was too fast."

He stayed seated, his gaze steady on her as she moved.

"What about Sadie? What about Brody?" The words tumbled out as she shoved her hands into her coat pockets. "Has anybody asked them what they would think about us kissing? Sadie had a fit when she caught us hugging." Her voice cracked. "Oh, Ethan. I just—I don't know."

He stood slowly, giving her space, then stepped forward and gently clasped her shoulders. "Hey, listen. It's okay." His tone was calm, grounding. "We're both dipping our toes into this uncertain pool, right? I don't know about you, but I haven't been on a first date in over a decade."

A shaky laugh bubbled out. "Yeah. It's been a while for me too."

"Let's pack up. But listen, Tisha . . ." He ducked slightly, catching her gaze as she tried to look away. "I really like you. I thought that was an amazing kiss, and I'll go as slow as you need to go. But I have to say two things."

She swallowed, her heart pounding. "Okay."

"At some point, we're going to have to talk to our kids about dating," he said gently. "Unless you're absolutely sure you want to be a single parent forever, which I hope isn't the case."

Her chest tightened. "I know," she whispered.

"And," he continued, lowering his voice, "I'm going to need Chase to step out of the way."

The mention of her late husband hit her like a punch, sharp and unexpected. *Oof.* Her heart pinched, guilt and longing warring inside her. She drew in a shaky breath. "I know. I know you do."

A muscle in his cheek twitched. "I sort of assumed when you took off those rings that you were signaling it was time to move on. Otherwise, I never would've accepted Charlie's help to make this date happen. Did I misunderstand?"

"No, of course not." She tried to smile. "The reason I took off my rings is because I—I am ready."

He tilted his head to one side. "Except you just told me we moved too fast. So it feels like maybe . . . not so much."

"Please be patient with me, Ethan," she whispered.

His gaze held hers, but then he nodded, his expression softening. "I will."

He glanced up at the night sky, where the auroras had faded, leaving wisps of clouds drifting across a pale half-moon. "Why don't we head home?"

She nodded, a lump in her throat, and together they packed up the basket and folded the blanket. He carried both items along with the lantern to the helicopter, his quiet steadiness a balm to her frayed nerves.

Once they were buckled in and the headsets secured, Ethan started the rotors spinning.

"Let me send a quick text to Luke to let him know we're on our way back," he said.

"I'll text. You fly," she said.

He nodded. "Deal."

She focused on her phone, terribly aware of the silence between them.

As the helicopter lifted into the starry night, its lights sweeping over the snow-covered ground below, she fidgeted with the hem of her jacket. "Thanks for, um, arranging the babysitting. I hope Sadie wasn't too much trouble."

"Like I said, my mom is great with kids. I'm sure they had a fun time," he said, his tone kind but measured.

"Thank you for telling me more about your story," she said. "That was really brave of you to share. I'm honored that you chose me."

"You're welcome." He managed a smile, but there was a tightness in his face that she couldn't ignore. Had she hurt him? She turned to the window, staring out into the darkness, her mind spinning with doubts and what-ifs.

Twenty minutes later, Ethan guided the helicopter smoothly to the ground beside the resort. They disembarked in silence, Tisha carrying the lantern and blanket while he held the basket.

When they entered the resort, the warm glow of the lights greeted them. Sadie stood in the lobby, clutching Ollie in one hand and rubbing her eyes with the other.

"Mommy, you're back!" Sadie ran into her arms.

Tisha pulled her daughter close, hugging her tightly before glancing up at Mrs. McGuire. "Everything go okay?"

"Yep, everything's fine." Mrs. McGuire offered a warm smile. She glanced at Ethan. "I sent Brody to brush his teeth."

"Perfect. Thanks, Mom," Ethan said, then turned to Tisha. "Walk you out?"

"That's okay. I'm good." Tisha forced a smile. "Thanks, I had a great time."

She ushered Sadie toward the door, avoiding Ethan's gaze.

Once outside, she couldn't help but replay the moment in her mind. Okay, maybe she had been rude. But what was she supposed to do? Her emotions were a mess.

She settled Sadie into the car and drove quickly back to the cabin. Her fingers tightened on the steering wheel as her thoughts churned. Thankfully, Tom and Melinda's house was dark. She didn't want to face them—or anyone else right now. Not that it was their business, but she was sure they'd heard about her impromptu date with Ethan. Knowing Chloe and Charlie, half the town probably knew by now.

When they reached the cabin, she said, "Come on, sweetie. Let's get you ready for bed."

Sadie chattered on about her evening, describing the chicken nuggets and french fries she'd eaten, the movie she'd watched, and how Brody had let her pick the film.

"Well, how about that?" Tisha pulled back the covers on Sadie's bed. "The McGuire fellas were gentlemen tonight."

"What's a gentleman?" Sadie asked, her eyes curious as she hopped onto the bed.

"A man who is kind and considerate."

"Oh, yeah. Well, that's Brody . . . some of the time."

Tisha laughed softly, tucking her daughter under the covers.

"Was my daddy a gentleman?" Sadie asked, her voice small.

"Yes," Tisha said, her throat tightening. "Yes, he was."

They said their prayers, and Tisha kissed Sadie and Ollie good night.

"Good night, Mommy. I love you," Sadie whispered, her eyelids growing heavy.

"I love you too, pumpkin. Sleep well." Tisha brushed a strand of hair from her daughter's forehead before padding softly down the hall.

In the dim glow from the lamp in the living room, her gaze landed on the framed photo of Chase perched on the bookshelf by the fireplace.

I'm going to need Chase to step out of the way.

Ethan's words echoed in her head. Her stomach clenched at the memory. He wasn't wrong. At some point, she'd have to figure out what she really wanted. But how? How could she choose between holding on to Chase's memory and opening her heart to something new? As much as she loved Chase, she didn't want to be alone forever. And Sadie deserved a strong, loving father figure in her life.

Her thoughts drifted to a moment etched in her memory—she and Chase sitting across from each other at a picnic table under an umbrella on a warm summer day. It had been one of those rare times they'd gotten away while her father was nearing the end of his life. They'd dropped Sadie off with Natalie and her family, then shared a simple meal of hush puppies and barbecue sandwiches.

The conversation that day had stuck with her.

Chase had brought up the subject of moving on, though she hadn't understood why.

"If anything ever happens to me, I want you to know it's okay to move on," he'd said, his tone serious.

She'd bristled, shocked. "Chase, why would you even say something like that?"

He'd smiled, reaching for her hand. "Because I want you to be happy, Tish. I want you to love and be loved, even if I'm not here."

She'd been upset, maybe even a little angry, accusing him of being morbid. But now, as she stared at his photograph, those words resurfaced like a lifeline.

"That's the problem, Chase," she whispered, her voice trembling. "I don't know what I want. At least, I didn't. Until today."

The truth gnawed at her. She'd uprooted her life, moved across the country, and built a world where Chase's memory could thrive—where Sadie would always know who her father was. But now? That kiss with Ethan had upended everything.

"Oh, Chase," she murmured, tears blurring her vision. "This is so hard. How can I know the right thing to do?"

Her tears fell onto the glass of the photo frame. She wiped them away with her sleeve, her shoulders shaking. Probably something she should pray about, but the idea felt distant, like reaching for something just out of grasp. God was there—she believed that—but sometimes it felt like He wanted her to figure it out on her own.

She held the photo in both hands, studying the face she'd known and loved for so long. Then, slowly, she crossed the room to the chest by the window. Lifting the lid, she carefully placed the frame on the bottom and covered it with blankets.

Shutting the lid, she sat on it, her chest heaving. What was the right thing to do? She didn't know. But one thing she did know was that she wouldn't be able to forget that kiss anytime soon. And maybe—just maybe—fighting to keep Chase front and center wasn't what she or Sadie needed anymore.

He had to stop thinking about that kiss.

The way Tisha's soft lips moved against his, that adorable hum of approval she'd made when he tunneled his fingers through her hair. Yeah, okay, so he'd been a little nervous about flying her to see the northern lights, but the crackling in the night sky had been the perfect soundtrack to—

"Hey, did you hear me?"

Luke's question pulled Ethan back to reality. They stood at the check-in desk at the resort, working through the never-ending to-do list to prep for the festival.

"I need you to make an airport run. We have two clients coming in on the noon flight."

"Got it. Can you text me their names and flight info?"

Luke shot him an odd look. "There's only one flight landing at noon, pal."

Ethan pulled out his phone. "Then it should only take you a second to send me the info."

Luke checked his laptop, then tapped a few things into his phone. "Coming at you."

His message arrived. Ethan looked at the screen. "Whoa, no way. The Tanners? Where are they coming from?"

"Um . . . They caught the short hop from Anchorage. Why?"

"No, I'm asking where are they from originally?"

"Home address? Let's see." Luke scrolled down. "Oh, how about that? They're from Palm Harbor, Florida. Is that close to where you lived?"

Ethan's legs turned to jelly.

"You feeling all right?" Luke pushed back his chair and stood. "You just turned a shade lighter."

Ethan swallowed hard. "Kaylee and Adam. They are . . . She was Adeline's best friend."

"Huh. Did you know she was coming?"

"Had no idea." He thought about the calls he'd thumbed away. The text messages he'd read but hadn't responded to.

"Um, all right." Luke raked his hand through his hair, then glanced at the computer again. "I mean, I'd love to take this one for you, but . . ."

Ethan shook his head. "I need to do this myself."

Luke sat back down. "Let me know how it goes."

"Yep." Ethan scrolled back through the messages as he walked out to the Suburban. Kaylee had texted and called him as recently as three days ago, but there was no mention of travel plans. Her last message had simply stated "I'm going to keep praying about this, Ethan, and I'm not giving up."

That was fair. It didn't mean he had to say yes though. But it looked like she was going to be true to her word. He would set some boundaries around their conversation, and it definitely wasn't going to be over pie at the café. Because as much as he wanted to see Tisha, he wasn't about to let her witness what was likely going to be a heated discussion he'd tried his best to avoid. No matter how far Kaylee and Adam had traveled, he wasn't obligated to give an interview.

A few minutes later, he eased into a parking place in front of the airport, pocketed his phone, and headed for the automatic double doors. They parted, and he walked a short distance to the baggage-claim area. It wasn't long before he spotted Kaylee's trademark auburn hair spilling over her expensive puffy jacket. Then she waved and strode toward him, towing a suitcase and a carry-on.

"Hi," he said.

"Surprise!" She stopped in front of him, uncertainty flashing in her hazel eyes.

Her husband, Adam, walked behind her, towing matching luggage. "Ethan, good to see you, man."

Adam held out his hand, and Ethan shook it. Adam wore a knit beanie featuring Florida's professional hockey team logo, a teal-green hoodie layered under a high-end parka, jeans, and black-and-green high-tops.

"Nice to see you both." Ethan leaned in and gave Kaylee a brief hug. "I didn't know you guys were skiers."

"We're not. We came to see you. We have reservations at the resort to stay for the weekend."

"Welcome to Redemption," Ethan said. "You want to head straight to the resort, or should we stop and grab something to eat first?"

"Wherever you'd feel most comfortable, Ethan. We want to talk to you, and I know this is going to be a challenging conversation," Kaylee said.

He sighed, his stomach already in knots. "Follow me."

He helped them load their baggage into the back of the Suburban. Then Adam circled around and opened the front door for Kaylee.

"You should probably ride shotgun, dear."

"Thanks!" Kaylee climbed inside. Adam got in the back seat.

Ethan got behind the wheel, secured his seatbelt, and eased the vehicle out of the parking lot.

"I don't think I've ever seen so much snow in my life." Kaylee stared out the windshield, mesmerized.

"According to my weather app, there's more coming," Adam said. "Maybe we should learn to ski while we're here."

Kaylee reached over and bumped up the heat for her side of the interior. "Does it ever not snow here?"

"Yeah, we have some clear cold days. It's beautiful when the sun's out and the sky is blue," Ethan said.

A shiver wracked Kaylee's athletic frame. "I think I'll stick to sand between my toes and Florida sunshine."

"Well, I can drive you back to the airport."

"Ha!" She leaned over and nudged his shoulder. "You can't get rid of me that easily."

He drove to the Copper Kettle coffee shop, silently praying that the more curious members of the community would be busy getting ready for the festival that started in a few hours. Or at least not lingering over their morning coffee, eager for gossip.

Snowbanks lined the streets, pushed high by plows, and the occasional gust of wind sent powdery flurries swirling through the air.

"How does anyone drive in this?" Kaylee asked.

"You get used to it," Ethan said with a shrug, easing into a parking space in front of the coffee shop. Banners in shades of red and pink hung from lampposts, fluttering in the breeze, and the scent of woodsmoke lingered.

"What's Love Is in the Air?" Kaylee tapped her red manicured nail on the window in the coffee-shop door where the flyer was posted. "That's this weekend, right?"

"Sure is." Ethan held the door open and let them enter ahead of him. "Starts tonight."

"Are you part of the festival?" Kaylee asked.

"The whole town gets involved. So, yes."

"Makes sense," Kaylee said. "I appreciate you taking time out of your schedule to meet with us."

"You're guests at my family's resort. You'd probably be hard to avoid," he said.

"I warned you I was coming," she teased.

The warmth of the Copper Kettle enveloped them as they stepped inside. Its mixture of cozy booths, raw-edged wood bar lining the far wall, and bright shiplap walls offered a welcome respite from the snow-covered world outside.

"What a gorgeous sofa." Kaylee ran her hand over the purple velvet sofa with at least a half dozen throw pillows scattered across tufted cushions. "I could sit here and drink coffee all day."

"That's probably the owner's intent," Adam said, guiding her toward the counter. "Let's order first."

They ordered bacon, egg, and cheese breakfast sandwiches and coffee. Ethan silently wished he could run down the street to the café and have pie and flirt with Tisha instead, but the coffee shop was nearly deserted. Thankfully. Since they couldn't all fit on the sofa, he sat down across from them in a corner booth with a blueberry scone and a cup of black coffee.

"So." He glanced between Adam and Kaylee. "What's on your mind?"

"I'm here to give you a stern talking-to." The paper on Kaylee's breakfast sandwich crinkled as she took a bite.

"I bet you regret not answering her texts, don't you?" Adam said, winking at him.

"Yeah, nothing like a good lecture to really motivate me to change my behavior."

"What would motivate you, Ethan?" she said, dabbing at her mouth with a napkin.

He hesitated, measuring his words carefully. "Honestly? Nothing. Because I don't want to do this."

Amusement vanished from Adam's blue eyes. "Why not?"

Before Ethan could speak, Kaylee sighed and put down her sandwich. "I don't get it. Adeline, as you know, was incredible. She did so much, not only for the other Coast Guard families, but for the school and the community. She was such a light, a beacon of hope."

"You're not wrong." He took a bite of his scone and chased it with a sip of hot coffee. She wasn't telling him anything he didn't already know, but why did the whole world need to hear about it? Adeline had never wanted that kind of attention.

"Then why do you not want to share her story?" Kaylee poured oat-milk creamer into her coffee. "No one expects you to go on a press tour or walk a red carpet. We're not making a documentary."

"Yet." Ethan eyed her. "I wouldn't put it past you."

Kaylee's lips twitched. "I deserved that."

"Look, I'm not going to lie," Adam said. "I'm well-connected in the podcast industry. Our culture is hungry for inspirational content—feel-good stories about people making a positive impact. A long-form interview, cross-promoted on the right platforms, could have a big impact."

"And that's exactly why I'm not interested," Ethan said. "She's gone. Why do we need content that potentially goes viral to remind us of what we've lost?"

Irritation sparked in Kaylee's eyes. "But—"

"Kaylee, I'm going to be real blunt. I lost my wife, and my kid has to grow up without a mom. Not every gloomy story has this perfect silver lining. So help me understand why I should agree to turning our grief into a feel-good, inspirational story?"

"We're well aware that she's not here, Ethan," Adam said quietly. "The point Kaylee is trying to make is there's value in spotlighting the fact that there are still good people in the world. Maybe Adeline's efforts will inspire somebody else to do something amazing and make their community a better place."

"Brody needs to hear about how amazing his mom was," Kaylee added.

"Brody already knows how amazing his mom was."

"Does he? Do you talk about her with him? Are there any pictures of her in your new place?"

Wow, she sounded like Tisha. Stalling, Ethan turned his coffee mug in a slow circle.

"He's eight," Kaylee said softly. "Don't you want to create something tangible he can look back on?"

"No, not really."

Kaylee threw her hands in the air. "You're being stubborn."

"You're right, I am, and so are you, because you're asking me to do something I don't want to do."

"I'm asking you to let somebody interview you. Maybe for a podcast, or if you're willing, a regional magazine with a Florida audience. You won't have to leave Alaska. I'll handle all the arrangements, and we'll set up a couple of video calls. I'm just asking for your permission to tell your amazing wife's incredible story. Why won't you let me?"

"Because it's hard." He pounded his fist on the table, drawing a curious stare from the barista. Coffee sloshed out of his mug. He leaned forward and lowered his voice. "Because it feels like you're ripping my heart wide open when the scabs have barely healed. All right? I finally . . ." He hesitated. He was not about to tell her about Tisha.

"You finally what? *Moved on*?" Kaylee's chin wobbled. "How nice for you."

Spots peppered his vision. Words he'd for sure regret later fought to break free from his pinched lips.

Adam covered Kaylee's hand with his. "Let's be respectful, all right? Emotions are running high."

Ethan rubbed at the tightness in his chest. "Whether I start dating someone next week or next year, it's really none of your business, Kaylee. The point is, I need to protect my son, and I don't want to dredge up the hurt all over again."

"Are you telling me you don't like pain and dealing with your feelings, so you're not going to let this story be told?" Kaylee leaned across the table, her face flushed. "That's incredibly selfish, Ethan. And what kind of example is that setting for Brody?"

"How I parent my son is none of your concern either." Ethan stood, his insides turning to molten lava. He needed air. "I'll be out in the car. Come out when you're ready, and I'll drop you off at the resort."

Adam followed him out onto the sidewalk. The wind picked up and whipped around them. Shivering, Ethan jammed his hands deep into his coat pockets and headed toward the Suburban.

"Ethan, can we talk about this?" Adam called out.

Stifling a groan, Ethan hesitated and then turned to face him.

"You know, when Kaylee told me she wanted to do this, I was skeptical." Adam stood near the hood of the vehicle.

"Really?" Ethan frowned. "Sure doesn't seem that way."

"I get that." Adam's breath formed little white clouds in the air. "She's intense when she sets her mind on something. But the more she talked about her ideas for telling Adeline's story, the more I felt like we needed to pursue this."

"Why?"

"Because I saw how much it meant to her, and because I know what it's like to believe that someone's story deserves to be told."

Ethan hesitated. "You lost someone as well?"

Adam nodded. "Not in the same way as you. The details aren't super important right now. But the thing is, maybe we need to honor Adeline to make sure nobody forgets her. So we can feel like her life mattered."

He winced. "Adeline's life mattered. We don't need a podcast or a story in a magazine to prove that."

"Maybe you don't. But Kaylee? She feels strongly that Adeline's commitment to her family and community is worth spotlighting. And when you shut her down, we can't help but wonder if you're just doing it because you're scared."

Ethan yanked his keys from his pocket. "You don't know what you're talking about."

"Don't I?" Adam moved closer. "Look, man. I get it. Talking about Adeline, thinking about her—it hurts. But what about when Brody gets older? When he has questions you can't answer because you buried them so deep—"

"I answer Brody's questions just fine, thank you." He paused, fighting to keep from saying something he'd regret. "I don't need someone else telling him who his mother was."

"We're not asking for a grand gesture," Adam said. "What I need you to think about is what you're really afraid of. Because if it's just pain? That's probably going to be part of your story for a while. What if this could be a way to make something beautiful out of a tragic loss?"

Gritting his teeth, Ethan kicked at a chunk of ice near the curb. Oh, how he wanted to walk away. To tell Adam and Kaylee to let it go. But Adam's words lodged in his chest. "I'll think about it."

Adam nodded. "That's all we ask."

Thirteen

ONE. PIE NUMBER TWENTY-FOUR, BAKED AND ready to go. Well, almost. The sweet aroma of molasses and cinnamon enveloped her as she slid the shoofly pie onto the cooling rack. The golden crust and buttery crumb topping looked perfect. Tisha pulled off her oven mitts, dropped them onto the stainless-steel counter, and did a dance. Yeah, okay, so she was the only one here in the café after hours celebrating her sweet victory, but she'd pulled it off. She'd done what had seemed almost impossible and made twenty-four pies for the festival.

She checked the time on her phone. Six fifteen. Yikes. She'd planned to meet Ethan and the kids outside the community center fifteen minutes ago. A knock sounded on the back door. She hurried across the kitchen, out into the corridor, and pushed the door open. Her heart did a little flip-flop in her chest when Ethan smiled at her from the other side.

"Hey," he said, holding the door as Brody and Sadie crowded the space beside him. "All set?"

"Mommy!" Sadie waved. "Are you done baking?"

"All done," Tisha said. "I'm sorry I'm running late. You want to come in for a second?"

Brody took a deep breath. "Whoa, that smells like sugar." He pushed past her, then turned in a circle. "Hey, I've never been in here."

Ethan clamped his hand on Brody's shoulder. "Please don't touch anything."

"I'm thirsty, Mama. Do you have any drinks?"

"Why don't we walk over to the festival?" Ethan said. "I saw a hot-cocoa stand. And I'm sure there's plenty of water and juice boxes."

"Ooh, hot cocoa. Yum." Sadie clapped her gloved hands together. "Is it your mama's hot cocoa?"

Ethan chuckled. "I don't know if it will be the same as what the resort offers. We'll have to see. Are you ready, Tisha?"

"Yes. I just brought my last pie out of the oven, and the ones I baked ahead are thawing. Let's go."

She slipped on her jacket and hat and tucked her phone in her pocket. Then she followed Ethan and the kids outside. After double-checking to make sure the door was locked, she pulled it shut.

"Bring on opening night." She grinned at Ethan, then herded the kids away from the café.

"Oh, excuse me." Mrs. Dawkins stepped into their path. "Would it be possible for me to use the restroom?"

"I'm sorry, we're not open right now," Tisha said.

"Oh, but those porta potties are just unsanitary, and I don't have it in me to hike all the way to the community center." Mrs. Dawkins's expression puckered. "No exceptions for loyal customers?"

"We can wait," Ethan said. "It's fine."

"But I need hot cocoa," Sadie said. "ASAP."

Tisha gave her daughter a pointed look. "The hot cocoa isn't going anywhere. We can be kind and let Mrs. Dawkins use the restroom."

She pulled her keys out and unlocked the back door. "I'll just wait right here."

A light snow had started to fall, and Ethan and the kids tried catching snowflakes on their tongues. Tisha couldn't help but laugh. Of course, Sadie and Brody had to make it a competition, arguing about who caught the best snowflake. Bless Ethan for staying in the game, refereeing their dispute and not getting aggravated.

A few minutes later, Mrs. Dawkins came out of the bathroom and met Tisha in the doorway. "You know, I haven't had a chance to tell you that I've really appreciated all the joy you've brought to Redemption."

"Me?" Tisha pressed her gloved hand over her chest. "I don't know about that."

"Well, you've made it fun to come here and enjoy some pie and coffee. It's a gift. And you listen without judging, and try to make people's day by serving them something as simple as pie that they'll enjoy. Have you considered a career in counseling? Not that I don't want you to serve pie, because I would miss you if you left."

Words failed her. Had their most finicky customer just given her praise? Tisha studied her. "I did major in psychology, and I have considered getting a master's in counseling, but my future's kind of up in the air to be honest."

"Well, give it some thought. I believe God's going to use you in a big way."

Um, not sure about that. Tisha offered a smile, then ushered her out the door. "I hope you enjoy the festival."

"You too, dear." Mrs. Dawkins walked slowly across the parking lot. Tisha locked the door to the café again, and they walked around the building, then onto Main Street.

"I don't know that these two need any more sugar," she said to Ethan as Brody and Sadie hopped and skipped and danced down the sidewalk, freshly cleared and salted to keep everyone from slipping.

"Maybe we could get them some small cups of hot cocoa. Come on. If we hurry, we can catch the ice-carving demonstration at seven thirty."

After getting four cups of hot cocoa, which Sadie persuaded them to augment with extra whipped cream and sprinkles, they made their way over to the parking lot in front of the community center. One of the ice artists yanked on a chainsaw and the motor revved up. His partner used a metal pick and chipped away at a giant block of ice. A woman stood nearby, answering questions from the spectators as a new carving took shape.

"Oh wow," Tisha said, scanning the gathering.

A line of brown paper bags with candles inside served as luminaries lighting the perimeter of the parking lot. Festive music played from the building's outdoor speakers, and vintage lights crisscrossed the pergola at the entrance to the community center's commons area.

"Brody and Sadie, which one's your favorite?" Tisha pointed to the six different sculptures on display.

"I like the pirate." Brody pointed to the man with the eyepatch staring through a spyglass facing the sea.

"I like the dog," Sadie said, gesturing to a sculpture of a playful puppy. "Which one do you love, Mama?"

"I like that one there," Tisha said. "Looks like a miner panning for gold."

Ethan reached down and quietly took her hand in his.

Her heart turned cartwheels. She smiled, then sipped her hot cocoa. Would Sadie make a scene if she turned around and saw Ethan holding her hand? He caressed her skin with the pad of his thumb, sending a delightful tingle zipping up her arm. On second thought, Sadie's irritation was worth the risk.

Sadie and Brody had pushed right up against the roped-off

stanchions. They had a great view of the sculptors chipping away at the massive blocks of ice.

"Clutch, my man!" Two guys Tisha didn't recognize sidled up to them. "How are you?"

"Can't complain." Ethan grinned. "You in town to enjoy the festival?"

"Since we heard you were back, we came to play in the alumni game. Didn't want to miss the opportunity. Rumor has it you still got it, big guy."

Ethan shrugged. "I don't know about that."

"Guess we'll see, won't we? Have a great night." The one standing closest to Ethan winked at Tisha and then moved on.

"Hey, I've been meaning to ask you, why do they call you that? That nickname, Clutch—where'd it come from?"

He sighed. "People started calling me that after my freshman year in high school, when I nailed nearly every three-point shot I ever took. But then I totally blew a three-point shot, and we lost a championship game at the state basketball tournament. Other than that one critical failure, I was pretty good from the three-point line."

"Well, Chase used to say you miss one hundred percent of the shots you don't take. Failures are the best way to learn."

Ethan quietly sipped his hot cocoa.

Uh-oh. She winced. "I'm sorry. Is it okay if I mention Chase?"

Ethan glanced down and gave her a slow, cocky smile. "I don't mind if you talk about Chase. I'm not threatened. By the way, it's Gretzky, a professional hockey player, who deserves credit for that quote. And Chase is a big part of your past, but I would sure like to be your future."

Her stomach dipped, and she tightened her grasp on his hand. The ice sculptures glistened under the strands of white lights, and laughter faded into the background. His words, that smile, and the intensity in his gaze sent her mind careening around hairpin turns. It was terrifying, really. She tipped her chin up, tilted her head to one side, and flashed a flirty grin. "I guess we'll find out, won't we?"

Something sparked in his eyes, like he saw past her façade, straight into the places she wasn't ready to drag into the light yet. But instead of pressing, he lifted her hand to his lips, the warmth of his breath sending a delicious tingle arcing through her.

And oh, how she wanted to savor this. All of it. The tender hope reflected in his eyes when he looked at her. The whisper of a kiss he pressed to the back of her hand. Because for the first time in ages, the future didn't seem like something to fear.

❧

The next morning, Ethan set a plate of fluffy, golden scrambled eggs with a side of crisp bacon and a cluster of juicy red grapes in front of Brody.

Last night, Tisha had let him hold her hand. She hadn't pulled away. Hadn't shut down. But her answer still echoed in his mind. *I guess we'll find out, won't we?*

Not exactly a promise. Not exactly a brush-off though. More like a woman standing at the edge of something new, uncertain about taking a leap.

He could relate. More than he wanted to admit.

Ethan reached for the plate of cinnamon rolls and set them on the table. "Happy Valentine's Day, pal."

"Thanks." Brody grabbed the pepper shaker and sprinkled some on his eggs.

As his son dug into his meal, Ethan fixed a plate for himself and joined him at the table. The scent of warm cinnamon and cream-cheese frosting filled the kitchen, but his mind was still on Tisha—on the way she'd looked at him, like maybe, just maybe, she wanted to believe in second chances.

"I know those cinnamon rolls are calling your name," Ethan said, shaking off his thoughts. "But let's make sure we get some protein and fruit in too. We've got a busy day ahead of us."

"'Kay." Brody slid his glass of orange juice closer. "Wait. We forgot to pray."

Ethan hesitated. "You're right. We did. Do you want to try?"

Brody's cheeks flushed, and he shot a quick look around the resort's kitchen.

"There's nobody else here. Grandpa and your uncles left for the festival already, Aunt Megan's still asleep, and Grandma's out at the front desk helping our guests."

Brody dipped his chin, then nodded.

Ethan reached across the table and gently clasped Brody's hand.

"Dear God, thank You for this food and our family and a new day. Please keep us safe. Amen."

He'd whispered the words, and they'd flown out in a rush, but Ethan still wanted to push back his chair and clap. "Well done, Brody."

Brody slumped back in his chair, eyes gleaming. "That wasn't so hard after all."

Ethan chuckled. "Praying out loud is not easy. You did a great job."

Brody took a long sip of his juice, then shoveled in a forkful of eggs.

"What are you excited about seeing today?"

"I hope we can see those ice sculptures again. That guy with the chainsaw has a gnarly job." Brody took a bite of his bacon. "How'd he learn to do that?"

"Good question. I'm sure he practiced a lot to be able to create such amazing sculptures. Maybe one day you'll find something that you're passionate about and want to practice all the time too."

"My passion is skateboarding," Brody said, talking around a mouthful of food.

Ethan opened his mouth to correct his table manners. But maybe he didn't need to focus quite so much on those right now. Or offer another shameless plug for their rec-league basketball team. "I can see that. You've put in a lot of hard work practicing already. That's awesome."

Brody's eyes narrowed and he stopped chewing for a second. Ethan just smiled and took another bite of his breakfast. Poor kid. He'd probably been bracing for criticism.

"What are you excited about today, Dad?"

He reached for his coffee as his brain delivered a replay of Tisha smiling while the lights from the luminaries flickered in the background, casting everything in a golden glow. The warmth of her fingers threaded through his, and her eyes lit up when he said something that made her laugh.

"Wait, don't tell me." Brody's fork clattered to his plate. "I bet I can guess. Holding Miss Tisha's hand, right?"

Ethan coughed, barely avoiding spewing coffee across the table.

"Uh-oh." Brody's expression grew serious. "Are you choking?"

Ethan cleared his throat and shook his head. "No, I'm fine, thanks for asking. You just surprised me is all."

"Why? I saw you holding her hand."

Ethan grew still. Oh no. He hesitated, his coffee mug halfway to the table. "Is . . . is it okay that I was holding her hand?"

Brody shrugged. "Sure, I don't mind. Sadie freaks out though."

"Yeah, I'm going to have to talk to Sadie."

"Are you going to hold Miss Tisha's hand some more?"

"I hope so."

"Huh. All right." Brody took another bite of his bacon. "Can I say something, Dad?"

"If you'll finish chewing your bacon first, sure."

He carved his fork through the edge of the cinnamon roll with the cream-cheese frosting oozing down one side and took a bite. The subtle spice mixed with the warm yeasty roll and wrapped in the gooey frosting hit the spot. How Mom found the time to make these and patiently help the guests with all their questions about the festival was beyond him. He'd have to thank her before they left this morning.

"You seem really happy," Brody said. "When we first got here, you were, like, all stressed out and angry and stuff, but lately you just seem mostly happy, and I'm glad."

Oh wow. Ethan took another sip of his coffee, measuring his words carefully. "Well, you're right, Brody. I was pretty angry when we first got here, and kind of sad, to tell you the truth. But I've been thinking a lot lately, and I realize that I need to let go of that anger and sadness and focus on making the best of this new adventure we're on."

He reached across the table and placed his hand on Brody's. "And I'm so sorry for hurting you with my words. Please forgive me?"

Brody glanced down at his plate. The silence hung heavy between them, only broken by the chatter filtering in from the front desk. Ethan's stomach twisted with unease. He had been looking forward to hanging with Brody this morning—just the two of them. But now he wanted nothing more than to escape. This was not how he'd imagined their conversation over cinnamon rolls would go.

Brody looked up at him for a moment before finally nodding. "I forgive you, Dad."

Ethan grinned as he squeezed Brody's hand. "Thank you, son. And thank you for pointing out that I seem happier lately. You know why?"

"Why?"

"Because spending time with Tisha makes me happy. She's a wonderful person, isn't she?"

"You seem happier with Miss Tisha than you were with Mom."

Ethan set his fork down and scrubbed his palm over his face.

Adam's words echoed through his mind. *What if this could be a way to make something beautiful out of a tragic loss?*

"Well, I loved your mom very much, but our relationship wasn't always easy," Ethan said, taking a sip of his coffee.

"I know. I heard the fights." Brody looked down at his plate, pushing around a piece of bacon with his fork.

"I was gone a lot for work, and she kept everything running so smoothly at home. That's why some stuff that goes along with being your dad, well, I'm just not that good at."

"I think you're doing fine, Dad."

Ethan nearly choked up at the compliment. He swallowed hard, trying to compose himself. "Thank you. That's very gracious. I don't keep track of details nearly as well as your mom did. She loved you so much, and I'm sorry that she's gone."

"Yeah, I loved her a lot. And I miss her too."

Ethan took another sip of his coffee, wishing it had the power to wash the tears right back out of his system. He loathed crying in front of anyone. Especially Brody.

"If you could pick one thing, what was your favorite activity to do in the wintertime with your mom?"

"We went out for breakfast, especially when you were working. She liked smoothies more than the sugary stuff, but she always let me get extra whipped cream on my pancakes. Sometimes we would go to the skate park or to the beach, but mostly I just liked being with her. What was your favorite thing to do with Mom?"

Ethan smiled. "Remember when we used to go out for pizza and just hang out? There was that sandbox and splash pad outside, and you'd play for hours. I miss those days."

"Me too." Brody drained the last of his juice. "Do you think you'll end up marrying Miss Tisha?"

Funny thing, he'd entertained that same thought. Especially after she let him hold her hand and they walked together while the kids looked at the ice sculptures. For a few minutes, everything had felt easy and right. Like they were a family.

"Whoa, buddy." Ethan held up his palm. "One day at a time, all right?"

"Just asking," Brody said.

"By the way, some of our friends from Florida are here today. Adam and Kaylee."

Brody's eyes widened. "They're here? Did they bring their kids?"

"No, it's just the two of them. They want someone to interview me about your mom."

"An interview for a TV show?"

"Probably for a podcast. A true-story kind of thing. They want to spread positive stories, and they thought something about the Coast Guard community might be good. And your mom was a big part of that."

"Cool," Brody said with a hint of a smile.

"So you'd be okay if somebody wrote a newspaper or a magazine article or posted something on social media that was all about your mom?"

"Can I be on the podcast?"

Ethan hesitated. He wasn't about to make any promises he couldn't keep. "I'm not in charge of that, but we could ask Kaylee and Adam if they're doing any family interviews."

"But are you going to do one?"

"An interview? At first I said no, but if you're okay with it and they still want me to, then yes."

"You totally should."

"Thanks for saying yes." Ethan fidgeted with the edge of his paper napkin. "It's not easy talking about what we've gone through."

Brody shrugged. "It's easy for me. Besides, Mom would want me to do the right thing."

Ethan blinked back hot tears. "Brody, I . . ." He cleared his throat. "I'm really proud of you."

Brody gave him a wary look. "Thanks, Dad. I'm proud of you too. Can I have a cinnamon roll now?"

"Of course you can." Ethan reached for a cinnamon roll and placed one in front of Brody.

The prospect of sharing memories of Adeline with others and sitting down for a lengthy Q and A still sent a chill racing down his spine. But Kaylee and Adam were right. And so was Brody. This was the right thing to do. No matter how much he struggled with handling his feelings. Maybe saying yes would somehow honor Adeline's legacy and pave the way for a fresh start.

Fourteen

They didn't call her the pie whisperer for no reason.

With a warm smile, Tisha handed the young brunette woman, a sweet mom of four who volunteered in Sadie's class at church, a white box wrapped in a pink grosgrain ribbon.

"There you go, Ayla." The enticing aroma of fresh berries and buttery crust lingered in the air. "Enjoy the festival and your new jumbleberry pie."

"Thank you so much, Tisha. Can't wait!" Ayla took the box, then guided her stroller with a sleeping baby around the line of people waiting to order kettle corn at the next booth. The hum of laughter and conversation echoed off the walls.

Tisha blew out a long breath as she reached for her water bottle. Oh no. Empty. She scanned the room for someone to sit at her station for a few minutes while she took a quick break. She spotted Chloe working her way across the crowded community center. Tisha gestured for her to come closer.

"Hey, girl." Chloe grinned, the tips of her pixie-style haircut dyed pink in honor of the festival. "How are things?"

"Never better," Tisha said. "I'm exhausted but nearly sold out. The pie walk has been a huge hit. You were right, twelve pies wouldn't have been enough."

"Glad to hear it." Chloe glanced at her phone. "If you need a quick break, I can sit here for a few minutes."

"Yes, please." Tisha grabbed her purse and her water bottle. "I need to check on Sadie. She's with my mother-in-law over at the quilters' booth. Then I'll grab a refill, use the restroom, and be right back."

"Perfect." Chloe sat down on the folding chair behind the table. "See you in a few."

Instead of cutting through the crowd, Tisha climbed the stairs beside the stage and walked across to the other side. If she went down the opposite stairs and out the exit, she'd be close to the restrooms and the water-bottle refill station. Then she'd have a few minutes to check in with Melinda and Sadie.

The backstage curtains swayed as she hurried past them.

"Hey, beautiful."

A strong hand curled around her waist.

She yelped as Ethan gently pulled her behind the thick black curtain, then tugged her against his firm muscular chest.

"What are you doing?"

The rich sound of his laughter and the mischievous spark in his eyes made her feel like she was floating. Oh, how she loved to see that gorgeous smile. A smile she hadn't been able to put out of her head for the last twenty-four hours. Especially after he told her he wanted to be her future.

Because she sort of wanted him to be her future too.

He cupped her cheeks with his hands as he surveyed her face. His gaze eventually landed on her lips. "I couldn't stay away another second. I saw you smiling and laughing and handing out pie, and I just got a little jealous. So when I saw you go up the stairs, I decided to surprise you and say hello."

"Say hello, huh? Is that all you want?" she teased, clutching both lapels of his navy-blue jacket. "By the way, there's plenty of pie for you, so no need to be jealous."

"That's good to know," he said, his voice gruff as he tilted his head to one side. "To be honest, I really just want to kiss you again. And here we are, alone, backstage, with these curtains offering the perfect cover and—"

She didn't even let him finish his sentence before pulling him closer and pressing her lips against his.

She needed this. She needed him. He eased his hands to rest under her jaw. She let her palms glide up over his collarbones, threading her fingers behind his neck, and anchored herself in the warmth of his touch. When Ethan deepened the kiss, her legs turned to liquid beneath her. The rough stubble on his jawline grazed along her chin, igniting a delicious sensation that rippled through her abdomen and down to her toes.

How long had it been since someone kissed her like this? Since she let herself want something just for her?

In the dim backstage lighting, tucked away from the chaos of the festival, she was swept up in the moment. All of her worries and heartache melted away, and frankly, she wouldn't mind staying back here for—

"Mama, no!"

Sadie's shriek cut through the air, vanquishing their thrilling little bubble.

Tisha's eyes flew open.

"Uh-oh," Ethan whispered, pressing his forehead against hers.

Oh no. No, no, no.

"I've got this," Tisha said quietly, although a sinking feeling in her stomach pushed aside all the effervescence she'd savored less than thirty seconds ago.

Sadie stood at the edge of the curtain, fists balled at her sides and her tiny body humming with fury. Her face was scrunched in horror, and her chest rose and fell.

"What are you doing? You can't kiss him!" Sadie howled and stomped her sneaker so hard that her pigtails bounced.

"Whoa, whoa, whoa." Tisha relinquished her hold on Ethan and slowly moved toward her daughter.

"You cannot kiss him anymore." Sadie leaned out of Tisha's reach. "What would my daddy say?"

Oh, baby. Tisha's stomach twisted. She sank to her knees. "Your daddy is in heaven now, and he's not coming back. I wish that weren't true, but there's nothing we can do to change that. We have to move on."

"No, I don't want to move on!" Sadie clamped her hands over her ears. "You said he was always with us."

"Sadie, you need to listen to me." Tisha fought to keep her voice even. "Your daddy loved you more than anything in the world. He wouldn't want us to be sad and lonely forever."

"I'm not alone," she wailed, her voice echoing off the walls. "I have you and Grandma and Grandpa and Ollie. We don't need *him.*"

Tisha winced and squeezed her eyes shut. *Lord, please help. I don't know what to do.*

Ethan pressed his strong hand against the small of her back. "Tisha, maybe we could talk about this another time?"

She opened her eyes and pinned him with a long look. "I said I've got this. Just give us a few minutes. Please."

Hurt flashed in his eyes. Then he nodded. "Okay."

She watched him walk offstage, then turned her attention back to Sadie. Poor thing. Her whole body trembled, and tears slid down her flushed cheeks. "Sadie, let's find your coat and get some fresh air outside."

"Not until you say you'll stop. Stop hugging and kissing him!"

Then Sadie turned and ran.

"Wait. Sadie, no. Come back!"

Tisha pushed through the double doors and rushed out into the hallway. How fast could one unhappy seven-year-old run? She glimpsed Sadie's hair bouncing against her back as she squeezed between the adults milling around the front door, then ran out into the parking lot.

"Sadie, stop!" She yelled, then collided with two older women walking side by side into the community center.

"Slow down there, sweetheart." The silver-haired woman on the right grabbed Tisha's forearm. "What's the rush?"

"M-my daughter. She just ran out into the parking lot." Tisha wrenched free from the woman's grasp. "Sadie!"

Oh, her sweet baby girl. She'd never forgive herself if something terrible happened.

Tisha fought her way through the glut of people blocking her exit, her heart thumping as she ran outside.

A colossal wall of water surged across the bay, bearing down on them. Its deafening roar reverberated through the ground under her feet.

Gut-wrenching screams pierced the air.

"Lord, have mercy," she whispered, pressing her hands to her cheeks. Leaves, sticks, and fish churned in the humongous, angry brown wave, tossed about like toys. A terrible stench made her gag. She pulled the collar of her sweater up over her mouth and nose to filter out the rancid smell.

People hollered and ran, eyes wild as they sprinted past her.

"Sadie!" She screamed again.

A lanky man in worn jeans, a plaid flannel shirt, and battered sneakers slowed down, his chest heaving as he caught his breath. "What do you need?" he gasped, his face pale and drawn.

"Sadie, my daughter—she's out here somewhere," Tisha yelled, her eyes stinging as she squinted against the sleet pelting them. "Please! You have to help me!"

"We'll find her. Right now you've got to run for higher ground." He tugged on her sleeve and pointed toward the hill. "C'mon. This way."

They cut around the corner by the bank. Blinded by sleet and terror, Tisha scrambled over the concrete, sucked into the throng that had bolted from the community center. People pressed in on all sides, filling the street like teeming salmon, desperate to escape. The cacophony of hurried footsteps and anxious cries filled the air, mingling with the thunderous sound of the impending wave. Hot tears stung her eyes at the thought of fleeing the spot where she'd last seen Sadie. The man in the plaid shirt turned to help a teenage boy who'd slipped and fallen on an icy patch.

"Go!" he shouted, waving her on as he slowed to lift the kid to his feet. "Go! Now!"

Tisha glanced over her shoulder. A horrendous scream crawled up her throat, raw and guttural. The water arced over the railing at the edge of the harbor, a curling wall of wrath and mud. It swallowed the docks, the boats bobbing there, greedily devouring everything it could.

Tisha's mind whirled as she turned and ran. Would she ever find her little girl? A sickening horror washed over her. She could barely make out the hill in the distance, her only hope. She'd never make it. The wave would catch her first. She'd lose Sadie and then herself.

"Sadie!" She screamed, then stumbled on the slippery sidewalk, her shoes sliding out from under her. The water slammed into the buildings lining the street behind her with a deafening groan.

"Head for the school!" a woman yelled, pointing toward the hillside where the junior-high and high school buildings sat on a plateau. Tom and Melinda had mentioned that the schools served as emergency shelters in case of earthquakes and tsunamis. They'd been built on the highest point in Redemption, but that had to be over a quarter of a mile away. She couldn't run there. The water would take her out.

Another desperate sob broke loose as she scrambled to find her footing and navigate the worst version of reality she could possibly imagine. Without her daughter.

Water licked at her heels as she tried to run faster. Her lungs burned, and her leg muscles protested. Somewhere behind her, a window shattered. Shouts echoed, and children cried out for their mothers. But still no Sadie.

The crowd surged, sweeping her sideways. A man knocked into her, spinning her toward a parked truck. Tisha clawed at the cold metal, her breath coming in gasps now as she fought to stay upright. Her mind raced with thoughts of Sadie, alone and vulnerable.

She had to find her.

Ice-cold water swirled around her calves.

"Sadie!" she choked out, but her voice was swallowed by terrified screams and the sickening roar of water gobbling everything in its path.

The day had gone from blissful to tragic in the span of two minutes.

Ethan stood on the hill outside the high school, the ground vibrating under his boots. The wind whipped his face, stinging his skin, but he didn't flinch. Below, Redemption broke apart as gray churning water swept away toys, furniture, chunks of buildings, channeling its way into every nook and cranny until it lapped at the base of the hill.

The air reeked of salt and wet earth and made his stomach twist. He glanced from one rooftop to another. A haze of mist and debris blocked his view. He couldn't find his family. Where was Brody? Surely he wasn't down there somewhere. Alone. Surely Mom had grabbed him, along with Dad, and made it up the hill in time. His hands shook and his breath came fast and shallow as he scanned the area for his son. What about Tisha? Sadie? Were they safe?

He should have done something—pushed harder, called the mayor, insisted his dad ask more questions. Why hadn't he thought about collecting sandbags? Or maybe he should've called their representatives in Juneau and warned them that Townsend Glacier threatened to wreak havoc.

"Dad, over here!"

Ethan whipped around at the sound of Brody's voice. His son sprinted toward him, his small legs pumping, hoodie flapping behind him.

"Brody!" Ethan shouted, then ran to meet him and sank to his knees in a mud puddle. "Oh, Brody, thank God. I was so worried."

He squeezed his eyes shut, breathing in the smell of his son's laundry soap and shampoo. Then he blinked away tears, eased back, and surveyed every inch of his precious boy. His cheeks were flushed, his hair damp. He wore a hoodie layered underneath a puffer vest, and his hands were red and cold.

"I was so worried I wouldn't be able to find you," Ethan said, his voice cracking.

"Dad, are you crying?"

"Yes." Ethan swiped at the moisture dripping from his nose.

"I'm fine, Dad," Brody said, wiping his hand across his face. "I was so scared, though, when the water started coming."

Ethan swallowed against the tightness in his throat. "Me too, pal, but I've got you now. You're safe." He kissed the top of Brody's head, then stood and lifted him into his arms.

"Ethan!"

His mother's voice sliced through the chaos. Ethan turned, his pulse kicking up as he spotted Mom hurrying across the high school parking lot. When she reached them, she pulled Ethan and Brody into a fierce embrace, gripping them as if she'd never let go.

"Mom, I'm so glad you're safe," Ethan said into his mother's shoulder. "Where's Dad and the others?"

Mom pulled back but kept her hand pressed against his shoulder. "They're okay. Your dad is with Megan, Tate, and Luke. They are all safe. By the grace of God, no water is rising out at the resort."

"We have to get down there," Ethan said. "What if people are trapped?"

Mom's brow furrowed. "Honey, the water hasn't receded yet. It's too dangerous."

"I can't just stand here and do nothing," Ethan said, shaking his head. "I knew—I knew this would happen."

"It's a natural disaster," Mom said. "No forecast for this."

"But I tried to tell Dad that I flew over Townsend. I saw the ice breaking off. I asked him about the last time there was a terrible landslide, and he didn't seem too concerned."

"Oh, son." Empathy filled his mother's eyes. "You can't blame yourself. This isn't your responsibility. Oil spills, fires at the cannery, earthquakes, tsunamis—this is life, especially when you live near the Pacific. God is in control; He knows what He's doing."

"I know He is, but . . ." He trailed off, scanning the roofs of the houses and severed trees again. Mom was right. Water still sloshed through town—an ugly, gray, soupy mess that would upend people's lives for months.

"Dad, what if there's another wave?" Brody trembled in his arms. "What will we do?"

Ethan shot Mom a pleading glance. *A little help?*

She reached over and squeezed Brody's leg. "There could be another wave, but it's not likely. Let's focus on getting inside, getting warm, and maybe finding something to eat. What do you think about that plan?"

"Good plan," Brody said. "Are there snacks here?"

Smiling, Ethan put Brody down, then crouched to look him in

the eyes. "Listen, I promise I'll be super careful, but I have to help. You need to stay here with Grandma, okay?"

Brody sniffed, then nodded. "Okay, Dad."

"I will come back for you. I promise."

"I know." Brody offered him a fist. "Love you, Dad."

Ethan's heart pinched. He bumped Brody's fist. "I love you too, pal."

He straightened and turned to face his mother. "Please keep an eye on him for me. I'll be back as soon as I can."

"Be careful, Ethan," Mom said, her expression sober.

Ethan jogged across the parking lot toward a small group of firefighters and police officers organizing near an emergency vehicle. The wind tore at his jacket and icy rain fell from a granite-gray sky. Maybe he couldn't stop a tsunami, but he could still try to save as many lives as possible.

A glimpse of a blonde woman holding a little girl's hand and weaving through the people clustered under the high school's portico halted his steps.

"Tisha!" he called out, his pulse already kicking into overdrive.

Her head snapped up, and when their eyes met, she burst into tears. They ran toward each other, splashing through the slush, with Sadie still clinging to her hand. Ethan closed the distance between them in a few long strides.

"Ethan," she said, her voice trembling. "I didn't know if you were okay. Is Brody here?"

"Hey, it's okay." He reached out, gripping her shoulders with both hands. "Brody's safe. He's with my mom right over there."

Her brow furrowed, Tisha craned her neck to see where he pointed.

Ethan glanced down at Sadie, hiding behind her mother. "Hey, kiddo, you all right?"

She nodded, but her chin quivered. "I'm scared. A lady from my church class picked me up and carried me here."

Tisha's eyes welled, and she cupped her hand to her mouth. He crouched down, eye to eye, then reached out and gently rubbed Sadie's shoulder. "We were all scared, sweetheart. I'm really glad someone was able to help you stay safe and find your mom. You're so brave, and guess what?"

Sadie gnawed on her thumbnail. "What?"

"You're in the safest spot right now, on top of the highest hill." He smiled. "I need you to do something for me."

She sniffed, her blue eyes wide. "What is it?"

"I need you to stay here inside the high school with your mom, where it's safe. People will take good care of you, and I'm coming back as soon as I can, but you need to keep an eye on your mom. Can you do that?"

Sadie nodded.

Tisha gulped back a sob, and Ethan looked up at her. She searched his face as a tear tracked down her flushed cheeks. "You're going back out there, aren't you?"

"I have to," he said, pushing to his feet. "There might be people stranded, or if I can get to a chopper, injured victims might need an evacuation. Time is short."

Her eyes welled with more tears. Then she reached up and cupped his cheek with her cold palm. "Come back, Ethan. Please."

He pressed a kiss to her palm. "I will," he said, his voice low. "I promise."

With one last glance at Sadie, still clinging to her mother, he backed away, then jogged toward the first responders assembling at the edge of the parking lot. Tisha's words lingered in his ears. He didn't look back though. He couldn't. But knowing that Tisha, Sadie, and Brody waited for him gave him strength. He would come back. He had to.

Fifteen

ELL, CLEARLY SHE HAD A THING FOR HEROIC aviators.

Tisha blinked back tears as Ethan hurried toward the emergency-response vehicle sitting at the edge of the parking lot. "Come on, pumpkin. Let's go inside." She guided Sadie toward the line snaking out from the entrance to the high school.

"Sadie, hey!" Brody trotted over with his grandmother not far behind him.

"Brody, look." Sadie held out her arm and pointed to an angry red cut stretching from her wrist to her elbow. "Cool, huh?"

"Sadie, what happened?" Tisha gently clasped Sadie's arm for a closer look. "We need to get that cleaned out."

"It's gnarly," Brody said. "Guess what?"

Sadie planted her hands on her hips. "What?"

"On the way up the hill, we saw a truck flipped over and floating in the water on its roof."

Sadie gasped. "No way!"

Mrs. McGuire offered a kind smile as she draped her arm around

Tisha's shoulders and pulled her in for a side hug. "It's hard to see him run toward danger, isn't it?"

Nodding, she swiped at her damp cheeks with the back of her hand.

"It's going to be all right," she said. "We're all going to pull together, and we'll get through this. Just like you have hurricanes in North Carolina, we have earthquakes and tidal waves and landslides here."

"Hey, Tom." Mrs. McGuire waved at someone behind her. "See? Here's your family."

Tisha turned, and the knots between her shoulder blades loosened a fraction as Tom and Melinda approached. Their pants were sopping wet and caked with mud, but they appeared mostly okay.

"Oh, thank You, Jesus!" Melinda swept Tisha and Sadie into a hug. "All I could do was pray that you would find your way up the hill."

Tisha exhaled, her body sagging into the embrace. "Thanks for telling me this is where we were supposed to go if there was ever an emergency. Somebody I recognized from church grabbed me and pretty much dragged me away from the community center."

She cringed at the thought of what might've happened if she hadn't listened.

"And somebody from church brought me," Sadie echoed, her small voice filled with a mix of relief and confusion.

"Yeah, about that." Tisha turned to Sadie and gently smoothed hair off her face. "The next time you're upset, I need you to not run from me. Do you understand?"

Sadie's lower lip trembled. "But I was angry with you for—"

"That doesn't mean you get to run." Tisha crouched, cupping Sadie's cheeks with trembling hands. The fear of losing her—even briefly—still rattled in her bones. She took a deep breath, forcing herself to stay calm. "I need you safe, Sadie. No matter what."

Sadie nodded. "Okay, Mama. I'm sorry."

"It's okay," Tisha said, pressing a kiss to her forehead. A few feet away, a young mother juggled a fussing baby and a preschooler tugging at her sweater. Tisha didn't hesitate. She stepped forward and touched the woman's arm. "Do you need a break? I can hold him for a few minutes if you want to use the restroom."

The woman's tired eyes flooded with gratitude. "Would you? I just—I don't want to put him down, and my little girl really has to go."

"Of course." Tisha reached for the baby, cradling him against her chest. He settled almost immediately, his tiny fingers curling into her sweater. Warmth spread through her, pushing aside the fatigue. There was still so much uncertainty and so much fear lingering in the air, but helping—caring for someone, even in a small way—gave her something to focus on besides worrying about Ethan.

Tom watched her quietly. When the young mother returned and took her baby back, they moved closer to the high school doors. Sadie and Brody had already started a game of freeze tag with the other kids waiting under the portico.

"You know," he said with a small smile, "you sure do have a soft spot for men who rush into danger."

She let out a quiet laugh. "And pilots, right?"

"Maybe," he said, his expression turning serious, "it's because you see their brave, generous hearts."

The words settled deep, wrapping around the aching parts of her soul.

She swallowed hard and turned her gaze back toward the crowd, where volunteers were passing out blankets. A man handed her one, and she draped it around her shoulders.

"Sometimes we do everything we can and suffering still visits us. It doesn't mean we're terrible people or we did anything wrong." Tom paused, holding the heavy metal door open. "But we've been hit hard like this before. And it's out of our suffering that we figure out what we are made of. Getting through the hard times is how we become what God wants us to be. Even in the water and the mud and the broken things, He's going to shape us and mold us."

"I know you're right," she said, waiting as the volunteer posted at the door logged each person's name and contact information in her phone. "But I don't want to be shaped and molded. I've had enough of that, thanks."

"You sure have, sweetie." He offered a tender smile. "And Melinda and I are proud of you. You've been so brave."

"It's because of Chase that I've learned to be brave," she admitted. "I know you and he didn't always see eye to eye, but he really wanted you to be proud of him. He felt like flying was his way of serving the Lord. I hope you know that. He truly felt a passion for all the things that you and Melinda taught him. Y'all raised a good man, Tom."

Tom's eyes welled and his chin wobbled. He wrapped her in a gentle hug. "Thank you," he whispered against the top of her head.

She smiled through her tears. "You're welcome."

He pulled a red bandanna from his pocket and dabbed at his face. Clearing his throat, he gave his name and address to the volunteer, then stepped through the double doors into the high school.

"As soon as we get the all clear, we can probably head back down the hill and check on the café," Melinda said. "The sooner, the better. That mud won't shovel itself."

"Mud?" Sadie trotted over to join them. "Where?"

"When the water retreats back into the ocean, it leaves us a parting gift. Thick, stinky mud." Melinda tugged on one of Sadie's pigtails. "Sounds super fun, right?"

"Ewww." Sadie scrunched her nose. "That's gross."

"Agreed," Melinda said, herding Sadie toward the door. "Come on, let's go in here and get warm."

Inside the high school cafeteria, Tisha and Sadie found a quiet corner and sagged against the painted brick wall.

"We'll go get some drinks and snacks," Melinda said, her voice soothing. "Brody, want to come?"

Brody nodded and fell in step beside Melinda as she crossed the beige-tiled floor to a makeshift snack stand on the opposite side of the room.

"Mama, can you sing me the song?" Sadie plopped onto Tisha's lap, looking up with hopeful eyes.

"Which one?"

"The one that Daddy always sang."

Tisha swallowed hard, feeling the weight of sadness. "I sure can."

She hummed a few opening bars of their favorite hymn, the beloved words that Chase had sung to Sadie since the day she was born. By now, they knew all the verses and all the hand motions by heart.

Through blurred vision and a lump in her throat, Tisha sat on the floor with Sadie and quietly sang, "He's got the whole world in His hands."

Yeah, okay, so Tisha knew the words were true, and she couldn't argue with the wisdom Tom had offered. Doubt still found a way to linger in the cracks of her heart though. But as they sang, the tension in her chest loosened just a little. The words were more than just a childhood melody—they were truth. Even in the chaos, the fear, and the heartbreak, God was still holding everything together.

She glanced toward the door, thoughts of Ethan spooling through her head. Maybe she didn't have to understand why men like him—like Chase—felt called to help others. Maybe it was enough to trust that God had given them that gift for a reason.

When they finished the song, she pressed a kiss to Sadie's hair and whispered, "God's got us, baby girl."

And this time, she truly believed it.

He'd assisted one woman who'd gone into labor onto a chopper bound for the hospital in Glennallen. Then he'd floated down Main Street in an inflatable raft from the fire department to assist a man trapped in his car with a broken leg. After that, he'd rescued three dogs, four cats, and one bearded dragon, returning them all to their families, who were spending the night in one of the school gyms.

Ethan stifled a yawn, then eased his Suburban to a stop behind the café. Thankfully, the water had receded some in the last hour or so. How the car still worked given all the water that had poured out of the driver's side door when he'd opened it, he had no idea. But he'd take a slightly waterlogged vehicle that smelled a little if it got him where he needed to go.

And right now, he needed to get to Tisha.

Electricity had been shut off, at least until morning, but the glow from a lantern or a candle through the window caught his attention.

Tisha. They hadn't spoken since they'd crossed paths outside the high school. That had only been six hours ago, but it felt like six hundred. He would have kept going, working through the night to help residents wade through the water to find their missing pets. But the fire chief saw him swaying on his feet as he shoveled mud out of the doorway to the police station and sent him home. Tisha and Sadie weren't at the high school when he'd stopped by a few minutes ago. And now he couldn't ignore the light in the window and just drive by the café. What if there genuinely was an issue? No one should be in there at this hour.

He worked his way across the disgusting parking lot, mud squelching under his boots, then knocked softly at the back door. No one answered. He clicked on his headlamp, turned the knob, and it opened.

"Hello?" He stepped inside. Movement caught his eye. Tisha appeared, eyes wide and red-rimmed.

His heart squeezed. "Hey. What's wrong?"

She wiped her face, smearing a streak of mud across her splotchy cheek. "Ethan. You shouldn't . . ." Her voice caught. "What are you doing here?"

He tugged off his headlamp so he wouldn't blind her. "You and Sadie weren't at the high school. Someone said she went home with Tom and Melinda, so I swung by here. I promised I'd come back for you," he said, his voice gravelly from giving instructions and talking nonstop to other volunteers. He had practically inhaled a peanut butter and jelly sandwich, a bag of chips, and some Fig Newtons, washing it all down with a cup of tepid coffee. He'd tried to stay hydrated, but the needs had stacked up—almost insurmountable. Everywhere he'd looked, mud mixed with snow, and devastated people waded through stinky water.

She let out a ragged breath. "I'm saving the pies I sold. At the festival today, people paid for all twenty-four pies, plus begged me to let them preorder if they donated to the fund for the playground equipment. So now I have to follow through. Besides, I thawed them out, and we're probably going to lose everything in the freezer anyway." She gave a half-hearted thrust in the air with her fist. "So I've got to save the pie."

"I'll help."

She shook her head. "You don't have to."

"But I want to."

"Fine. Here they are." She turned and shone the beam of her flashlight on neat stacks of white boxes on every square inch of counter space in the café's kitchen.

"My Suburban is parked out back. There's not much in it, believe it or not. Where are you going to take them?"

"To the cabin, I guess. Between space in my fridge and some at Tom and Melinda's place, I think I can save a lot of them, and there are a few that'll just have to sit out. I'd deliver them myself if I could, but that's probably not safe."

He scrubbed his hand over his face. "Will you let me help you move these?"

She hesitated. "Ethan—" Her face crumpled, and she pressed the back of her hand to her mouth.

Oh no. He reached for her, but she shook her head and took a step back. "No, don't. I—I have to say this."

He stilled. "Say what?"

"I messed up. Backstage at the festival with Sadie. I should've handled it better. She was so upset, and then she ran, and the tidal wave . . ."

Sighing, he rubbed at the tightness in his chest. "No, I get it. I'm a dad, and sometimes we have to be careful how we respond. Especially in the middle of a crisis."

"I'm really sorry." A tear slipped down her cheek. "I don't want to hurt you, but I can't ignore her feelings."

"She's not ready." He reached out and skimmed his palms against the shoulders of her puffy jacket, now pocked with splashes of mud and grime. "Listen. You deserve a happily ever after, and frankly, so do I. But you and Sadie need time, and I'm not about to push my way into your life."

Sniffing, she gave a helpless shrug. "She's scared, and I don't know how to make her not scared."

"We don't have to fix this tonight," he said. "Or tomorrow. But as much as I'm into you, and as much as I want this, want us, Sadie has to be comfortable with a fresh start."

"I know," she whispered.

"And I don't think that means never." He gave her a small, sad smile. "But it means not right now."

Fresh tears welled in her eyes. "I hate this."

He leaned over and pressed a tender kiss on her forehead. "Let's get these pies rescued."

They loaded the pies into their vehicles, the only sound the slosh of water and emergency generators humming in the distance.

"I'll see you at the cabin in a few minutes," she said. Their head-lights cut through the darkness. It was eerie driving down Main Street with no lights and evidence of the destruction lurking in the shadows. The ice statues had been toppled over. Only the pirate was still standing, but he looked disfigured and sad.

Ethan turned the corner and headed up the hill toward the Binfords' place. When he got there, Tisha had backed into the driveway, so he mimicked her parking.

Tom came out on the porch to help.

"Let's see how many I can put in the cabin," Tisha said.

"All right." Ethan followed her around to the bungalow-style structure behind the Binfords' home. "Wow, this is nice."

"You've never been here?"

He shook his head. "Is it new?"

"Built within the last five years maybe?" Snow crunched under her boots as she carefully held two pie boxes in one hand, then fumbled with the doorknob. "It's quite lovely. Sadie and I are glad to have a space of our own."

"Yeah, I bet." He scraped his muddy boots on the welcome mat.

"Don't worry about the mud; it's inevitable."

"If you're sure." He stepped inside. Pictures of Chase greeted him—on every surface and every empty space on the wall. Art-work related to planes. Pictures of Chase, pictures of Chase and Tisha. More pictures of Chase and Sadie. He tried to keep his eyes focused straight ahead, but man, the guy was everywhere. So this was why Sadie reacted the way she did. If Chase was still this much in their lives, then Ethan had made the right decision.

"Here you go." He handed her a stack of three boxes, determined to keep his expression neutral. It wasn't his place to criticize or comment. There was nothing he could say that would make this situation any easier.

Between Tom hauling pies into the house and Tisha and Ethan bringing in the rest from their vehicles, within thirty minutes, they'd made space for almost every pie. Except for four that she stacked neatly on the counter.

"These will be okay without refrigeration. I'll try to find their new homes tomorrow," she said, facing him in the dim glow of the lamplight. "Ethan, I—"

He held up his palm to stop her. "Tisha, I think I need to go before I can't walk away. So let me know if you need any more help with the pies."

Then he turned and left the cabin. Thankfully, Sadie and her grandparents did not come outside, and he made a quick escape in the Suburban. He cranked up the U2 station on satellite radio and drove through town, the windows down and songs playing loudly. When he got to the resort, he parked and trudged toward the back door. What a blessing to be able to sleep in his own mud-free bed. He needed a hot shower and a bowl of cereal, and then he planned to sleep for about two days.

Luke greeted him at the door. "Hey, man, I was getting worried about you. Everything all right?"

"Yeah. I just helped Tisha with a pie rescue."

"Oh? How'd that go?"

"Not great."

"Uh-oh."

Ethan hesitated, then craned his neck, looking around. They didn't have any scheduled guests tonight, but they had opened up the rooms for anyone who needed them. Three couples sat by the fire, talking quietly.

"If you're looking for Brody, Mom put him to bed about an hour ago. The kid was wiped."

"Yeah, I know the feeling."

"Come on in the kitchen. Tate went to grab more pop out of the garage."

Luke had the most delicious-looking sub-style sandwich packed with lettuce, tomato, and some kind of deli meat sitting on the counter. "Here, I made this for you."

"Wow. Thanks. I'm starving."

"Thought so. There's some grapes, chips, and plenty of cookies."

"Yeah, I'll take the grapes, thanks."

He dragged himself to the table, pulled out a chair, sat down, whispered a quick blessing, then dove in.

"So, things with Tisha are . . . bumpy?" Luke set the bowl of grapes in the middle of the table. "I heard about that kiss."

"Did you also hear about Sadie's epic meltdown?"

Luke palmed the back of his neck. "Yeah, I might have heard something about that. She'll get over it."

"That's the problem," Ethan said. "I just told Tisha I'm taking a step back because she and Sadie need some time."

Luke stared at him. "What?"

Ethan paused, his sandwich halfway to his mouth. "Sadie's not ready for me to be a part of their lives."

Luke's mouth drifted open.

Ethan pinned him with a look. "What?"

"I'm proud of you, man. That's a selfless move." Luke leaned his elbows on the table. "But what are you thinking? She's seven. You've got to win her over. How hard can it be?"

Ethan shrugged. "Not as easy as you might think. Sadie isn't ready to say goodbye to her daddy yet. And I can't barge into her life. I need to be invited in."

"Huh." Luke ripped open a bag of barbecue-flavored chips and popped one into his mouth. "Guess I'm just surprised you're going to give up so easily."

Ethan sighed. "I'm not giving up. It's called being patient."

Shaking his head, Luke reached for another chip. "Good luck with that."

Sixteen

I*'M NOT THREATENED . . . CHASE IS A BIG PART of your past, but I would sure like to be your future.*

Ethan's words from three nights ago when they'd walked hand in hand near the ice sculptures spooled through her head. Tisha sat on the sofa in the cabin, savoring her morning coffee. Sadie was sprawled on the floor by the fire, on her tummy, chin propped on her hands while she watched an animated movie on Tisha's iPad.

Again.

School had been closed indefinitely due to water damage, so Tisha should probably be spending her Monday morning teaching Sadie something new. But she just didn't have it in her.

Besides, she couldn't get past her conversation with Ethan when they'd rescued the pies. If Ethan wasn't threatened by Chase, he'd kind of acted like he was when he came by the cabin. Or had Sadie's melodramatic reaction to their last kiss aggravated him enough that he'd decided she wasn't worth it?

She winced. Hopefully that wasn't the case. But she hated that maybe she'd let a good man get away because she liked her

Chase-shaped cocoon a little too much. Her eyes roamed the cabin walls. There were a lot of photos in here. Jennifer and Melinda had every right to decorate the place however they wanted, but if she were in Ethan's shoes and walked in here, well, she would have had questions too.

There was no way she'd want to see fifteen different photos of Adeline because, let's be real, Tisha had done a deep dive on the Internet, and the woman was *stunning*.

But on the other hand, if she closed this chapter of her life, what would it mean for her? She hadn't really loved being a McDowell. Oh, she'd loved her father, adored her sisters, and deep down, she did love her mother, but marrying Chase and taking the Binford name had been such a delight. He'd really given her the freedom to be herself, to be joyful, and to love others well. But even in losing him, she hadn't really learned to sit in her sad feelings. Not yet, anyway.

"Oh, how did I mess this up?" Tisha murmured.

Sadie paused the movie, then looked over her shoulder. "Who are you talking to, Mama?"

"Myself." Tisha dragged a hand across her face. "Sadie, come up here and sit with me for a minute."

"But my movie's not done."

"We'll finish your movie after we chat."

"Okay." Sadie dragged herself, her blanket, and Ollie over to the couch and climbed up next to Tisha.

"Why are you just sitting here, Mama?"

"Listen." Tisha took another sip of her coffee, her own version of liquid courage, then set the mug on the coffee table and pulled Sadie close. "Sweetheart, you know that your daddy loved you very much, right?"

"Of course."

"And he loved me."

"Yes."

"But just like we talked about the other day, he's in heaven now. And we believe that we'll see him again someday."

"When we're with Jesus too, right?"

"Good job. And that means we can't keep holding on to him here."

Sadie stared up at her, confusion swimming in her eyes. "What do you mean?"

"I'm a little bit worried that we've held on too tightly to all these pictures."

Sadie looked around slowly. "But I like these pictures."

"I do too. They're very nice. But remember we talked about making a fresh start?"

"We can make a fresh start and still have pictures. What's wrong with that?"

"I think that you and I need to pick one or two of our favorite photos of your daddy, and then we're going to need to put the rest away."

"But it will be so boring in here."

Tisha laughed softly. "Don't worry. You're a super-talented artist. I bet you can come up with some pictures that we can frame. And I know I have photos of our friends and family back in North Carolina. Trust me, there are lots of things we can fill these walls with. But we don't have to have this many pictures of your daddy."

Sadie sat for a moment, her little feet bouncing. "Okay, Mama."

"Good." Tisha squeezed Sadie's hand. "Now, let's do this together." They stood and began taking down the photos of Chase, carefully placing each one on the table. Sadie's eyes lingered on the photos, her lips forming a small pout.

"You can pick two to keep, sweetheart," Tisha reminded her.

Sadie walked over to the table and selected two photos—one of Chase holding her as a baby and another of him smiling with Tisha on their wedding day. Tisha's breath hitched at the sight, but she nodded, swallowing her emotion.

They put the rest away in a box together, both of them quietly acknowledging this new step in their lives.

Once the box was closed, Sadie looked up at her mom. "What do we do now?"

Tisha smiled and ruffled her hair. "We move forward, sweetheart. We make room for new memories. And there's something else," Tisha said as they settled back on the couch.

"What is it?"

"I need to talk to you about Ethan and Brody."

Sadie sighed and dipped her head. "I'm gonna have to apologize, aren't I?"

"Well, I'm not as concerned about the apology as I am about your feelings. Sweetheart, Ethan is a very good man."

"And you like him."

"I do like him. And I think he likes me."

Sadie twisted her blanket in her hands.

"I'm sorry that you and Brody had a tough time at first. But I think that you might have to get used to the idea of Ethan and Brody being around more."

Sadie looked up, eyes wide. "Will there be more hand-holding and kissing between you and Mr. Ethan?"

Tisha laughed. "Yes. *Not* between you and Brody."

Sadie giggled. "Oh, Mama, you're silly. Of course not."

"Would you be okay with that? Ethan and me as boyfriend and girlfriend?"

"Yeah, I would." Sadie grinned. "You know, I think my daddy would have really liked Mr. Ethan."

Tisha clapped her hand over her mouth to hold back a sob. Sadie looked horrified.

"What? What did I say?"

"You said exactly the right thing, honey."

"Oh." Relief washed over her little face. "Can I finish my movie?"

"Yes."

"Can I build a fort?"

"On one condition."

Sadie's expression sobered. "What?"

"We sit in the fort together and eat a sweet treat."

"Do you have any funny cake?" Sadie looked at the ceiling, then released a blissful sigh. "Because that would be perfect."

Laughing, Tisha patted her leg. "It sure would."

Tisha stood and went to the stack of pies Ethan had helped her carry into the cabin last night. She'd owe someone a funny cake if she cut into the one she had here. But that was a small price to pay in exchange for quality time with Sadie.

"Are we gonna do anything else today?"

"That's a great question. It's pretty messy out there. As soon as Grandma and Grandpa are ready, we'll probably head over to the café and try to get things cleaned up. Come on, let's build this fort."

She dragged chairs over from the kitchen table, and Sadie went and pulled the extra blankets and quilts off their beds. They stretched the blankets over the chairs until they had the cutest little A-frame fort. Sadie tucked her special blanket and Ollie inside and then brought the iPad over.

"This is a movie about Rapunzel, Mama. You'll love it."

"Great. I'll be right back." She transferred her coffee to an insulated mug with a lid, cut two slices of funny cake, and carried them into the fort.

"May I have some milk, please?"

"Absolutely." Tisha went and filled a cup with cold milk, added a lid and a straw, and grabbed two forks. And just as she was returning to the fort, she heard footsteps on the porch, followed by a knock.

Maybe he should have called first.

Ethan stood on the porch outside the cabin, gripping two bouquets of roses so tightly his knuckles turned white. Pink for Sadie and red for Tisha. His legs felt like jelly, and sweat trickled down his back despite the frigid morning air.

Luke's words had echoed through his mind all night—*I'm just surprised you're going to give up so easily.* So he'd crawled out of bed at dawn, spotted the flower arrangements his mom had made for the gala that wasn't happening, and explained his plan. She'd handed him two of the most beautiful bouquets, kissed his cheek, and sent him on his way.

Now, as the door opened, Ethan sucked in a sharp breath. Tisha stood there in red-and-white plaid pajamas and a sweatshirt adorned with hearts and baking utensils. Her hair was in a loose ponytail, and her cheeks were rosy from the warmth inside. She looked *real.* Comfortable. Like home.

His throat went dry, and he almost dropped the flowers.

"This is a nice surprise." She tilted her head, her lips curving into a faint, teasing smile.

"You're adorable," he blurted.

She raised a brow, clearly amused. "Thanks. Did you come all the way over here to tell me that?"

"Actually, I came to see Sadie. But these are for you." He extended the red roses.

Her fingers brushed his as she took them, and his heart stuttered.

"Thank you," she said, holding them to her nose and inhaling. "Sadie's in the fort watching a movie. She may not be thrilled about the interruption, but you're welcome to try."

Ethan stepped inside, his boots thudding awkwardly against the wood floor as he toed them off. The living room was dominated by blankets draped over chairs and stacked cushions, with soft light spilling out from within. He crouched, ducking inside.

Sadie sat cross-legged, wrapped in a blanket, with a

chocolate-smeared face and a stuffed killer whale clutched against her side. She looked up, startled but curious.

"Hi, Sadie."

"Hi, Mr. Ethan. Want to watch the movie?"

"Maybe later. I was hoping we could talk for a minute."

Sadie frowned, carefully setting her plate on the floor. "I guess. My mom interrupted me too. Maybe I just need to learn to be flexible."

Ethan chuckled, his nerves easing a little. "Thanks for fitting me in. This is really important." He held out the pink roses, watching as her eyes widened in delight.

"For me?" she whispered.

"Yep."

"Mama!" she called. "Mr. Ethan brought me flowers!"

Tisha's voice floated in from the kitchen. "I know. Isn't that sweet?"

Sadie beamed and cradled the bouquet in her lap. "Why?"

"Well . . ." Ethan cleared his throat, the words catching for a moment. "I need to ask for your permission for something."

Her brow furrowed in confusion. "Permission? What for?"

"To love your mom."

From the kitchen, Ethan heard the faintest gasp.

"Yeah, I know you love her. I saw you guys kissing." Sadie examined a rose petal. "I get it, and it's okay."

Ethan smothered a grin with his hand. "Here's the thing. I know you miss your dad—I do too. He was a great guy, and I'll never try to replace him. But if you're okay with it, I'd really like to be here for you and your mom. To make sure you're both happy and safe."

Sadie hugged her stuffed whale tighter, her gaze searching his face. "I think my dad would've liked you."

Ethan blinked rapidly against the sting in his eyes. "Thank you, Sadie."

Her serious expression softened into a small smile. "You're

welcome." Then she giggled. "But does this mean Brody and I have to get along?"

He laughed, shaking his head. "One thing at a time, kiddo. No marriage plans yet. I'm just starting with you. By the way, Brody is next door at your grandparents' house with a puppy that was rescued yesterday."

Sadie grinned, then sprang to her feet, destroying the fort in the process. "Can I go see the puppies at Grandma and Grandpa's house?"

"Sadie!" Tisha rushed over, wiping at her cheeks. "Please don't smear pie on the carpet."

Sadie practically danced toward the door. "Mama, can I go?"

Tisha sighed, a mix of amusement and exasperation in her smile. "Boots and coat first."

When the door slammed behind Sadie, Tisha turned back to Ethan, still clutching her bouquet. "You didn't have to do that, you know."

"I did." He stepped closer, his voice low and steady. "Because I meant every word."

Her lips parted, and her eyes shone with unshed tears. "Ethan…"

"I'm in love with you, Tisha." He reached for her free hand, threading their fingers together. "And I want to be part of your world. All of it. I'm terrified, but I'm not letting that stop me this time."

She set the flowers on a nearby stack of books and closed the distance between them. "I'm in love with you too," she whispered, her voice trembling. "And I'm not going anywhere."

Ethan gently cupped her face, his thumbs brushing her cheekbones in a delicate, almost reverent caress. Her skin was soft beneath his touch, warm and slightly flushed. He hesitated, his gaze searching hers for any sign of doubt. The world seemed to hold its breath as her eyes softened, inviting him closer. Leaning in, he let the scent of her—vanilla and a faint trace of cinnamon—wash over him. When their lips met, the kiss was tender, slow, and filled with unspoken promises. The soft pressure of her mouth against his sent a hum of electricity through him. Her hands slid up to the back of his neck, her fingertips grazing the edges of his hair. The gentle tug anchored him, drawing him closer as the kiss deepened. The quiet crackle of the fireplace faded into the background.

When they finally pulled apart, their foreheads rested together, their breaths mingling in the quiet.

"You're very sweet," she murmured, her lips curving in a soft smile. "And a little dangerous. Like chocolate peanut-butter pie."

His laugh rumbled low in his chest. "Lucky for you, anything chocolate peanut butter is my favorite."

"Lucky for me," she echoed, before he kissed her again, this time with the quiet certainty that they were building something real.

Seventeen

THE FOLLOWING WEEK, TISHA SAT AT THE counter in the café, her laptop open before her. They'd cleaned the place up and passed health inspection, but customers had been slow to trickle in. Thankfully, she was able to use the downtime to complete her application for graduate school. She'd planned to take classes online once she got settled in Redemption, but Sadie's challenges at school and making pies for the festival had all shoved her plans aside. Now, with life returning to a semblance of normalcy and spring on the horizon, she decided to go for it.

The door opened and she turned, her heart lifting in anticipation. It wasn't just any customer—it was her favorite. Ethan strode in, his presence lighting up the room as he scanned the café.

"You here by yourself?" he asked, a warm smile spreading across his face.

"Owen is meeting the grocery-delivery truck from Anchorage out back. Right now it's just me. Charlie's still helping her family clean their place up."

Ethan brushed his lips against hers.

"I love that you can kiss me almost anytime you want."

"And I love you," he said.

She'd never tire of his kisses. Or his tender words. They were a balm to her soul. How could she have ever doubted their connection?

"What are you doing?" He sat down beside her, glancing at her screen.

"I've decided to apply for graduate school. I really want to get a master's degree in counseling," she said, her voice tinged with both excitement and trepidation.

"I'm sure you can do that. Do you want to say why? And maybe tell me about it over a slice of chocolate peanut-butter pie?"

"I'll get that for you in just a minute," she said, pushing her hair behind her ear. "We need a local counselor around here. Pie doesn't solve everything."

"Are you sure? I feel like pie has played a significant role in our lives lately."

She gestured to the mailing envelope he carried under his arm. "What's that?"

"Oh," he cleared his throat, opening the tab and pulling out a gorgeous magazine.

"Oh wow. What's this?"

"The latest issue of *Florida Living*." He slid it across the counter, his expression serious.

"Oh, is this Kaylee's story about Adeline?"

He nodded.

"May I?"

"Please do. I put a sticky tab on it. It's the cover story." She flipped open to the marker, gasping at the beautiful picture of Adeline carrying a surfboard out of the water. The inset photo showed her reading to children, and another featured her enjoying drinks with friends.

"It's well written," Ethan said, his voice thick with emotion.

The two sat quietly as she read both pages, absorbing the impact of a generous human gone too soon. When she closed the magazine and carefully handed it back, she gently squeezed his arm. "I'm really glad you said yes to that. Have you shown it to Brody yet?"

"No, I brought it to you first. I'll let him look at it after school."

"I'll be curious to hear how he reacts." She saved her progress online, then shut down her laptop. "And I'm sure her parents are very pleased about the article."

"Very. We just FaceTimed. Her dad couldn't hold it together, but I can tell he's thrilled. They thanked me for letting Kaylee do it."

"Have you heard from Kaylee or Adam?" Tisha asked.

"Just a short note with the magazine." He blew out a long breath. "I'm sorry that she's gone, but they were right. It's important that we let her legacy live on, and that her generosity is evident to those around her."

"This does, in fact, call for pie."

"Wait." He reached for her hand, his touch sending warmth coursing through her. "If you ever want to know more about her, you can ask."

"All right. Would you like some whipped cream with your pie?"

"Please."

"How about coffee?"

"Of course."

"I'll be right back."

As she moved into the kitchen, she felt a rush of gratitude for this moment. She was finally pursuing her dreams, and Ethan was right there with her, encouraging her every step of the way. The thought of becoming a counselor filled her with hope, not just for herself but for the community she loved. She wanted to help others find their way, just as Ethan had helped her find hers.

When she carried out the pie and coffee, she found Ethan frowning, scrolling through his phone.

"What's the matter?" she asked, careful not to spill his mug of coffee.

"Oh, the news station in Anchorage is doing a story about Trevor's plane. Evidently, the landslide after the glacier calved moved some things around, and they've identified the plane as belonging to him."

Tisha gasped. "Babe, that's a big deal, right?"

"Yeah." Ethan nodded, thumbing the story away and putting his phone in his pocket.

"But I'm guessing no remains?"

"Not yet."

"So the mystery isn't really solved?"

"No. But I'm going to go speak to his mom anyway."

"Oh, that's very brave of you."

He lifted one shoulder, then reached for his napkin and fork. "I don't know about brave. We both need closure."

They sat in comfortable silence for a few minutes.

"So how did you know that chocolate peanut butter would be my favorite flavor?" he asked, his fork loaded and halfway to his mouth.

"Well, it's rich."

"Ha, that's cute."

"I didn't mean monetarily." She nudged his shoulder with her hand. "I meant deep. Textured. Sweet on the inside, but a little bit of a crust—"

"Yeah, this is not exactly the swoon-worthy description I'd hoped for."

"I'm a baker, not a romance novelist."

He leaned over and brushed his lips against hers. "Have I mentioned lately that I love you exactly as you are? You are the best surprise of my life."

She kissed him back, savoring the sweet taste of chocolate and peanut butter lingering on his lips. Sitting in the café on a quiet morning, sharing an ordinary slice of pie, a wave of emotion swept over her and nearly took her breath away. She had never imagined she could feel so deeply for someone new, not after losing Chase. And the thought of building a life with Ethan filled her with a renewed sense of purpose. She squeezed his hand, knowing that together, they could face anything.

It had to be here somewhere.

Ethan stood in front of the closet in his childhood bedroom, scanning the boxes stacked high on the shelves. His parents had done a great job saving relics from his past—trophies, quilts stitched from T-shirts from all the basketball tournaments he'd played in, and photo albums Mom had started in a valiant effort to keep up. Now things were stashed in shoeboxes, saved on flash drives, or lost in the ever-elusive cloud.

But MJ's piece of jade . . . He must've hidden it somewhere out of sight to avoid the sting of how Mrs. Kelly had reacted the last time he tried to reach out.

Today would be different.

The wreckage of Trevor's plane had been identified, and Ethan had worked hard to process his feelings. He'd embraced a new relationship with Tisha, God had mended the broken places in his heart, and now he felt emotionally fortified to try again.

He found a box marked with his old address in Florida. It wasn't the one he'd been searching for, but curiosity tugged at him. He found a pocketknife from middle school on his dresser and slashed open the packing tape on the cardboard. He froze when he recognized Adeline's handwriting on a note addressed to his parents.

Hey, I felt like you guys should have this, just in case things go south for me. I don't know that Ethan will have *the presence of mind to save some of the most precious notes and cards and letters. So just in case no one reminds him that he's an amazing husband and a wonderful father, I know you'll take up the mantle. XOXO Adeline.*

He blinked back tears as he slowly pulled out the stack of papers inside. Drawings from Brody—stick figures of them at the beach, playing basketball, even a remarkably decent rendering of a helicopter hovering over the ocean.

There were cards too. Adeline had included romantic notes he'd given her over the years—for Mother's Day, her birthday, and their anniversary.

Thank You, Lord, for Adeline, he prayed silently. *Brody and I were blessed to have her, even for a little while.*

He sifted through more. Church crafts and Father's Day cards, memories etched in construction paper and crayon. One stood out—a framed photo of Brody and Ethan in Halloween costumes. He smiled through the ache. Darth Vader and Luke Skywalker. That had been a good year.

Setting the photo aside to show Brody later, he refocused on the task at hand.

He reached for the box labeled with the year MJ and his dad had passed away. His stomach churned as he opened it. There it was—the piece of jade. Its edges were worn smooth from the months he'd carried it in his pocket after MJ's accident.

Ethan picked it up and held it for a moment, letting the weight of it settle in his palm.

"Lord, give me the words. I need Your help with this."

He slipped the rock into his pocket just like he used to when he was a teenager and headed downstairs.

Dad was at the desk, reading glasses perched on the bridge of his nose, the newspaper spread out in front of him. His brow furrowed as he scanned a page, the soft rustle of paper filling the quiet space.

"There you are," he said, glancing up. "I was just about to come find you. Did you see this article about Trevor Kelly's plane?"

Ethan nodded, his chest tightening at the mention. "I did. I'm actually on my way to visit Mrs. Kelly. Does she still live in the same place?"

"Same place." Dad's expression shifted, his usual stoicism softening into something more tender. "Proud of you, son. Good for you. Give her my best, will you? Tell her we're praying there's a miracle, that she gets to see Trevor again."

"I will." Ethan hesitated, his hand gripping the back of a chair. "I'll be back in time to pick up Brody from school. No worries."

Dad smiled faintly. "I'm sure you will."

Ethan climbed into the Suburban and worked his way through town. He drove a few miles north to a quiet, established neighborhood. People were out moving damaged household goods and picking up debris. The subdivision was a patchwork of winter stillness and bustling recovery efforts.

Ethan drove three blocks straight back like his parents had driven him countless times when he'd been dropped off at the Kellys' house for movies, an overnight stay, or a pickup game of basketball out in the cul-de-sac. The hoop was still there, the net gone and the rim rusty. He parked behind a well-loved minivan. The driveway had been cleared and the pathway to the door shoveled. A heart-shaped wreath made from rustic branches and a burlap ribbon with the word *LOVE* carved in wooden letters hung on the front door.

After he cut the engine, Ethan sat in the silence of the Suburban. His fingers brushed the smooth jade in his pocket as he whispered, "Lord, be with me. Let my words be Yours, not mine."

He climbed out, the crunch of his boots on the icy path breaking the stillness. A sharp yip came from the other side of the door, followed by muffled footsteps. When it opened, Mrs. Kelly stood there, a Chihuahua nestled protectively under her arm. Her silver hair framed her face in a stylish bob, and her chin trembled as recognition dawned.

"Ethan McGuire," she said, her voice catching. "My goodness, is that you?"

"Yes, ma'am." He smiled softly. "How are you, Mrs. Kelly?"

"I'm fine, fine," she said, though the words sounded reflexive, not entirely convincing. "Just surprised, is all. Come on in."

She stepped aside, the warmth of the house enveloping him. Praise music drifted faintly from the kitchen, the notes a balm to his nerves.

"Don't mind Oscar," she said, nodding toward the growling Chihuahua. "He's all bark, no bite."

Ethan chuckled, though the sound was strained. "I'll take your word for it."

He hovered near the door. "I don't want to intrude. I just . . . I have something I need to say."

Her brow furrowed, and she gestured toward the living room. "Sit, please."

"No, ma'am. I won't stay long." He swallowed hard, his gaze dropping briefly before meeting hers again. "I came by years ago, right after . . . after you lost your husband and MJ. I didn't handle that well."

Her face softened, the pain in her eyes tempered by understanding. "Oh, Ethan, you were just a boy. No one expects a child to know what to do with grief like that."

He reached into his pocket, pulling out the piece of jade. Its green surface gleamed in the soft light as he extended it toward her.

"I'd like to try again," he said quietly. "This belonged to MJ. He always talked about carving it into something, and I thought . . . I thought it should be here, with you."

Her hand trembled as she took it, her fingers brushing against his. "Oh, Ethan," she whispered, her voice breaking. A single tear slid down her cheek. "That's so thoughtful of you. Are you sure?"

He nodded. "Yes, ma'am. I lost my wife less than two years ago—melanoma. And now it's just me and Brody. I can't imagine what it's like to lose a spouse and a child, but . . . I know grief. And I know I didn't say or do the right things back then. I'm so sorry if I hurt you."

She clutched the jade between both hands. "Ethan, you didn't hurt me. You were grieving, just like we all were." She gave a sad, soft laugh. "MJ always did have big dreams, didn't he? I don't think anyone could've carved this stone, but I'll treasure it. Thank you."

He cleared his throat, his own tears threatening to spill.

"If it's God's will, we'll find Trevor. But if not . . ." Her voice faltered. "I've made peace with my losses. It's taken years, but I've learned to trust that God can use even the worst things for good."

Mrs. Kelly's gaze was steady despite the tears streaming down her face. "He's a good, good Father, Ethan. I believe that with all my heart. And I believe He has plans for you and Brody, more than you could ever imagine."

Ethan stepped forward, pulling her into a hug. They stood there, bound by shared sorrow and unshaken faith. When they finally pulled apart, Mrs. Kelly patted his arm, her eyes shining.

"You're a good man, Ethan McGuire," she said. "Thank you for coming. And thank you for loving my boys like they were your brothers."

He swallowed the lump in his throat and nodded. "Always, Mrs. Kelly. Always."

Eighteen

TISHA SCRAPED ANOTHER SHOVELFUL OF MUD off the linoleum inside the community center, her muscles aching but determined. She carted it out the front door and dumped it into the plastic bin Tom had left outside. Sunlight peeked through mottled gray clouds, illuminating the chaos surrounding Redemption. The sounds of life filtered through the air: lively conversation, the consistent *beep beep beep* of heavy equipment backing up. Redemption would slowly rebuild, but first they all had water damage and mud—so much mud—to remove.

Sadie sat on a canvas camping chair nearby, Ollie in her lap as she read one of Jennifer's old Baby-Sitters Club books. Squinting, Sadie glanced at Tisha. "How much longer?"

"Not too much, sweetie," Tisha replied, wiping her brow with the back of her hand. "It's almost time to go watch Brody and Ethan's basketball game."

"Yay!" Sadie's eyes sparkled, her excitement bubbling over. "I drew Brody a picture. It's in the car. Except I want it to be a surprise."

"Oh, that's very sweet." Tisha smiled. "I'm sure he'll love it."

Just then, Megan picked her way across the parking lot, her expression brightening the dreary scene. She wore an old Redemption High sweatshirt over leggings and rubber boots, her hair pulled back haphazardly.

"Hey there," Megan greeted, holding a cardboard box in her hands. "Do you have a minute? I want to show you something."

"Sure. I wouldn't mind taking a break from mud removal," Tisha said, leaning her shovel against the wall.

"I know, right?" Megan wrinkled her nose. "It's gross and a little smelly."

"You're not wrong." Tisha swiped her nose with the sleeve of her shirt.

"Miss Megan," Sadie said. "What are you doing here?"

"Well, I have a couple of things I want to share with you girls. First for you, Sadie." Megan set the box on top of a plastic crate nearby and opened the flaps. "I was wondering if you might like to wear a shirt I wore when I was your age. It says Redemption Pirates."

"Oh, that's cute," Sadie said.

"Sometimes people wear the names of their favorite teams on their shirts when they go to the games and cheer, right? What do you think?"

"Sure! Can I put it on now, Mama?"

"Of course," Tisha said, smiling as Sadie put her book on the chair beside Ollie, then tugged the T-shirt over her head. It fell past her hips but looked adorable with her red leggings and layered over her white long-sleeve shirt.

"Hey, we almost match!" Sadie beamed at Megan.

"And for you, Tisha." Megan's eyes lit up, her voice animated. "You are not going to believe this! I was in the attic putting some stuff away, and I came across this box. I wanted to make sure there weren't any pictures getting damaged, and I found this instead."

The smell of wool and leather filled the air as Megan pulled out a varsity letterman jacket, holding it up with pride.

"Oh wow." Tisha clasped her hand to her mouth as she took in the sight. Pins and special icons were attached to the letter *R*, and when she turned it around, she saw *McGuire* stitched in bold letters. "This must be Ethan's."

"It is. I was wondering if you would like to wear it to the game today," Megan said, her tone earnest.

"Oh, I don't know," Tisha hesitated, an internal battle raging. "Seems kind of extra."

"Well, sometimes my brother needs people to show him that they are for him. Do you know what I mean? I think you guys are adorable together. And I know Brody's team is just little kids playing rec-league basketball, but like everything Ethan does, he takes it very seriously. I wish you could have seen his face when he looked for you after Brody made that basket."

"How do you know he was looking for me?" Tisha asked, her pulse quickening at the thought.

"Because I'm his little sister and I know things," Megan replied with a wink.

Tisha laughed, the tension in her chest easing just a bit. "All right. I'll put it on."

"Okay, and you'll do it, right? You'll wear it to the game?" Megan pressed, her excitement infectious.

"Of course."

"And don't forget, the game starts at two. We moved it to the high school gym."

"Got it. Thanks."

"Perfect. I'll see you there." Megan picked her way across the muddy parking lot, the empty box wedged against her hip.

Tisha grabbed her shovel again, but her focus was elsewhere now. Did Ethan need her to wear that jacket? Would it mean that much to him?

"Mom, are we going to eat lunch soon?"

"Yes, I've got ham-and-cheese sandwiches and chips, and we've got lots of pie," Tisha said, pointing toward the small cooler she'd packed.

"That is a nice jacket. Mr. Ethan will be happy to see you wear it," Sadie said, her innocent insight stirring emotions within Tisha.

Tisha smiled, warmth spreading through her. "I think you're right."

She meant what she had said to Ethan; she was ready to move forward. Chase was her past, and she wanted very much for Ethan to be her future. This was her declaration, a public gesture of affection that she needed to make—not just for Ethan, but for herself and for Sadie. As she stood there, the jacket heavy in her hands, Tisha felt a surge of hope. Today would be different. Today, she would embrace her future.

⌇

Wow, this place was packed.

Ethan stood at the end of the bench, the familiar smells of hot dogs and popcorn wafting from the concession stand, taking him right back to his high school days when he played in this very gym. But he couldn't get distracted. They were down by four points with only two minutes left in the first half. The kids were playing hard. Brody was happy to be there, which was already a win. And Sierra—Ethan's little powerhouse—had taken control of the game. What a feisty point guard she had turned out to be as she dribbled down the court.

"Let's go, Ninja Narwhals!" he called out, his heart racing. Wait. He heard a familiar voice and glanced over his shoulder. Tisha sat with his family in the bleachers. His breath caught. Was she wearing his high school varsity jacket? She grinned and waved with both hands. He couldn't help but smile back, nodding in approval before shifting his focus back to the game.

Good thing he was paying attention, too, because Sierra passed Brody the ball. "Brody, shoot!" she urged. "You can do it! Shoot, Brody, shoot!"

The kids on the bench clapped and yelled, their energy infectious. Brody glanced at his dad, uncertainty flickering in his eyes.

"You've got this. You can do it," Ethan called out. The clock ticked down as Brody took a deep breath, launching a gorgeous jump shot that sailed through the air.

"Come on, come on," Ethan said.

But the ball clanged off the front of the rim.

"Oh, unlucky, unlucky." Ethan clapped his hands.

The scoreboard buzzed, signaling the end of the first half.

"All right, bring it in, bring it in." Nicholas motioned for them all to move down to the end of the bench. "Great job, team."

Brody slumped into a chair, wiping the sweat from his forehead. "I missed."

"Hey." Ethan sank down in front of him, placing both hands on Brody's knees. "No big deal, man. It's okay. You'll get it next time. Super proud of you."

Brody bit his lip, disappointment evident.

Ethan caught Tisha's eye again. Her smile, the way her face glowed in the gym lights, and the way she pointed to his jacket made him smile back. Man, she looked good.

Ethan hung back, letting Nicholas give the kids pointers. He handed out water, listening patiently to their commentary, including little Jet's insistence that he needed to sub in for a three-pointer.

"That's the spirit, my man." Ethan ruffled the kid's sweaty hair. "I bet you've got a three in you."

The kid was the smallest on the team but perhaps the most enthusiastic. "Sub me in, Coach, please!"

Ethan and Nicholas exchanged glances. "Good plan. Be smart about the shots you take."

As time ticked on, both teams traded leads back and forth. Folks must have put their disaster-relief efforts on hold to attend this game because Ethan had never seen a gym this full for a rec-league basketball game featuring second graders.

He tried to stay focused, but he couldn't shake the thought of Tisha in that jacket.

"Come on, Brody, shoot!" Sierra passed him the ball again. Ethan had spent so much time daydreaming that he hadn't realized the clock was winding down. They were down by one. Brody managed to dribble toward the basket, but the other team had a tall kid down low, waving his hands in the air. Brody executed a clever little turn, dribbling back out.

"Come on, come on, you've got this," Ethan whispered, clenching a towel with both hands. "Take the shot, pal."

With the clock ticking down from five, Brody flung up a wild shot. The ball swished through the net. "That's the way!"

The buzzer rang—they'd won!

Ethan ran onto the court and swept Brody into his arms, twirling him around in a circle as if they'd just won state. "I am so proud of you!"

Brody flung his arms around Ethan's neck, and Ethan reveled in the joy radiating from him. "That was awesome, Dad!"

Ethan didn't want to let him go, but they needed to show good sportsmanship and shake the other team's hands. "Come on, pal, line up. Tell everybody good job, okay?"

The kids lined up, slapping hands. Ethan shook the other coaches' hands.

"Way to go, Clutch! Your kid's got your sweet shot."

He laughed. "I don't know about that. He's still young yet."

They herded the kids off the court. One of the moms had brought granola bars and tangerines. The kids settled down, all chatting about who had the best shoes. Honestly, Ethan couldn't get their pep talk over with fast enough. He reminded them about their next practice, encouraged them to help their parents with cleanup, and promised to see them soon.

When he finished, Tisha waited at the edge of the court, her eyes sparkling. "Great game," she said, giving Brody a high five. "That was a beautiful shot, my man."

"Thanks," Brody said, looking around for the hoodie he'd discarded.

"Nice jacket," Ethan remarked, nodding toward Tisha.

"Thanks. Megan brought it over. She thought I might want to wear it."

"Huh. Never thought you'd be the kind of girl to wear a guy's letterman jacket."

Her brows sailed upward. "Well, that depends. Are we a couple?"

"What kind of question is that? We are *absolutely* a couple."

"Well, I only wear the jackets of my favorite players." She tilted her head, a teasing smile on her lips.

"If I'm your boyfriend, then you can only have one favorite player."

"I was kind of hoping this said Clutch." She tried to look over her shoulder. "I'm pretty happy to wear something that says McGuire though."

His mouth ran dry, his skin flushed. What he wouldn't give to sweep her into his arms and kiss her senseless right there.

"I know what you're thinking," she said, her eyes sparkling.

"I'll behave," he said, his gaze drifting to her lips. "For now."

"You are a rule follower after all, right?"

Sighing, he laced his fingers through hers. "Come on, let's go find a closet somewhere."

"No, we can't," she said, her cheeks flushing. "Seriously, Ethan,

I'm super proud of you. I know you were hesitant to coach, but you and Brody were a joy to watch."

"Thanks. That means a lot."

"How will you celebrate the big win?" She looked around, probably making sure Sadie hadn't gone far. Ethan spotted her sitting on the bleachers, speaking with a girl from her class at school.

"Good question. I'll leave that up to Brody." Ethan shook his head. "I still can't believe we won."

"What a sweet bonus that Brody made that winning basket."

Pride coursed through him. It had been a leap of faith to take on coaching the Ninja Narwhals, but watching the kids—especially Brody—grow and improve with each game had been its own reward. And having Tisha there, finally, supporting them made it all the more special.

Epilogue

SHE COULDN'T HAVE ASKED FOR A MORE PER-
fect day to spread Chase's ashes in the shadow of Mount Greer.
Snow still clung to the jagged peak and blanketed the mountain's
foothills, all the way down to the edge of the lake. A dense forest of
evergreen trees stood alongside the stately birches and cottonwoods
with their bare branches dancing in the breeze churned up by the
helicopter. Ice still rimmed the edges of the lake, but the water in the
middle had thawed and rippled in the sunlight, reflecting the expanse
of blue sky and the mountain's breathtaking facets.

Ethan guided them over the lake, then set the chopper down in
a flat clearing not far from Jess and Shannon's cabin. The meadow,
still covered in snow, sparkled like scattered diamonds.

Ethan reached over and squeezed her hand. "Are you ready?"

Tisha looked down at the urn nestled in her lap. She'd suggested
that Melinda and Tom keep the urn with them. They'd driven out
to the cabin from Redemption along with Sadie. Chase's siblings
Tyler and Jennifer, along with Tyler's wife Skye, planned to follow
in their own vehicles. But Tom and Melinda had insisted that

Chase needed his final journey to include a flight. And who better to make that possible than Ethan—the best at the stick.

She gave Ethan a small, grateful smile. "Thank you for doing this. Not too many men would fly their girlfriend to spread her late husband's ashes."

He smiled, brushing a strand of hair from her face. "I'm not just any man. Thought we'd established that." He leaned closer, pressing a tender kiss to her forehead. "This is going to be a beautiful day, and I'm honored that you included me."

He climbed out and circled around to open her door. She shifted the urn to the crook of her arm, gathered the hem of her floral maxi dress, and reached for his hand. Ethan's strong grasp steadied her as he lifted her down, setting her gently on the soft ground.

Ahead, the small group had gathered near the dock. Tom and Melinda stood close together with Sadie between them, her ever-present Ollie tucked under her arm. The cabin's owners, Jess and Shannon, along with their two kids lingered nearby, flanked by Chase's siblings and Luke. Sadie looked adorable in a navy-blue-and-white-striped dress, her wide eyes reflecting an innocent understanding of what this all meant.

Tom cleared his throat. "Thanks for coming. I have a brief passage I'd like to read."

He flipped open his well-worn Bible and carefully draped the ribbon marker over the side. The breeze picked up, tugging at Tisha's hair and carrying the familiar fragrance of evergreen trees. She brushed her hair back, and Ethan's hand, warm and steady, found her shoulder. She leaned into him.

Tom began to read, his voice firm yet laced with emotion. The verses resonated in the stillness broken only by the gentle lapping of the lake against the dock and birds chirping beyond the cabin.

When he finished, he closed his Bible and looked up. "Tisha, if you would do the honors."

She hesitated, clutching the urn. "Are you sure?"

Melinda stepped forward, her expression peaceful. "We're sure. Chase would want it this way."

"Go ahead, Mama," Sadie said. "I'll watch."

The dock swayed gently under her feet as she walked out slowly to the end. Her heart thrummed and the urn felt heavy in her hands. At the edge of the dock, her fingers trembled as she loosened the cap. Then she tilted the vessel and the ashes spilled out, caught instantly by the wind. They swirled in the sunlight, a soft gray plume against the winter sky, before drifting out over the water until the lake embraced them.

Behind her, someone sniffled.

Tisha closed her eyes, tears slipping down her cheeks. She looked out over the lake, where the ashes had disappeared into the endless blue, and whispered, "Goodbye, Chase. We'll see you again one day."

The soft thud of footsteps broke the silence, and Tisha turned. Sadie was running toward her, clutching Ollie tightly to her chest, her face pink from the cold air.

"Mama!" she called, skidding to a stop in front of her. "I think Daddy's part of this place now. Just like the trees and the lake. And did you see the way the ashes danced? They were flying. He'd love that."

Tisha's heart swelled, and she smiled through her tears. She knelt, pulling Sadie into her arms and pressing a kiss to her daughter's temple. "That's beautiful, sweetheart. You're right. He sure did love to fly."

Ethan walked out on the dock and joined them. "I'm proud of you," he said softly.

Tisha looked up at him, her smile widening. "Thank you. Now it's time to focus on what's ahead. On the life we're building."

Sadie beamed, holding Ollie high in the air like a flag. "We're going to do this together, Mama. Right here in Redemption!"

Tisha laughed, the sound light and unburdened as she stood

and reached for Ethan's hand. Together, they walked back toward the others, sunlight streaming through the trees.

For the first time in a long time, Tisha felt the weight of her grief lifting, replaced by hope—a promise of love, faith, and the future waiting for them all.

Thank You!

Thank you so much for reading *The Other Side of Goodbye*. We hope you enjoyed the story. If you did, would you be willing to do us a favor and leave a review? It doesn't have to be long—just a few words to help other readers know what they're getting. (But no spoilers! We don't want to wreck the fun!) Thank you again for reading!

We'd love to hear from you—not only about this story, but about any characters or stories you'd like to read in the future. Contact us at www.sunrisepublishing.com/contact.

Read on for more of the

WELCOME TO
REDEMPTION, ALASKA

series

Return to Redemption for
Luke and Emma's story in
The Long Way Back to You.

Sometimes the life you're meant to live is the one you left behind.

Emma Carlisle built the perfect life in Boston—successful career, surgeon fiancé, everything mapped out. But when unpaid property taxes force her back to Redemption, Alaska, she has one goal: sell the family house, settle the debt, and escape before the past can destroy her again.

She didn't count on Luke McGuire.

Luke never stopped loving the woman who vanished without explanation fifteen years ago. Now he's desperately fighting to save his family's failing resort while watching Emma prepare to disappear again. The stakes couldn't be higher—his family's legacy hangs in the balance, and losing Emma a second time will destroy him.

But Redemption holds devastating secrets about Emma's criminal father and the family shame that drove her away. When shocking revelations about her past surface and her perfect Boston life begins to crumble, Emma faces an impossible choice: return to the safe life that's slowly killing her spirit, or risk everything for the messy truth of where her heart belongs.

With Luke's unwavering love and her own buried dreams calling her home, Emma must decide if she has the courage to embrace the life she was always meant to live.

A story about second chances, buried secrets, and the courage to come home.

One

THESE THRILL-SEEKERS WERE EITHER FEARLESS
or fried.

Every time extreme skiers boarded his chopper, Luke Mc-Guire had to remind himself that the resort needed the money. Because their quest for epic powder only made his job harder.

Luke gripped the cyclic control, the steady thrum of the chopper vibrating under his hands, and tried not to think about all the ways this trip could go sideways. Through the windshield, he surveyed the endless, jagged expanse of Alaska's Chugach Mountains. An unforgiving, steep wilderness cloaked in miles of pristine snow. The sun glinted off razor-sharp peaks, dazzling white against the brilliant blue sky, but he wasn't in the mood to appreciate the view.

"Yo, Captain Luke." One of the skiers' voices crackled through the headset. "Are you taking us to the secret backcountry location or what?"

The guy reeked of marijuana and sweat. His two friends weren't any better. Super rowdy with their crude jokes, and laughing like hyper middle schoolers instead of taking it seriously that they were minutes from hurling themselves down a near-vertical slope.

"Slow your roll, fellas," Luke said, leaning forward to gauge the best place to land. "If you want to ski, you'll stay put until our skids touch the snow."

His brother Ethan, riding in the copilot seat, shot him a look. "Relax. They're just pumped. It's going to be okay."

Luke huffed, his grip on the controls tightening. "I'm counting the minutes until we're on the ground."

"Don't you remember how it was when you were young and wild and free?"

"Hmm. I wasn't quite *that* free," Luke said.

In the back, one of the skiers let out a whoop and slapped his buddy's shoulder. "Bro, this is gonna be *sick*! Best heli-skiing in the world right here!"

Luke dragged his hand down his face. "We'll be on the ground in just a minute."

"You're such a buzzkill," the third guy grumbled.

Laughing, Ethan shook his head. Luke glared at him.

Ethan turned his laugh into a cough. "At least they paid up front. Right?"

Luke didn't respond. Instead, he focused on the controls, guiding the helicopter toward a plateau carved out like a cereal bowl between surrounding peaks. Tight landing, but he'd done it a hundred times before. His gut told him not to waste time finding a better spot.

"Hold on. We're coming in."

The skiers barely acknowledged him, too busy shouting at each other about who would drop first, how the powder looked "gnarly" and "wicked," and who was going to film what on their GoPro.

Luke ignored the noise and eased the skids onto the snow with a delicate bounce.

"All right, out," he said, flipping the switches to keep the rotor spinning at idle. "Grab your gear and stay clear. Got it?"

"Yeah, yeah, we got it. We're professionals, man," one of them said, laughing.

The trio spilled out onto the snow, still laughing and jostling each other as they pulled their skis and gear from the cargo rack.

"Hey, I'll pick you up at Lookout Point at three thirty," Ethan called, leaning out the door. "Don't be late."

"Chill, dude," one of the guys called back, waving a gloved hand. "We won't stand you up."

"Somehow I'm skeptical." Luke blew out a sharp breath, his patience fraying. "They seem like they kind of enjoy ignoring deadlines and itineraries."

Ethan slid the door closed. With a wave, Luke lifted the helicopter off the ridge. The skiers turned into specks below them.

"Man, stoned adrenaline junkies are not the way to go," Luke said, adjusting his headset.

"You say that, but these guys are keeping the lights on. No clients, no income. You know the math."

Luke gritted his teeth. "I know the math. I've seen the numbers. Doesn't mean I have to like it."

"Last time I checked, it's not like we've got a line of tourists waiting to book accommodation in March," Ethan said. "Not with Redemption still half-wrecked from the tidal wave."

"Don't remind me." Luke altered their heading, cutting around a fog bank drifting in off the bay. "Dad shouldn't have let those volunteers who came to clean up stay for free. It's killing us. We barely had enough money to fix the generator last month."

"Dad's tenderhearted these days. You know that. Ever since he got hurt . . ." Ethan's voice softened, tapering off as if he was unsure how much to say.

Well aware, thank you very much.

Luke swallowed back the snarky words. Ethan had spent twenty years saving lives—rescue swimmer, aviator, Coast Guard hero. Luke was proud of him. Really, he was. But sometimes, when he thought about everything his older brother had accomplished, it was hard to ignore the ache of what could have been.

Ethan had flown off to adventure and purpose, while Luke had stayed behind, trading his own dreams to keep the resort operating after the fire. Someone had to step up. And Luke didn't regret the choice. How could he? Family came first. But that didn't mean it was easy.

"To your point, that's why I booked as many extreme skiers as I could. But I'm regretting my decision. They're trashing the place and getting high. Did you see the mess that last group left? Beer cans everywhere, a hole in the drywall . . ."

Ethan exhaled, shaking his head. "Repeat after me: This is all temporary. We have to make it to May. Once the tourists show up, we'll be back on track."

"You think Dad's going to let people keep staying for free all summer?" Luke tightened his grip on the cyclic. Part of him felt bad about complaining. He didn't want to admit how much it worried him—how much Dad's generosity, while admirable, made him feel like they were teetering on the edge of a cliff.

"Hope not," Ethan said. "Are you planning to talk to him, or should I?"

Luke hesitated. "I'll try."

They fell into silence, the sound of the rotors filling the space between them. Below, mountains gave way to dense forests and half-frozen creeks that fed into the bay.

As they passed over a peninsula jutting out into the water, Luke spotted a house sitting alone, shingles missing from the roof and windows boarded up. The old Carlisle place.

That ache in his chest, the one he worked so hard to ignore, flared to life. *Emma.* He hadn't thought about her in months, but seeing her family's property brought it all back. Her laugh. Those gorgeous eyes. The freckles on the bridge of her nose.

Where was she now? Did she ever think about Redemption?

About him? He hadn't set foot near the place since she left town almost two decades ago. Redemption had chewed her up and spit her out, so she and her mother had fled. He couldn't blame them. Not really. But she'd left him behind and never looked back. And that part still stung.

He should've been over it by now. Should've let go of the hope that she might come back, that they could ever be what he'd once imagined. But some stubborn, irrational part of him still clung to the notion, like a splinter he couldn't dig out. And now, here he was, thirty-five years old, single, childless, and clinging to a failing business.

What a legacy.

"You okay?" Ethan's voice broke into his thoughts.

"Yeah. Just noticing the Carlisle place. It's a mess."

Ethan raised an eyebrow. "Didn't you, uh, have a thing for the girl? You're not still hung up on her, are you?"

"No," Luke said quickly. Too quickly. "It's just weird, you know? Feels like another lifetime. I don't understand why they're letting it fall into disrepair."

Ethan didn't push, thankfully.

The peace didn't last long though.

"Hey." Ethan leaned forward, pointing through the windshield. "Do you see that?"

A thin column of smoke curled up into the sky. It was coming from the direction of their resort. Luke's stomach dropped.

"That's us," Ethan said, his voice tight.

Luke adjusted the controls, bringing the helicopter around for a better view. "Maybe somebody's burning trash."

"That doesn't look like a trash fire," Ethan said grimly.

Squinting through the fog, Luke kept his eyes on the faint orange glow flickering through the trees.

The smoke was thicker now, black against the sky. That wasn't just a pile of burning debris—it was a cabin. One of *their* cabins.

"No," Luke muttered, his pulse racing. "Hang on. I'll have us on the ground in a minute."

Ethan grabbed the radio, already calling it in. "Redemption Base, this is Helo One. We've got a structure fire on the south side of the property. Repeat, structure fire. We'll need assistance."

Luke's mind spun, tamping down memories of the last time they'd battled a fire at the resort. He couldn't think about that. Not now.

But the same old fears pushed to the surface. No amount of repairs or blind faith seemed to be enough these days. A single thought echoed. Relentless. Unshakable.

How much longer could he hold this place together?

⚊

Boston's rush-hour traffic was about to ruin her Friday night.

Blasting his horn, the Uber driver pumped his brakes to avoid rear-ending a luxury SUV. Snow fell in thick wet flakes, forcing the windshield wipers to work overtime. Emma Carlisle tugged a black cocktail dress over her sports bra, then tipped sideways in the back seat when the car suddenly sped up. She smacked her elbow against the window, wincing as pain shot up her arm. The silky fabric snagged against her leggings, and the semi-sheer insets clung to her torso.

Ugh. This thing was so not her style. But her future mother-in-law had given her the designer dress and insisted it was perfect for tonight's celebration.

Sighing, Emma shimmied the fabric over her hips, then peeled off her leggings and stuffed them into her black knockoff Birkin handbag.

The driver glanced at her in the rearview mirror. "Everything okay back there?"

"Just fine," she said, struggling to free her curls from the keyhole closure at the nape of her neck. Oh brother. She untangled her hair with one hand and dug through her bag for her earrings with the other. Maybe staying late at the gym to help one of her favorite clients finish that last set of ten burpees had been a questionable choice.

The car jolted to a stop at another red light. Gritting her teeth, she glanced at the digital display on the dashboard. Seven minutes until Kendall's party. At this rate, she'd be lucky to make it before dessert.

Emma shivered. The sleeveless dress offered all the warmth of tissue paper, and her short suede boots, still stuffed in her bag, weren't going to help. She should've worn the emerald-green pantsuit—her style, her color, and her choice—but no. She'd caved. Again.

The bitter thought lingered as her phone buzzed against the seat beside her. Emma grabbed it, half expecting the usual check-in from her fiancé, Nathan. Instead, it was Abbie, one of her best friends from middle school. Emma tapped the screen to accept the call, then held the phone to her ear. "Hey, girl. What's up?"

"Don't panic," Abbie said. "But my bridesmaid's dress is back-ordered. Until July sixth."

"Oh. Wow. That's—"

"Less than a week before your wedding. I know." Abbie sighed. "I called three other stores, but they all said the same thing."

The car lurched forward, tires spinning on the snow-slicked street. Emma clutched the overhead handle.

"Emma? You there?"

"Yeah. Listen, um, don't stress. It's not a big deal." Emma forced a laugh. "I'm sure it will all work out."

Abbie paused. "Really? That's not what I expected you to say."

"Well, to be honest, that dress is the least of my worries. I stayed late helping a client hit a personal best. She just got divorced and wants a fresh start. Long story. Anyway, now I'm rushing to a party for Nathan's sister, Kendall. She made partner at her law firm."

"That's nice of you," Abbie said. "I'm looking forward to meeting Kendall at your shower in June."

"Yeah, that will be fun." Emma cradled her faux-diamond earrings in her palm. Frankly, the thought of her Alaska friends meeting her East Coast people made her palms sweat.

"I'm sorry about the dress. I'll keep you posted," Abbie said. "Are you sure you're okay?"

Emma hesitated. "Yeah, I'm fine. Why?"

"You don't sound like you. Oh, hang on." Abbie muffled the phone, but Emma still heard her welcoming kids as they got in the car. "School's out. Gotta run."

"I'll call you soon," Emma said. "We need to catch up."

"True. Love you."

"Love you too."

She ended the call as a new message popped up.

Nathan
____

Running late. Save me an
appetizer?

She stared at the text. No apology. Just clinical efficiency. Typical.

"Almost there, miss," the driver said, slowing to turn onto the street leading to the Prescotts' neighborhood.

"Great." Emma fastened her earrings, slipped on her boots, then jammed everything else back into her bag. She used the selfie camera on her phone to check her makeup. Brushing a stray curl from her face, she practiced making a genuine smile. The reflection portrayed a woman she barely recognized—Nathan's polished, sophisticated fiancée.

Fake it till you make it, right?

A few minutes later, the Uber pulled up in front of the Prescott family's brownstone, its grand facade glowing against the dark, snowy night. She added a generous tip in the app for her ride. After all, she had changed in the back of his vehicle.

"Thank you. Have a great night." Emma closed the door of the car and draped her heavy bag over her arm. A gust of wind bit through the flimsy fabric of her dress as the Uber drove away. She slipped into her secondhand wool coat, then hurried toward the towering double doors. Her stiletto heels clicked against the salted sidewalk, and snow clung to her curls.

Squeezing her eyes shut, she drew a ragged breath. Only a couple of hours. Smile, make polite small talk, and celebrate Kendall. No problem.

She tapped the brass knocker, but when no one answered, she went inside. Warm air greeted her, along with muffled sounds of classical music and the hum of lively conversation. A uniformed staff person stationed nearby greeted her with a polite smile.

"Emma, darling." Sylvia Prescott's voice floated across the foyer like a silk ribbon, and she glided toward Emma wearing a gorgeous mauve gown that hugged her toned figure. Her tennis bracelet and matching teardrop earrings sparkled under the light from the chandelier. The sleek bun at the nape of her neck was so perfect, not a single hair dared to slip out of place.

"We were wondering if the weather had gotten the best of you." Sylvia's voice was smooth yet tinged with the kind of warmth that felt forced. Emma caught the subtle once-over her future mother-in-law gave her.

"Sorry I'm late." Emma shed her coat and resisted the urge to tug down the hem of her dress. "I stayed late to help a favorite client push through a challenging workout."

"Of course." Sylvia's smile faltered as her dark eyes lingered on Emma's bare legs. "You should've worn tights, dear. It's too cold to go without."

Emma blinked and glanced down at her bare legs. Tights? She wasn't five.

Before she could respond, Kendall Prescott appeared at Sylvia's side, her shoulder-length silky black hair reflecting the light and her aubergine pantsuit flowing as she moved. The deep V-neck and gauzy cape screamed power, and she wore the chic outfit effortlessly.

"Glad you made it," Kendall said, giving her a quick hug. "Thank you for coming."

"Wouldn't miss it." Emma hugged her back, then offered a bright smile. "That's a fabulous color on you. Oh, wait—" She fumbled in her bag and pulled out a small wrapped box. It was a charm bracelet from a local designer. A splurge she couldn't really afford, but she knew better than to arrive without a gift. "I brought something for you. Congratulations on making partner. That's a huge accomplishment."

"Oh, you didn't have to do that." Kendall added the gift to the pile on the glass console table nearby. "Thank you for thinking of me. We need to—"

"Honestly, these caterers are the worst." Frowning, Sylvia craned her neck and surveyed the formal living room. "They claim they're shorthanded this week, but the lack of adequately trained servers is untenable."

"I'd be glad to help," Emma said. "What's wrong?"

Kendall and Sylvia stared at her. An awkward silence stretched between them.

"That's so kind. Thank you, dear." Sylvia's brittle smile accompanied an obligatory pat on Emma's arm. "You're wonderful with people, and I know everyone here would love to see you. Put your things in the closet under the stairs, then check with the staff in the kitchen."

"Of course." She scooted past Sylvia and Kendall. Where was Nathan? He probably wouldn't be thrilled that she'd volunteered to sub in and serve appetizers, but nobody wanted Sylvia to be unhappy. And Kendall deserved to have a wonderful party.

Emma spotted him walking into the room. He looked incredible in a dark blue suit with a matching tie and crisp button-down shirt—monochromatic from head to toe. Grinning, he paused and spoke to a tall blonde woman wearing a trendy black cocktail dress and sky-high red heels. Courtney? Sydney? One of his classmates from back in med school. Emma hesitated, but he didn't notice her, and the weight of Sylvia's hawkish gaze propelled her into action.

After tucking her coat and bag out of sight in the closet, she went searching for further instructions. Emma found the caterers in the kitchen, where a frazzled woman handed over a tray of champagne flutes. The glasses wobbled as Emma adjusted the tray. She hadn't done this since college, when waiting tables had been her escape from mean-girl politics. Now, it felt like she was back in their crosshairs.

She stepped into the living room, where guests in tailored suits and glittering formal gowns circled the room, their laughter and chatter mingling with the string quartet's live performance.

Emma plastered on her best smile and began circulating.

"Champagne?" she offered to a group of older men huddled near the fireplace. One of them took a glass, barely acknowledging her presence, while the others continued their conversation about hedge funds. She moved on, approaching three women she recognized from the club.

One of the women waved her tray away, but another guest smiled warmly and took a flute. "Thanks, hon. You must be Emma, yes? The personal trainer and fiancée."

Emma nodded, her smile tightening. "That's me."

"Sylvia showed me the wedding invitations," the third woman said. "They're stunning. And just four months to go. Are you nervous?"

Before she could answer, Nathan appeared at her side. Relief swept through her.

"Hey," she said.

"Hey, you." He leaned in and kissed her temple, his hand resting low on her back. "You didn't have to do this."

She gave a half-hearted laugh. "I offered. Your mom mentioned that the caterers were short-staffed, and I figured . . ."

Nathan looked at her, his expression softening. "You don't need to prove anything to anyone, Emma. Least of all my mother."

"I know," she said, shrugging. "But it's your sister's big night."

He took the tray from her and set it on a table nearby. "You're more than enough. You always are." He kissed her again, this time letting his lips linger on hers.

Her pulse sped and she pressed her palm on his firm chest.

When he pulled away, his chocolate-brown eyes roamed her face. "As much as I'd like to keep kissing you, I think we'd better find our seats. Come on."

They made their way to the table, and just as Emma settled into her chair, a familiar voice called out from behind. "I thought that was you."

Emma turned and blinked. "Mom?"

Her mother, elegant in a silver sheath dress, stepped closer with a glass of champagne in hand. Her brown hair styled in a chignon, her lipstick, and her designer beaded clutch purse were all flawless.

"What are you doing here?" Emma gripped the wooden back of the upholstered chair. "I didn't know you were invited."

"Sylvia and I ended up playing in a pickleball tournament together last week. She insisted I attend. Said it would be lovely for the families to connect before the wedding." Her mother's smile didn't quite reach her green eyes. "I thought, why not?"

Emma forced a smile. "Right. Of course."

Nathan reached over and offered his hand. "Mrs. Wendel. It's good to see you again."

Her mother's face lit up. "Likewise, Nathan. And please, call me Pam."

Just then, Nathan's phone buzzed on the table. He glanced at the screen, frowning. "Sorry," he said. "I need to take this. It's about a patient. I'll be right back."

Emma watched him disappear into the hallway before turning back to her mother. "So . . . you and Sylvia are friends now?"

Mom chuckled. "Hardly. But we move in the same circles. And I do like to keep up appearances."

No kidding. Emma sipped her water, hoping the conversation would stall there.

But her mother leaned closer, lowering her voice. "Besides, you and I need to talk."

Uh-oh. Emma hesitated. "Everything okay?"

"Not really. I didn't want to tell you this way, but I got another notice from Redemption. I haven't paid the property taxes on our house."

Emma's mouth went dry. "What do you mean? As in you haven't paid this year's taxes yet or . . ."

Her mother sighed. "As in never."

Emma gasped. "Never? Why didn't you say something sooner?"

"I didn't think it would be an issue. But now there's talk of liens and legal action." Her mother shrugged, then took another sip of her champagne.

Emma's stomach twisted. Maybe she should've seen this coming. "You couldn't stand that house. Why have you hung on to the place all these years if you can't afford the taxes?"

Something unreadable flashed across Mom's face. "I never said I couldn't stand that house."

"Then why did we leave?"

Her mother huffed out a laugh. "After what your father did? And what happened between you and Luke?"

Emma's breath hitched. *Luke.* "He didn't—"

Mom held up her palm. "Don't, Emma. Don't romanticize it. Alaska ruined our family. Your father ruined us. And now he's exactly where he belongs. Thankfully, his parole was denied."

Emma squeezed her eyes shut. The words stung like lemon juice in a paper cut. No point in defending her father's behavior though. At least not to her mother. Instead, she drew a calming breath, then opened her eyes. "So you just . . . what? Let the place rot?"

Her mother drained the last of her champagne. "It's not my fault Redemption is grappling with mud and water damage and flooded houses. Somebody at town hall probably decided they had an axe to grind, and now they're coming after me for these stupid taxes."

Emma stared at her, stunned. "You're unbelievable."

"I'm realistic," her mother said. "And I'm not going back there. Not now. Not ever."

"Then I'll go," Emma said, the words tumbling out before she gave them much consideration. "I'll reach out to Gavin. He'll help me figure out what to do."

"Will he though?" Her mother smiled, but there was no warmth in it. "I think you need to just let it go, but if you decide you're going back, I won't stand in your way. And I'm not about to cancel my honeymoon."

"Honeymoon?"

"Egypt," she said, her smile widening as she reached for her cloth napkin. "It's a bucket-list destination. We've waited long enough since the wedding. Richard and I leave next week."

Richard. Right. Husband number three.

Emma massaged her aching forehead with her fingertips. What was happening? How could she possibly be responsible for that house? She leaned back so the server could set a kale, quinoa, and avocado salad topped with candied walnuts in front of her.

A text message from Nathan popped up on her phone.

<u>Nathan</u>
Sorry had to leave quickly.
Patient coded.

"Oh no." Emma pressed her fingertips to her mouth. No point in texting him back. He wouldn't read the message anyway.

Mom glanced at her from across the table. "Everything okay, love?"

No. Not at all. Because somehow she'd have to explain to her fiancé that she was headed to Alaska to sell a house.

Acknowledgments

With all my love and deepest gratitude to my husband and our three sons. Thank you for your unwavering support, encouragement, and remarkable patience. Living with a writer (who also happens to be navigating perimenopause) can't be easy. I love you guys to the moon and back!

To my mom, my mother-in-law, and my sister Heather: Your constant encouragement and belief in me means so much. Thank you for cheering me on every step of the way.

A huge thank you to Susan May Warren for the incredible opportunity to write this story and for so generously sharing your wisdom, guidance, and brilliant plotting insight. You are a gift.

And to the amazing team at Sunrise Publishing: Thank you for producing beautiful books, creating a space where authors can grow, and helping us connect with readers in the most meaningful ways.

About the Author

Heidi McCahan writes uplifting inspirational romance novels set in small towns. She is the bestselling author of sixteen books, including *Her Alaskan Family* and *A Baby in Alaska*. A perfect day for Heidi includes a cup of good coffee, dark chocolate, and reading stories with happy endings. She makes her home in North Carolina with her handsome husband, three amazing boys, and the world's greatest Goldendoodle.

Heidi enjoys connecting with writers and readers, so please visit her website at HeidiMcCahan.com.

It's time to come *Home* to *Heritage*

"A heartwarming and inspiring story of second chances, renewed faith, and the enduring power of love."

—SUSAN MAY WARREN

USA Today bestselling author

We solve the problem of what to read next.

YOU MAY ALSO LIKE...

When Noah Hebert inherits the struggling Blue Pirogue Inn, he must solve a puzzle left by his grandfather to save it from his family's nemesis, Isaac Bergeron. Teaming up with Elisa Bergeron, the café manager and his rival, they must navigate family feuds—and unexpected sparks—while racing against time.

Where I Found You **by Besty St. Amant**

Working together to keep Fox Bakery from going under, Robin and Sammy find that something more than friendship is simmering between them. But will Robin follow her old dreams back to the glamor of Paris, or will she discover how sweet it is to be loved in Deep Haven?

How Sweet It Is **by Andrea Christenson**

Dani Sullivan is determined to revive Jonathon Island's fading charm and reunite her fractured family. Her plan? Reopen the Grand Sullivan Hotel. But without the funds to restore the hotel, Dani's forced to accept help from Liam Stone—a big-city hotel developer whose sleek, modern vision is everything she's trying to avoid.

Meet Me at the Grand **by Lindsay Harrel**

We solve the problem of what to read next.

WHERE EVERY STORY IS A FRIEND,
AND EVERY CHAPTER IS A NEW JOURNEY...

Subscribe to our newsletter for a free book, the latest news, weekly giveaways, exclusive author interviews, and more!

Shop paperbacks, ebooks, audiobooks, and more at
SUNRISEPUBLISHING.MYSHOPIFY.COM